RED ROSE BOUQUET

JENNIFER RODEWALD

ISBN: 978-0-9978508-0-2

WORDS THAT EDIFY
Rooted Publishing

Printed in the United States of America

First Printing, 2016

Edited by Dori Harrell of Breakout Editing

Roseanna White Designs, www.RoseannaWhiteDesigns.com
Images from www.Shutterstock.com

Author photo by Larisa O'Brien Photography

Published by Rooted Publishing
McCook, NE 69001

Table of Contents

JENNIFER RODEWALD

So that I might learn compassion.

"I want you to know you can hold my hand."

I looked up to the woman, confused. "Why?"

After a long, maybe meaningful look, the woman shrugged and turned away.

"Will it hurt?"

No answer.

"What about later?"

With her back still turned, the woman spoke. "You'll never have to think about it again."

~1~

Cheryl stared at the affidavit in front of her. She couldn't see the words written on the document. Instead, Andrew's handwritten letter—who did that anymore?—floated before her mind.

Please, please forgive me.

Those words had branded themselves into her psyche, and she couldn't banish them. Why would *he* write her? During the months they'd been together, she had never been anything more significant to him than a beauty on his arm—or in his bed. Never. In the beginning, he'd shown signs of being a more decent human being. He'd been nice to her cat, had felt guilty when one of his clients wasn't anywhere in the region of innocent and he had to defend him anyway. But those little blips had proven to be merely white flakes of snow on an otherwise black heart. They melted, absorbed into the darkness, and left the unobstructed truth.

And the truth was he, like all the others she'd been with, was not a good man.

Horrible people didn't beg for forgiveness though.

Her eyebrows pinched together as her head continued to pound. She hadn't heard from him in two years, and it wasn't even like he had a reason to apologize. What was he going to gain? He was married. To *her*—the hometown sweetheart from his childhood, whom she'd been forced to meet on her last trip to Denver.

Did his wife know he'd sent the letter?

Cheryl's eyes slid shut, and the rest of the words written by Andrew's hand scrawled before her vision.

I have no excuse, Cheryl. I behaved horrible, treated you terribly. I have asked God to forgive me for everything I did to you, to others, and for the rebellion I've waged against Him, and He has given me grace upon grace. But I know that I hurt you—I saw it in your eyes the day you told me good-bye. Please forgive me.

Was his letter part of a twelve-step program? Rehab required such things.

Her chest tightened as hard anger curled its hostile grip. She didn't want to be part of a checklist. And besides, if God had forgiven him, then why bother asking her? Didn't God trump? What was he talking about anyway? Andrew was an atheist.

Her hands covered her face as she rubbed her eyebrows. None of this mattered at the moment. She was sitting at her desk with a mountain of work that wasn't getting done.

If Andrew wanted her forgiveness, he was in for disappointment. She didn't have time to deal with it. He was a lawyer too. Surely he'd understand.

She scrubbed her face one more time, making a mental note to check a mirror before she left her office, and refocused on the testimony before her.

When I came in, I found the woman on the stairway, her clothes torn...

Cheryl's stomach turned sour and hot. Even after ten years of prosecuting the bad guys, every despicable account like this ignited fire in her gut. She'd been able to convince herself, back in prelaw school, that she'd make a difference and that it would matter.

She had lived in a fairy world—shattered first by a man who'd shown himself to be as blackhearted as Andrew, and then by the despicable realities of human nature. This world was ugly, and no one knew it better than she.

Case in point. The perpetrator in the criminal case she was working on would walk. Guaranteed. The account she was reading was the DA's only solid piece of evidence, and it had been rendered by a convicted felon—a questionable witness whose past cast him into serious doubt because of a very probable agenda against the defendant. Every other shred of evidence the police had been able to scavenge was circumstantial. Worthless.

Didn't matter if she believed every word of her client's story—that the woman had been attacked by her boyfriend while he was stoned out of his head, raped, and then tossed down the cement stairway and left for dead. Only what she could prove mattered—and that wasn't much.

Head once again in her hands, she groaned.

This job. This life.

This everything.

Her throat swelled, and unwelcome hot liquid pushed against her eyelids.

She couldn't do it anymore.

~*~

Brock sliced the water with the aluminum oar and pushed, his solid stroke sending the kayak into the current. The cool mountain air from the crisp May morning filled his lungs. The kids would be up from the city by ten, and he'd need to be on hand to help unload the bus, but for what was left of the early morning, he had the Yampa River to himself.

The water slithered through the valley with deep S curves and a current whose gentle surface belied the strength beneath. He couldn't check out mentally, but he could relax as he prepared for another week. A week full of eight- to twelve-year-old kids, of hiking, fishing, campfires, and goofy camp songs. Who would have guessed the hometown snowboard-cross star would end up a full-time youth camp director? Not him. He'd lived for thrills, which had made the races attractive in the first place, and he'd lived for himself. Right up until Mexico went and undid everything he'd ever been sure about.

Praise God. Even if there was some pain with that one.

Coming home had been good. And finding himself in the offering to others hadn't a parallel. Not on the slopes. Not in fame.

Even with that, sometimes the praising God part was harder than others. The snowboarding dream wasn't the toughest to turn loose of. Kayla...well, she was a whole different story. It wasn't fair that he still thought about her. She'd found herself another rising star, and that was that. Pictures printed within the pages of *Sports Illustrated* drove the point in solid.

At least the dude hadn't shattered Brock's record. Yet.

Things not worth thinking about. Brock had an hour's worth of river to paddle before he'd need to port and call it a day. Or a morning. Time that would be better spent praying over the kids he'd take charge of for the week—for their safety and for their hearts. Not time to waste feeding bitterness.

His heart would be just fine. No thanks to Kayla.

When I was small, I always thought what you did was amazing. Rock climbing? Pretty awesome. I never took into account how risky it was, how fearless you were. And how reckless.

After, though... I never told anyone how angry I was. At you, because I needed a mother and you weren't there. I guess I figured I'd get over it, especially since it wasn't right for me to be mad.

I never did.

~2~

Therefore, it has become essential that I resign...

Cheryl stared at the cursor flashing against the words she'd typed. Essential? That might be a little overstated. She was good at her job. Not many women had accomplished what she had in the criminal trial world or had lasted quite so long. Sheer determination had propelled her—she wasn't going to be a statistic in her profession. And she needed to offer something to the Great Judge...

She'd stepped into a world of the profoundly ugly. Wicked hearts, twisted systems. It had helped that she'd mastered stone-cold indifference before she'd graduated law school. A necessity. Not just for her career, but for every part of her life.

All things considered, she should feel proud. Except she wasn't truly successful.

She was a survivor—in life and in her profession—but that was all. Surviving wasn't the same thing as succeeding.

The familiar tension gathered in between her shoulders and gripped the back of her neck. Next, the strain would move up to the base of her skull, and from there...

Her headaches had been unmanageable. Stupid doctors. Surely there was something they hadn't tried. Something different they could do.

Sleep. Dr. Reef said consistent sleep would help. Easier said than done, even with the horrible numbing pills he'd prescribed. She'd stopped taking them. All the medication had really accomplished was to lock her in the hazy world of semiconsciousness, holding her hostage to the terrors that tortured her in the place of dreams.

She'd take migraines over those nightmares every time.

Blinking, Cheryl pushed away her spiraling thoughts. Time to decide: resign or not to resign. *Quit fingering the issue and grip a choice.*

What should she do?

She could go into civil law. It was easier to transition from a criminal to a civil practice than the other way around, and she'd known a couple lawyers who had done it. That would get her out of the district attorney's office and maybe away from the scum of the earth.

A flash of some daytime courtroom show passed through her mind—programs she'd avoided since law school. Away from scum? Maybe not.

There were other things she could do. Didn't have to be law related.

She scanned her condo. Clean, modern, minimalist in decorating style. Expensive. Not extravagant, because she was a public prosecutor, not a private-practice senior partner at some big, fancy firm. Not like Andrew had been. Money wasn't dripping out of her faucet. But she did pretty well, even at that. Going back to school, finding a different vocation, would cost her a steady paycheck. Even if she found a place half the size and half as nice, rent would still be expensive in LA. What else could she do that would allow her to keep up with the life she'd worked for? Not to mention her bargain with God.

If she was to quit law, how could she even try to appease the Great Wrath?

The cell sitting next to her laptop buzzed its rhythmic alarm, signaling an incoming call. Turning it face up, the caller ID spelled out *Ethan.*

He called maybe twice a year. It wasn't her birthday, and Christmas was over six months away. What could her brother want?

"Hello?"

"Hey, sis. How are you?"

He didn't really want to know. "I'm good. I'm fairly busy though. What's up?"

"Always busy."

The pause felt like a silent rebuke.

"Yes. Well..." Her voice became crisp. Ethan knew nothing of her world, and they both preferred it that way. He had no business calling out her lies. "That's my life, E. I've got about two minutes before I need to go."

"Fine. I'll make it snappy, Sherbert."

Her teeth set on edge as she closed her eyes in a harsh scowl. Holdovers from her childhood just about sent her screaming. There wasn't any going back to those days, so remembering them was a waste of time and emotion. However, scolding Ethan would only extend this conversation.

"Here's the short of it," Ethan continued. "Nana needs help, and I can't do it full time anymore. You need to come back."

No. Absolutely not. "I have a job here. A life. That's not an option."

"No, Cheryl. It's not option*al*. Time to grow up, quit chasing whatever it is you've been chasing the past ten years, and take on some real responsibility. You owe Nana that."

Quit chasing things? He was one to talk. Mister dropped out of college three times before he finally got an associate's degree, because he couldn't concentrate on anything other than girls, slopes, and pot. Yeah. He was totally one for a lecture.

But Nana...

"Time to come home, Cheryl."

Home? The small town of Hayden hadn't been home for a very long time. She'd made sure of it.

Her eyes moved from the computer she'd been staring blankly at to the letter still sitting open on the other side of the desk. Andrew's. That would be ironic.

He'd be floored to discover she'd grown up in the Colorado mountains too.

"Cheryl, I mean it. We need you to come back."

"What's wrong with Nana?"

"You'll have to see for yourself, kid."

Vague answers always hinted a lie. Ethan's track record supported that suspicion. But if something was actually wrong with Nana...

She scanned the letter she'd been composing. Resignation. Maybe that wasn't necessary. A leave of absence due to family affairs. That was legit. And it would get her out of a decision for the moment.

So, she'd go back. Even if Hayden wasn't home—and she intended to keep it that way.

~*~

Steam swirled over the mirror as Brock towel dried his shaggy head. Twenty-six kids, ranging in ages from eight through twelve, were settling in the cabins scattered along the curved drive beyond his grandpa's home. No, it was Brock's home now. Still hard to grasp. Gramps had died so suddenly, and his leaving the ranch house and fifty acres solely to Brock had been equally unexpected.

But blessed. Even the timing, as emotional as it had been, had been of God. If Gramps had died even a year before, the house and land would have gone to auction, because Brock hadn't yet grown up. *God does, in fact, know what He's doing, even in the hard things.*

Good to remember. Because going out with the boys tonight wasn't on Brock's *can't wait to happen* list. Not for a bachelor's party. How had E landed a girl like Brandi anyway? He was the wild child of the West; she was the cultured sweetheart of the South. Two more different people couldn't have picked each other if they'd been blindfolded, given a dart, spun around, and told to fire.

Huh. That was basically dating in a nutshell. Take a shot and hope you hit a winner. Not good odds.

Brock had hit a gold digger. Or a fame seeker, more aptly put. What did that song say about drawing the queen of diamonds? Yeah, she'd beat you, for sure. Or leave you the second you decided a more humble life might be your calling.

A growl curled from Brock's throat. What was with this resurgence of bitterness today? *Let it go, dude.*

Besides, Ethan was happy. Finally. A good friend would be stoked for his childhood pal.

Stoked. Yep, totally stoked to go out and party with the boys.

Brock tugged on a pair of dark-blue jeans and slid a thermal shirt over his head. Good enough for a bachy in Hayden. After a quick check in the mirror, he slid his feet into his boots and headed out the door. He stopped at Cammy's living quarters, his on-site cook-slash-stand-in-grandma, to let her know he'd be out for the night and then pointed his Bronco down the one-lane drive toward town. The cabins, all six of them, illuminated in his headlights as he approached and passed each one. A sense of purpose and satisfaction billowed in his chest. He met his own eyes in the rearview mirror and grinned. Okay, so the past may have had some bumps, but this—*this*—was worth it.

Eight mud-slathered vehicles—five of them trucks—gathered in front of the Hi Way Bar & Restaurant in downtown Hayden. *The gang's all here.* And not one of the guys would have wagered they'd be at *this* kind of gathering for Ethan. His best friend had moved from girl to girl, then woman to woman since puberty. No kidding. Who'd have thought?

God does work miracles.

Brock snorted a laugh and then prayed for Ethan and Brandi with his next thoughts. Because really, all marriages that made a go of life were miracles. Two naturally selfish people pledging to live for one another for the rest of their lives, come good or bad? That'd take an act of God to see it through. He knew. Not that he'd made that pledge, but still...

Brock passed through the heavy wood front door, and the horn that sounded like it belonged in an arena rather than a sports bar blared above his head.

"Hey!" Ethan stood from his stool at the bar and threw up his hand. "There he is! My best man, last guy to the party. Go figure that. Can't even blame it on the slopes anymore."

"Sorry, man. I have grownup responsibilities." Brock shook Ethan's hand and then pulled him into a man hug. "You know, since I don't live with my nana anymore, like some guys I know."

Ethan elbowed him. "Yeah, I know. I'm soooo pathetic, taking care of the elderly and all."

They strode back to the bar where Ethan had been sitting, and the other guys circled around.

"How's that going to work out, E?" Jeff, the resident make-a-life-plan man, leaned on the counter next to Ethan. "Nana Grace needs help, right?"

Ethan snorted. "Don't tell her that. But yes. My baby sis is coming back."

"Whoa, what?" Adam slid closer. "Sherbert the knockout is coming back? Glad I stuck around."

"Dude, she's my sister."

"Grow up, E. Cheryl certainly did. Last I saw, she did it *well*." Adam hung on that last word as if they all needed help understanding what he meant.

No one needs a translation, idiot. They were all red-blooded males with eyes that worked just fine, thank you very much. And Cheryl Thompson had definitely grown up. Then again, none of them had seen her for like a decade, so who knew?

"She ever get married?" Jeff asked.

Brock had wondered the same thing—in passing—when Ethan told him he was engaged.

"Not your business." Ethan shot Jeff, and then Adam, the *don't touch my sister* look he'd perfected when they were in high school. They'd all known he was serious too. Ethan was a slope junkie and a player when it came to the girls, but he was dead serious when it came to his baby sister. It was kind of the two of them against the world for a while, especially after their dad had remarried, so Ethan's over-the-top protectiveness was understandable, if not admirable.

"So she didn't."

Didn't what? Brock shut off the family history lesson in his brain and worked to catch up to the conversation.

"No. She's not married." Ethan fisted his drink and took a long swig. "That I know of."

Adam busted out laughing. "Ah, so you're close, huh? Dude, what are you getting all worked up about if you don't even know what's going on in her life?"

Brock squeezed the tender spot in between Adam's shoulder and neck—the spot that made grown men wince. "Drop it, buddy. We're not here about Cheryl. Bachy night, remember?"

"Bachy!"

"Bachy!"

Gage and Shane both raised their mugs as they called out together. Leave it to the two married guys to move the night forward.

Jeff raised his mug. "To you, E." He clanked his mug against Ethan's and then drained the beer. "Except, you gotta explain this deal to me. Aren't bachelor parties supposed to happen the night before your wedding? We're a whole week ahead of schedule."

Ethan shrugged. "Brandi wants to do something different. A party together."

The guys went still. Brock fought the urge to laugh. The things they got all bent out of shape about...who cared? Not like Ethan's life was going to end after Brandi slipped a ring on his finger.

"Dude..." Jeff shook his head.

"Bro." Adam slid an arm around Ethan's neck. "It's starting already. She's gonna change your whole life."

Ethan looked him right in the eyes. "I hope so."

That look. Ethan's dead-serious expression grabbed hold of something Brock had pushed way down deep and had tried to forget about. He had to glance away because he knew exactly what it was.

Nope. Not true. He was good single. The last thing he wanted was a woman turning his world upside down.

Landing in Denver was always bumpy. The 747's cabin shuddered and jolted as the plane made its final descent. Cheryl's throat tightened, and she fisted the seat arm on her right.

The man in seat B tipped his head toward her ear. "We'll be fine, little missy."

"Of course. Denver's never a smooth landing."

One side of his mouth tipped in a crooked grin. "Feel free to hold my hand."

"I'm fine."

Men. So predictable. Be nice to the pretty girl. Pour out a little charm. Buy her a meal. Wake up with her in bed. Formula romance. She wasn't in the mood, even if she could use the distraction.

The plane rocked two more times, and then the thrust of the brakes pushed Cheryl against the seat. After she drew three deep breaths, the squeal of rubber tires against the asphalt runway reported their landing.

Safe on the ground, Cheryl blew out a slow breath. The relief was short lived, however, as she switched her cell from airplane mode to receive calls. Ethan had texted her.

Ethan: *Why didn't you fly into Yampa?*

She was over thirty years old. Did she really need to clear her plans with her older brother?

Except, maybe she should have flown into the tiny regional airport. This plan about confrontation looked less and less like a good idea as she gazed over the Denver valley. She should have just torn up the letter and been done with Andrew Harris for keeps. What possible good could come out of her seeking him now?

No. He didn't deserve to wiggle off the hook with a little *I'm sorry* note. And she wasn't going to let him appease his guilt, or his new wife, or whatever it was that had motivated him to write the stupid thing.

Cheryl: *I have an appointment in Denver.*

The cabin attendant came over the speakers, letting the passengers know the gate number where they would deplane and their assigned baggage claim carousel. Important information, but it was all on her e-ticket, stored safely in her phone, so she ignored the overhead voice.

Ethan: *With who? You haven't been to Colorado in years.*

She'd been to Colorado more recently than he knew, but it had been a while. Details not necessary for Ethan to know.

Cheryl: *Never mind. I'll rent a car and be up later.*

Ethan: *Rent a car? For how long?*

How long was this going to take? She scowled, muting the growl that threatened to escape her throat.

"Boyfriend troubles?"

She looked sideways at the nosy man sitting next to her. "Fish much?"

His ears turned crimson.

Good. Maybe he'd give up. Back to the other irritating conversation.

Cheryl: *Don't worry about it. I'll figure it out.*

Ethan: *Why don't you call me and we can talk about this?*

He'd apparently figured out that she wouldn't answer if he called her. Finally. Only took two days of leaving voice messages. Texting was easier. She could say what she wanted and not have that awkward *I'm disappointed in you* silence weigh against her conscience.

Cheryl: *No. I'll see you sometime tonight. Don't be a pest.*

Ethan: *Can't wait.*

Then again, maybe she could read disappointment in a text, because that was definitely not heartfelt. Why'd Ethan have to go all big brother on her all of the sudden? They were just fine as near strangers. Family reunions hadn't been a part of their calendars for years. Life had taken them down opposite paths, and it was easier to leave it that way. This whole coming home deal—no, going back to Hayden, which was *not* home—was a bad plan.

She could skip it. Catch the next flight out of Denver, never even leave the airport, and forget all of it.

Her phone buzzed against her palm. Another text.

an: *I'm serious, sis. I can't wait to see you again. It's been way too*

Not sarcasm. Guess that meant she was seeing this stupid thing through. Which meant all of it, starting with Andrew Harris.

~*~

Good thing she'd done some preliminary research. Andrew had once again uprooted his life. If she'd come unprepared, it would've taken days to figure out he'd moved into the foothills, started his own *little* (read: pathetic) practice for weird cases he'd never even given a thought to before. She'd unearthed all the dirt on him while still in Cali, and there'd been quite a little bit. Not the kind she'd expected though.

Forced out of his big-time job because he took on a shaky, politically incorrect case. That didn't sound like the Andrew she'd known and loathed at all. What exactly had happened to the man she'd left standing in his downtown loft fighting a massive hangover two years ago? Reform?

Not even possible. Reform like that would take an act of God. Andrew hadn't been interested in God, which had initially hit her as a good thing. If he didn't believe, then she could pretend she didn't either, and they'd carried on their...well, whatever they were, without guilt. That'd been the whole goal from the beginning.

Cheryl pushed that path of thought away. Too deep for a day like this. Too deep for any day. She and God weren't on speaking terms anymore, and she was pretty sure they both preferred it that way.

More murky thoughts not worth thinking.

She focused on driving. The little rental she'd procured from the airport—which took forever—handled well enough, even if it was a bottom-rung economy car. It'd do for now, although she wasn't sure taking on the two mountain passes she'd need to climb to get to Hayden in the little rabbit-mobile was a good idea. She might need to renegotiate.

One problem at a time.

Flowing with the traffic zipping over the interstate, she took the curve that separated the valley from the foothills and passed through the Hogback. Her grip strengthened on the wheel. Once upon a time the mountains had represented shelter. Home. But like all storybook tales, the pages had turned until the final words pronounced "The End." The difference between a book and real life was that she couldn't go back. "The End" meant exactly what it said, and she'd had to go on. In her case, life wasn't about a new chapter. It wasn't even about a new story. It was simply surviving the cliff fall that came after "The End." Every time she thought she'd hit a spot to land on and start over, the edges crumbled, and she was falling again.

She hated it.

A familiar knifing pain speared the base of her skull.

Not now.

Letting her shoulders droop, she focused on relaxing the muscles in her neck and back. Deep breath in. Long breath out. Repeat, but pay attention to the road. Man, had it always been this curvy? And busy?

For twenty more minutes, Cheryl attempted to perform her deep breathing exercises while driving. The sharp pain continued its threat, but it didn't spread up and over the rest of her brain, so she counted it as a win. For the moment.

Reaching a little village carved into the mountain next to the river, she followed the GPS until the feminine computer voice announced that she'd reached her destination. Careful to park away from the front door, and beside a large SUV that would give her cover, she shut the engine off and sat back.

Sometimes spying came with her job. But this time... Her heart squeezed hard and irregular, and the warmth that flowed through her veins wasn't adrenaline. She called it anger, even though she knew it wasn't that either.

She'd never confronted an ex-boyfriend like this. They did what they did—stayed with her until the thrill was gone or until her sharp edges pushed them away, and then left. She'd let them go. Men weren't faithful creatures, and she knew better than to expect an exception. So what was she doing here, waiting to face Andrew?

None of the other exes had ever asked for forgiveness. That was the boiling point.

Come on. Let's get this over with...

Cheryl checked her watch. Three minutes till noon. Her source said he always left the office for lunch. Met his wife on Tuesdays. Went out to a small café on Thursdays. Otherwise, he ran the pathway by the river for twenty minutes and then ate from a brown bag at the park.

She'd picked Thursday to fly in on purpose.

The door popped open, and the profile of the man striding out looked all too familiar. Tall, built like an all-around athlete, caramel-brown hair. And she didn't need to see his smile to remember how charming it was.

Andrew let another man pass out of the door before he let it go and reached to shake his hand. A client, probably. Apparently he was making it in this new life of his. The men ended their conversation and parted ways, Andrew turning her direction to walk to the café across the street. Her first glimpse of his face caused her breath to catch.

Whoa. That was quite a scar.

He passed by her little Flintstone car without a glance. She watched him until he crossed the street and ducked into the café. *Who spends their lunch every Thursday at the same restaurant?* No wonder he was an alcoholic. He was predictable, a surefire creature of habit.

Played well for her today. And now was the moment. Time to put the knife back where it belonged.

Cheryl snatched the letter, now bent and rumpled, as if she'd poured over it countless times. She hadn't. Just a few reads, that was all. She wasn't obsessed or anything.

Jamming the envelope into her designer denim pocket, she scurried across the road and breezed through the same door she'd just watched Andrew enter. A quick scan told her he sat alone at a table by a window, hunched over, as if reading.

Brooding, probably. He did that a lot too.

She moved to the counter and caught a waitress's attention. "I'm joining someone." Pointing to Andrew, she fixed her best sultry little smile and winked. "He'll want a Fat Tire. Give me whatever daiquiri in a bottle you have."

The woman's forehead wrinkled. "Is Mr. Harris expecting you?"

Cheryl pushed out a suggestive laugh. "He's never sorry when I show up."

Red tinged the waitress's ears as she glanced between Cheryl and Andrew. All small towns worked the same, didn't they? Perfect.

"Just bring the drinks, and don't worry about the rest, okay, sweetheart?" Cheryl patted her arm. "He's a big boy."

Score one for the ex-girlfriend. Cheryl wiggled her shoulders straight and sauntered to Andrew's table. Without a word, she pulled out the chair across from his and slid onto the seat.

He glanced up and froze.

"Miss me?"

With growing eyes, he simply stared.

"I know. They all do."

After a visible intake of breath, he sat back, a shield of caution dropping over his expression. "What are you doing here?"

Cheryl extinguished the flirty look and narrowed her gaze. With one fluid motion, she removed the letter from her pocket and slapped it onto the table. "Explain yourself."

He studied the crinkled envelope, and Cheryl wished she'd kept it pristine, as if what he'd written hadn't mattered to her at all. Of course, if that was the truth, she wouldn't be there, would she?

The waitress saved him from answering, delivering the drinks Cheryl had ordered. She set the Fat Tire in front of Andrew with a little more force than necessary, making the bottle clunk a hollow announcement onto the table.

Andrew's eyes fixed on that brown bottle and didn't move. "Sage, what's this?"

"Your *friend* said you wanted it."

He moved to look at the waitress.

"What else, Mr. Harris?" the woman clipped.

Andrew looked back at the drink. "Give me a couple more minutes, okay?"

"Right." She spun away.

Cheryl sat back, crossing her arms, and watched the man sinking across from her. Satisfaction would have been the right emotion for the moment. It wasn't there though. Her heart turned as he fingered the beer, rolling it on its base. Slowly, he removed his grip and pulled out his cell phone. It was dark—off—but he didn't tap the Home button. Instead, he stared at the blank screen.

"What are you doing?"

He brushed at the scar running along his nose and looked at her. "Remembering."

Sage, the waitress, moved with a full tray nearby. Andrew stopped her with a small wave. She paused to turn a chilly look on him.

"I'm sorry, Sage. I know you'll just have to dump this, but I don't want it." He nodded toward the bottle. "I'll pay for it, but I need you to take it away."

The woman's pinched expression relaxed as she removed the beer. "Sure, Andy. How about a Coke?"

"Yep. And a chicken sandwich. Make one to go for Jamie too, okay?"

"You got it." Sage turned her eyes toward Cheryl, and the coldness in her expression resettled. "And you?"

"I'm not staying. But *Andy* here will take care of my drink as well, won't you?" She lifted a brow, knowing she was pushing every hot button he had.

Andrew shrugged. "Sure."

Sage nodded, her dislike for Cheryl evident with every move. Who cared?

"So you won't drink with a friend anymore, huh? Or is it just not with me?"

He pushed a hand through his hair and sighed. "I'm an alcoholic, Cheryl. And you know better than most that for me, one is never enough."

"So what, this Jamie woman reformed you, and now you've got your happily ever after? Just needed to unload some baggage, is that it?"

His gaze settled on the letter still resting on the table between them. "No."

Cheryl snorted. "Right. Listen, let me make this real clear for you. You are *not* forgiven. Got it?"

"Okay." His voice came soft. Regretful.

"That's it? Okay?"

"What else should I say? I am sorry—"

"No." She leaned forward as fury exploded in her chest. "No. You don't get to do this, Andrew. I didn't come here to give you a chance to apologize in person."

"What did you come for?"

Her heart stalled. He didn't have any right to ask that. None. She grabbed the letter and crumpled it in her fist. Shaking it, she hissed, "This means nothing. Nothing!"

"Then why are you here?"

Cheryl swallowed. Hard. She hadn't been able to answer that question for herself yet.

"Look. I know I don't know your past. I don't know why you—"

She pierced him with a sharp look. "No, of course you don't. You never asked. Never cared."

His head hung, and he nodded. "I know." He looked up and made eye contact. "I know I didn't, and I'm sorry. I'm so sorry for everything. But, Cheryl, whatever it is that has your heart caught in this cage of ice, you need to know that there's freedom. You don't have to live—"

"You know what?" She leaned across the table, her voice low. "Shut up, you hypocrite. You think that just because you've been sober a year or two that you've actually changed? Ha." She settled back again. "People don't change. We're a product of our pasts—our choices and mistakes and the people who have used us. That doesn't ever change. So don't think that since you've gone through some overblown twelve-step program or whatever, and you've managed to hypnotize that woman into marrying you, that you're somehow better than me. You're not."

He stared at his hands lying on the table. "I know."

She stood, her fists clenched. The crumpled paper in her hand bit against her palm. "Don't contact me again, Andrew. Ever."

"Okay."

She moved to stomp past him, but stopped when her name came from his broken voice.

"Cheryl." He looked up at her. "I hope someday, for your sake, you find out that you're wrong."

Cheryl glared at him for a breath. She'd never seen him so sincere— or broken. Not once in the fifteen months they'd been together. He meant every word.

Emotion clawed her throat. She swallowed it back, straightened her posture, and set her stride toward the door. Didn't matter what he believed. He didn't know.

There wasn't any way a man like him—or any man, for that matter—could know her hell. Or the fact that it would never change.

The little car put all four cylinders into the mountain pass.

The mountain was winning.

She should have exchanged it before she headed up and over.

She inched along at almost fifty miles per hour, the SUVs swishing past her to the left. Good thing the state had put some work into widening the highway, or she'd be getting the bird from every traveler stacked up behind her.

At least the ride downhill would be fun. And the road was dry, so she could let it fly. Maybe the speed would whip away her residual fury.

Probably not.

Why couldn't she let it go? She'd said what she'd gone to say. Andrew wasn't absolved. The end. He could live with it.

He would, too. Just fine. His life had carried on, smoothed out, and gotten good. She was still stuck with the rottenness. Granted, it wasn't all from him. She'd had a good share of the load strapped to her back long before she'd met him.

You don't have to live like...

How had he intended to finish that?

Didn't matter. He didn't know about her life, her past.

Cease and desist with the Andrew garbage.

"Come on..." Cheryl leaned forward against the steering wheel, wondering if it'd help her little vehicle crawl up the final bit of incline if she rocked back and forth. How weird would that look? "Just a little bit farther..."

The view opened on her right, and she caught a glimpse of the meadow stretching gently upward to the peak south of the highway, and the steep slope that flowed down toward Winter Park. Below, the highway snaked with wide switchbacks until it slipped out of view beneath the evergreens in the valley. One pass halfway done. The worst was behind her.

If only that were true of life. At one point, that was exactly what she'd thought—that the worst was behind her. She'd be able to leave her biggest problems, and life would move on.

She hadn't banked on the fierce grip of captivity.

Hard emotion locked in her chest, and a seething whisper pricked against her conscience.

Unforgivable.

A tremble shook her core, and she pulled in a breath to bolster against the surge of pain. Squeezing the steering wheel, she steeled herself against the voice, numbing her heart until the feelings died away.

There is freedom...

Maybe for Andrew—which wasn't exactly fair. She gripped harder, letting anger drown the claim he'd made.

Her cell, tossed onto the passenger seat, chirped. She glanced at the lit-up screen. Ethan. Again.

She snatched the phone just as she approached the first hairpin turn, and accepted the call.

"What now?"

"Hey." Ethan paused. "That's how most civil people answer their phones. Or *hello*. Or *what's up?* You know, so at least people get a good first impression before you go sinking your jaws into them."

"Cute. Why do you keep calling me?"

"I was just checking on you. How's the drive?"

"It's fine, Ethan."

"Which way did you go?"

She wanted to growl. They weren't the chatty kind of siblings. This was ridiculous. "I'm almost to Winter Park. I should be there sometime between six and seven."

"Good. We'll wait on supper for you."

"That's not necessary."

"That's not necessary," he mocked, using a sharp, girlish tone. "I'm your brother, not some witness you get to snap at. We'll wait for you.

How about you meet us at the Hi Way in town? Just text me when you get to Rabbit Ears."

There wasn't a point in arguing. "Fine. Now can I concentrate on the road?"

A drawn-out sigh hissed from Ethan's side of the line. "Okay, Sherbert. Drive safe."

Stop calling me that. Ugh. Already this had been a long trip, and she hadn't even reached her destination yet.

~*~

"It's been a good week, Brock. The kids all have that *this place is magic* glow."

Brock grinned as he wiped down the last of the eight tables. "Must be the cookin'. You spoil all of us." He stood and turned to face Cammy. "You did save a piece of that Twinkie cake for me, right?"

"Of course. I like my job—have every intention of keeping it." Cammy winked.

Like he could do without her.

Cammy tilted her head. "So, that redhead..."

Should have guessed. The female counselor with fiery hair had made no secret of her interest. From the moment she'd stepped off the bus, Brock knew she was the dart to avoid for the week. Seemed like more often than not there was at least one. Made him tired.

"You noticed, did you?"

Cammy's laugh cracked through the mostly vacant main lodge. "Kind of hard to miss." She turned serious with the next breath. "You're never interested in them."

Yes. That was true. And obvious, which didn't command a response. Brock finished with the table and backed his way through the swinging door into the kitchen.

With a determined stride, Cammy trailed behind him, her hands jammed onto her hips. "Come on now, Brock. You can't blame them. You're a good-looking single guy doing a job that makes women all gooey inside. Maybe you should give one a chance."

"You forgot former Olympian. That's why half of them come up for this little *field experience*." With the rag still gripped in a few fingers, he framed *field experience* with air quotes. "Sorry. Not interested."

"You don't know that for sure."

No, he didn't. Not for sure. But even the possibility of a woman hitching a ride with a bunch of foster kids, pretending to care just so she'd have the opportunity to flirt, was enough to make him keep to himself.

Brock dropped the rag into the sink of hot water, rinsed his hands, and moved to pick up the plate of cake Cammy had saved for him.

"One of them might be really nice."

He shoved a bite into his mouth and nodded. "Could be," he mumbled around the oh-so-sweet confection.

"You won't know unless you give them a chance."

After brushing the crumbs from his lips, he nodded again. "True."

"So you'll talk to her tonight at the bonfire?"

"Nope."

Cammy's shoulders slumped. "Brock."

He chuckled and wrapped an arm around her. "I've got all I need, Cammy. You keep food in my stomach. The kids that come up here keep me humble and on my toes. Nothing's missing for me, so let it go." With one last squeeze, he dropped his hand and returned to the cake.

"Mr. Kelly." One of the male counselors popped his head into the kitchen. "You need to get out here. One of the girls just got hurt."

Great. Last night of her week, too. Poor kid. Brock set his empty plate on the stainless steel counter and moved for the door.

"Let me know if I need to call Doc," Cammy called behind him.

"Give Brandi a heads-up." He waved without looking back. Not their first rodeo.

Following the younger man, Brock listened while he rattled an account of the accident.

"She was running near the fire pit—the girls were playing chase."

"Near the fire pit? I thought I made myself clear..." He'd built a fire as the kids were finishing their dinner. Final-night tradition. The kids had all been carefully instructed about his expectations, as had the adult leaders. Number one rule: don't run near the fire pit.

The counselor's jaw tightened. "Yes, sir. I'm sorry. She's got a pretty good burn on her arm."

Brock ran. Nearing the pit that sat fifty yards off the pond, he assessed the gathering. The area buzzed with guilty silence, broken only by a small, girlish whimper. He finished his sprint at the edge of the circle, and without instruction the group broke to allow him access.

The little girl sat in a huddle, her back to the woman clearly trying to help.

"Don't touch me," she hissed, adding a salty name to the end of her command.

Baggage often came out in a moment of crisis. Brock hoped the woman had been armed with that understanding. Didn't look like it, given her narrowing eyes and the tightening of her jaw. Touching the counselor's shoulder, he urged her aside.

"Let's see," he said.

"Good luck," the counselor mumbled.

Brock ignored her, focusing on the injured girl. "It was an accident, I know. I'm not mad, and I only want to help you."

"It wasn't an accident. She pushed me! She's always trying to do something."

"What?" the woman behind him stabbed the circle of silence with her irritation.

Brock eyed the indignant leader, knowing she had done no such thing, but giving her a stern look. She snapped her mouth shut and took another step back.

"Okay." He squatted beside the injured kid, maintaining her safe bubble of space. That had been one of the first phrases he'd learned when he began training for this program. Safe bubbles—these kids needed that more than most. "Listen, you're Sonja, right?"

The girl nodded.

"Do you remember my name?"

She drew a breath and swallowed. "Mr. Brock."

"Right. How about you tell me where we are."

Her eyes, lit with a blaze of insult, turned up to him. "I'm not stupid, Stupid. I know where I am."

"Okay, good." Brock sat back on his haunches. "How about you tell me?"

She rolled her eyes. "We're at some dumb mountain camp where we're supposed to sit around the fire and sing and forget everything else that is crappy about our lives."

"Good. We know exactly where we are. Now, tell me what happened."

Sonja paused and looked at the fire. The hardness in her expression melted a bit, and Brock watched as she sorted through her realities. Most of these kids had a couple—the one where memories played and replayed without mercy, confusing what was presently real with what was history, and the one that was, in fact, presently real. Some had an added reality, worlds in their minds—worlds that were theirs alone, the places to which they escaped.

Brock waited, and the crowd began to disperse. Within a few moments, only the redheaded leader was left standing at a distance that said she didn't want to interfere but had reason to be in on this situation. That meant she was Sonja's cabin leader, and more than likely hadn't been doing her job.

Brock set aside his irritation, focusing on the girl in front of him. "What happened?"

Sonja sniffed. "It wasn't Shaylee."

Shaylee...the counselor she'd indicted. Brock nodded.

"We were playing tag, and I tripped."

"What hurts?"

"My arm."

Brock held out a hand. "Can I look at it?"

Sonja lifted her eyes to his, suspicion lacing her expression.

"I won't touch it."

"They'll move me," she argued.

From her current home. He wanted to promise they wouldn't. It wasn't a promise he could keep. On average, a foster kid would spend at least two years in the system, many bouncing from one home to another for reasons as varied as the children themselves. Sonja may very well have had legitimate grounds for her fear.

"How about we make sure that you're going to be okay right now, and we'll save other worries for later?"

"I'm fine."

"Did you burn your arm?"

She pressed her lips tight.

"How does infection sound? We don't treat it, bacteria has a party in the wound, and then you lose your arm. Sound good?"

She huffed, glared at him, and then thrust her arm forward. "See? It's fine."

Not so much. Brock caught her hand, careful to keep his promise not to touch the burn, and turned her palm up so he could examine her forearm. A long welt bubbled dark and angry against her light-brown skin. Second degree, at least.

"Ouch, kid." He let her hand go. "That burn is pretty bad. It needs a professional, Sonja. We have to go see a doc."

"No."

"Okay, tell me how you think we should treat it."

"I told you—I'm fine." She huddled away again, tucking her injury close to her body.

"I heard that part. Did you hear the part about losing your arm?"

"Did you hear the part where I said they'd kick me out?" Preteens had such a universal way of coating their voices with a jerky tone that grated, and Sonja employed it with precision. "Doctors are expensive."

Brock wondered if she was replaying real conversations—the possibility of which sent a flare of rage streaking through his mind. Foster kids fell under Medicaid, so that was crap. Or maybe she was reflecting on pre-foster events. Or she was inventing fears, because those things had a breeding program that rivaled the bacteria he was worried about. Hard to know.

"This visit is on me, okay? I've got it covered, and I'll be the only one who sees the bill. Promise. I'd really hate to see you lose a limb."

"What makes you think your promise means anything to me?"

He shrugged, pretending her words didn't hit his heart like shards of broken glass. What kind of world jaded a kid like this before she was even twelve years old?

"Doesn't have to mean anything to you, I guess. But it means something to me. I keep my promises."

Another girl crept out of the shadows, where apparently she'd been listening, and crawled toward them until she reached Sonja's side. "He's not the lying kind, So-J," she whispered. "Remember, I have a superpower. I can see their hearts. His is good."

So-J. Good name. Brock locked gazes with the other girl. Her velvety dark skin reflected the dancing firelight as he watched her take Sonja's good hand.

"Felicity, you didn't tell me you had a superpower."

She only looked at him.

Brock shifted so that he could sit on the ground. His knees popped as he moved, reminding him that he'd officially moved another step closer to forty years old next month. "What do you see in my heart?"

"You want to help, even if you don't always know how."

Maybe she did have a superpower. "How can I help So-J?"

Felicity looked at Sonja and then back to Brock. "Let me go with you."

He looked from Felicity to Sonja and back again. "Done. Is that a deal, So-J?"

Sonja leaned toward Felicity, and Brock could see Felicity whisper to her friend.

"Yeah, I guess."

"Good. I'll get the truck." And the redhead. Because he'd need another adult with him as standard protocol, and Cammy would have to stay at the camp in his place until Ethan and Brandi could get out there.

Guess he'd end up talking to the woman after all. Not the conversation Cammy was shooting for though. At all.

When we first met, I felt lost.

But then you noticed me. In a lecture hall filled with smart, ambitious students, you noticed me. It was heady. Who was I? This small-town girl in the middle of a big-time school, studying to be something I felt was way beyond myself—why would you waste your attention on me?

That attention built, and somehow we became entangled. But you never told me about your family. Your commitments. You said you loved being with me. I took that as you loved me.

It took the truth hammering my soul before I knew how badly I'd misunderstood.

Cheryl drew a deep breath as her small car came around the last curve. The valley opened below, wide and amazing. Steamboat Lake glittered in the evening glow, and the Yampa River wound wide, graceful curves through deep green pastures, the scene framed by peaks on all sides. Breathtaking. She almost forgot why she left.

Driving through the town of Steamboat, she felt the familiar sense of home—the one that she didn't want. This quaint ski town had been a part of her life for as long as she could remember, all the way up until she was twenty-one. Until the day she'd decided to remove Colorado from her bloodstream. Apparently, even after ten years of purging the valley from her existence, she hadn't been successful.

She continued through old town, noting the minimal traffic. Late May was part of the down season, although the area never really had a dead time. It was too pretty and too family friendly not to have at least a handful of tourists at any given time. As she passed the tourist area, the businesses and homes thinned, and Cheryl's stomach knotted. Twenty more minutes. That wasn't much to prepare herself, but at that point, it was way too late to turn around.

Twenty more minutes and she'd be standing in Hayden. Facing Nana and Ethan. Facing the life before...

She pushed her shoulders back and lifted her chin. It was an appointment, nothing more. She'd done hundreds of meetings, many unpleasant, in her time as a prosecutor. This didn't need to be any different. Go. Get it done. Move on.

Her phone rang from the seat beside her. Knowing the caller, she glanced at the dashboard clock—6:50. *Good grief, E. I said I'd be there around seven.* He hadn't been this annoying when they'd been teenagers. What was his deal?

With a huff, she picked up the phone. "I just passed Steamboat."

"Okay. Hi to you too. Listen, we've got a change of plans. I have to head out to Brock's, so just meet us out there."

"Brock's?" Shouldn't that guy be living in some multimillion-dollar lodge built on his own mountain by now?

"Yeah. You remember how to get to his grandpa's place, right?"

They'd spent a fair share of their summers out there—the boys fishing or tubing the river, and she, as always, Ethan's little tagalong sister following them. Yeah, she remembered. Still didn't answer the whole *what on earth was Brock still doing in little Hayden* question.

"Look, Ethan, I've been traveling since four o'clock this morning. I'm not up for it. I'll just head to Nana's, and we'll catch up in the morning."

"No can do, sister. I'm taking Nana with us, and I'll need you to pick her up. Brock called while we were waiting at the Hi Way, and he needs us to hang out there while he takes care of a kid. Nana won't want to stay that long, so just keep driving. It'll only be a little bit longer. You're a tough girl. You'll manage."

Kid? Why would Brock King-of-the-Slopes Kelly need help with a kid? Men...and children. Neither her favorite types of people.

But there wasn't a loophole in this kink. If Nana needed her to pick her up, then—wait. If Nana wasn't well, what the heck was Ethan doing taking her out?

"Hey. Are you still there?"

"Yes." Cheryl spit out the word like a mouthful of ocean water. "Why is Nana out?"

"I thought I already explained that."

"You said she wasn't well."

"I said I needed your help with her, and I do. So get out here and help."

Clearly she wasn't going to get any real answers over the phone. Fine, Ethan Pain-in-the-Butt Thompson. But they weren't done with this.

"Are you coming?" he asked, clearly all patience and false excitement over their reunion gone.

"Yes."

"Good."

"Fine. See you in twenty. Have Nana ready. I'm not staying."

"Gotcha, Captain Party Pooper."

Cheryl shook her head. "Glad to hear that you've grown up over the years."

"Right back at you, kid."

His end clicked, and her phone made that little *call dropped* sound. Cheryl clenched a death grip on her steering wheel. Two weeks was definitely way too generous. She'd be gone in a matter of days.

Five miles before the Hayden town limits, Cheryl gently applied the brakes. Gramps Kelly's turn had always snuck up on her, and more than once as a teenager, she'd had to back up on the highway to make the turn. That'd been forever ago, so who knew how hidden the little drive was now.

Not very, that was how much. Two substantial posts, hewn out from large lodgepole pines, supported a sign over the dirt turnoff. *Kelly's Ranch* had been branded into a rough plank of wood spanning the space.

Well, that sounded like Brock. Never one to blend in, he always made a statement. In school. On the slopes. Now, apparently at his grandfather's ranch. Clearly he hadn't lost any of his flair for life—or himself—along the way.

She followed the three-quarter-mile drive toward the heart of the valley where the river bent and rolled. The quickly fading dusk settled a pink hue over the bright-green grass of the spring pastures. Once, several years back, she would have sat back and released a sigh of contentment.

The muscles at the base of her neck tightened. She hunched over the steering wheel and groaned. One day. Just one day without the tension would be amazing.

When a small cabin came into view at the final bend that was supposed to lead to Gramps's home, Cheryl sat up straight. What the heck? Another identical structure sat on the opposite side of the road just a half a football field length away. And then another. She counted six before she pulled up to a lodge that overshadowed Gramps Kelly's modest ranch home.

Anger locked her biceps tight. What was Brock doing? Hayden hadn't wanted to become the little Steamboat down the road. The people liked their quaint town, their "normal" lifestyle, and their familiarity. Gramps Kelly had been one of the most vocal about that opinion.

Clearly, Brock had his own ideas.

Tired, tense, and now ticked, Cheryl jammed the gear into park, popped out of her little rat-mobile, and slammed the door shut. Cool, crisp air hit her full on, fresh, thin, and tainted with the definitive musk of wood smoke. A faint tickle of laughter drifted from the east side of the new lodgey building. She directed her stride in that direction, certain she'd find her brother entrenched by his circle of friends, and Nana waiting in a lonely chair off to the side.

She did not expect to find a host of kids circled around a stone fire pit. Or Ethan in the midst of them, laughing and handing out marshmallow sticks. Or Nana perched on the edge of a bench playing some clapping game with a tenish-year-old girl.

"Sherbert!" Ethan left his distribution post and strode toward her, his arms open wide.

Cheryl cringed and braced herself for an exuberant impact. What happened to the irritated brother she'd spoken with on the phone?

He didn't give her a chance to examine it before he crushed her in his arms. It took a moment for her to command her stiff body to embrace him back. Her arms circled his torso, and she patted him twice on the back.

"Hello, Ethan."

He snorted. "One of these days, Sherbert, we'll find the fun girl again."

She'd never been "fun." Not like Natalie Rice, who had a punch line ready in the blink of an eye, or Amanda Clipp, who had never met a dare she couldn't put down. Cheryl had been reserved in high school, even before her life went sideways.

"Good luck with that."

With one long arm draped over her shoulders, Ethan laughed again, shaking her at his side. "The fam's together again. Come on now—that's gotta make you smile a little."

Sure. Cheryl arranged a small grin.

Moving them toward the campfire, Ethan inhaled. "Take that in, sis. You can't buy air that pure in LA."

"How would you know?"

He glanced at her, his look almost pleading. For what? This wasn't a homecoming for her—not the way Ethan was playing it. It was more like torture, not that he'd know or understand. He could hold on to the good times they'd had, keep their moments of joy. Her personal timeline had been slashed with a razor. Before and after. Everything that was before was unreachable, and trying to grasp at it meant digging into that moment that had changed everything.

She couldn't. Forward was her only option.

They reached the warm circle of people, mostly short people, gathered around the bonfire, before Ethan dropped his arm. Nana stood, hugged the girl she'd been doing clapping games with, and came toward the reunited siblings.

"My girl." Nana brought Cheryl into a hug, her thin arms belying the strength of her grip. The arms of a baker, one who still kneaded her own dough and lifted the long sheets of yeasty goods from a hot oven.

There was nothing wrong with this woman.

Cheryl curved her arms around Nana's shoulders, and at once her irritation melted. Nana held her as if she *knew.* Not the substance of the secret, but the ache of it.

"I've missed my girl," she whispered.

Emotion clogged Cheryl's throat. She inhaled, long and silent, and willed the unexpected feelings away.

Collateral damage. She hadn't banked on these sorts of shrapnel wounds back then.

The sound of gravel under rubber tires saved Cheryl from the hollow moment. Swallowing, she lifted her chin and dropped her arms.

Nana was not so willing to let go. She kept an arm snugged around Cheryl's waist. "My sweet girl, you've come home." Another squeeze.

Torture.

Cheryl clenched her teeth.

A car door slammed, followed by two seconds of silence and then another report of a door.

Ethan pinched Cheryl's shoulder and turned to walk back up the walkway. "That was quick, bro."

"Doc was on it, dude."

Brock. Had to be him. The tenor of his voice was deeper than she'd remembered, but then again, she hadn't seen him in years. He'd be all man by now—even if he did still carry a hint of the slope-junkie swing in his speech. "It's minor. So-J here will be fine."

Both men stopped just behind Cheryl, and the air paused before someone tugged on a strand of her dark hair.

"Who do we have here?"

Cheryl turned her neck, lifting an eyebrow at the man standing directly behind her.

"Naw-uh." His smile quirked. "Bro, you said your sister was coming back. This beautiful woman can't possibly be the little Sherbert who used to follow us around."

Ethan laughed. "The one and only."

"No." Cheryl turned to meet Brock's gaze with a serious warning. "That girl is gone."

"I see that." He winked.

Flirt. And she knew flirts.

Filling her chest with air, she reached for Nana. "We were just leaving."

"Oooh." Brock made a face that would have befitted a serious crash on the course. "Sherbert, I think somewhere along the way you got frost bit."

Cheryl straightened, lifting her chin as if she were cross-examining a snarky witness. "Do *not* call me Sherbert."

With her hand on Nana's arm, she marched toward her car. Behind her, she could hear Brock suck in air through his teeth. "You're right. Definitely not the same girl."

Good. Just so they were all clear on that matter.

Brock frowned as he concentrated on the fire. Holy frozen tundra. Someone needed to take a heating blanket to that woman. Or stand her close to the flames that were dancing in the semidarkness.

That was not the Cheryl he'd known.

Didn't matter that much, and he wasn't sure why it bothered him to the extent it did. Rolling his head from one shoulder to the other, he mentally shrugged it off. Or tried.

Ethan nudged him with an elbow to his arm. "She's *special*, isn't she?"

Was he that transparent?

"What happened?"

Staring at the fire, Ethan blew out a long breath. "Not sure, exactly. She just snapped, you know? Somewhere in the first couple years of law school, something happened, and she seemed to freeze up. I have some ideas, but nothing concrete. She won't talk about it."

Something twisted in Brock's stomach. When kids turned upside down like Cheryl had seemed to, alarms started ringing. Usually it was a sign of something dark and awful.

The knot of pain moved into his heart.

With an intentional mental heave, he shoved it away. He had more than enough to deal with on the ranch. And he was done with women. If Ethan couldn't break through to his own sister...well. Just well. Brock wasn't involved.

Crossing his arms, he played at indifference. "How'd she respond to the news?"

"Didn't tell her. Didn't even introduce her to Brandi."

"Why?"

"Because you saw about as much of her as we did." Ethan shoved his hands into his pockets. "It'll keep for tomorrow. She'll have to come back out here though. Unless you're going to give Brandi the day off."

"Wish I could, bro." Truly, he did. The thought of having Cheryl back on his property gave him chills. Literally.

"I know. It'll work out." Ethan shook his head, lifting a hand to rub his hair. "I just have to keep reminding myself. It's going to be fine."

Brock nodded, but not because he felt confident in Ethan's hope. Now he knew why E hadn't told his sister over the phone. Nothing concerning Cheryl Thompson would be easy.

"Sign here." The woman tapped a line at the bottom of the page.
"Why?"
"Because it says that you understand."
I paused. I understood, right? It was okay. Happened all the time.
The woman huffed. "Hurry up."
Tension gripped my shoulders. Rolling them back, I eased it away.
Who wouldn't be nervous? Totally normal. It was going to be fine. With
a good grip on the pen supplied beside the paper, I signed.
Perfectly legal. Which meant it was all okay.

If her room hadn't been dust-free, Cheryl would have sworn it hadn't been touched over the years. The same pictures on the wall, same gray-and-blue spread on her bed. Even her corkboard, tacked with 4H ribbons and her acceptance letter to UCLA, still hung slightly crooked. Exactly as she'd left them.

Cheryl dropped her travel bag—the only luggage she'd unloaded from the rat-mobile's trunk, because she wasn't staying nearly as long as she'd thought—and moved back into the hall.

"Nana?" She lifted her hand to tap on the older woman's door. "Are you okay?"

"Yes, sweet girl, just changing out of these smoky clothes. I love a good campfire, but I don't want to sleep with it." She cackled a laugh, and a few moments later her door opened. She looked Cheryl up and down. "Now, come on, my girl. You didn't even bother changing. How are we going to enjoy a *Dr. Quinn* rerun if you're still stiff in that business outfit? Can't be comfy."

Dr. Quinn wasn't on Cheryl's radar. Who cared if she'd been obsessed with the show back in high school? "I'm sorry, Nana. I just wanted to make sure you're settled in before I go to bed."

"It's only seven thirty."

Cheryl shut her eyes. "I know but..."

"I'm not that old, girl. Come on now. I set back some of my cinnamon knots. We'll douse them with maple frosting. Girl's gotta eat, right?"

Cinnamon knots...oh, so not fair. "I don't indulge the way I used to, Nana."

Nana poked at Cheryl's lower ribs. "I can see that. Ridiculous, child. God did not intend for us to show our skeleton through our skin. Food nourishes our bodies and our spirits. I think yours are both a little too lean."

Cheryl rolled her eyes. "Gluttony is a sin, right?"

"So is self-obsession." Nana raised her eyebrows. "Can't be any fun either."

She wasn't self-obsessed. Everyone she knew counted calories, steps, sleep patterns, work-out intervals... Cheryl looked away, rubbing her neck. How had this conversation happened anyway?

Nana laughed again. "Okay, girl. You live your own way. But, me? I'm too old to submit to self-inflicted torture. I'm having a cinnamon knot and a sit-down on the sofa. I've worked all day doing what the good Lord made me capable of doing, and I've earned it." She patted Cheryl's hand and began to move down the hall. "You're welcome to join me if you decide."

That was that. Nana descended the stairs, and Cheryl moved back to her childhood bedroom. After changing into those comfy clothes Nana had been talking about, she pulled out her tablet and surfed the social networks. Nothing good—situation normal. Candy Crush it was, until she ran out of lives. Then...nothing.

Cheryl stared at the ceiling for over an hour. Sounds from the television drifted from the front room downstairs. *Dr. Quinn*, no doubt. She should have sat with Nana. Shouldn't have bickered about something as stupid as cinnamon knots. Shouldn't have been her normal, icy self.

Why did protecting her heart have to mean wearing this frozen armor?

She didn't know any other way. To warm up would mean to feel again, and to feel again would mean to feel *all* of it again. She couldn't. She would be crushed under the weight.

The closing music signaled the episode's end. Cheryl listened, waiting to hear Nana's shuffled footfalls in the hall. They didn't come, even several minutes after the television fell silent. Sitting up with the covers wrapped around her waist, Cheryl strained to hear.

Snuffling.

She'd made Nana cry.

Setting aside the comforter, Cheryl placed her feet on the floor, pulled a sweater over her head, and moved from her bedroom. After softly descending the stairs, she paused and listened again. This time silence. She crept around the wall dividing the stairway from the front room and found Nana still perched on the sofa, staring at the black TV.

"Nana?"

The older woman didn't stir. Cheryl stepped into the room. Nana sat transfixed. With a hand to her shoulder, Cheryl gave her a small squeeze.

Nana looked up. "Oh, hello there, dearie. Did you find what you needed?"

What?

"We're out of most goods, I'm afraid, but if you come back in the morning, I'll have more cinnamon knots ready." She chuckled, shaking her head. "My granddaughter, she loves those things. She'd eat three or four in one setting, bless her."

"Nana—"

"That's right. You probably don't remember her. She's been away for a while. I keep praying she'll come back, like her brother did, but something happened..." Nana's eyes glazed. "Do you know, sometimes the worst hurts are the ones we can't see?"

Cheryl's heart thudded hard. Nana didn't know. There was no way Nana could know, was there? Breathing suddenly became difficult.

"She'll find her way back." Nana squeezed her hand. "She's a good girl, my little Sherbert is. She'll come home."

Flustered, Cheryl cleared her throat and reached for Nana's elbow. "How about we go to bed?"

Nana looked up, though she still had that far-away quality cloaked over her eyes. "Of course, sweetheart. You know I always go to bed right at nine. Lots of work to do in the morning, and I'm going to keep doing it until they put me into the ground."

"Okay then." Blinking, Cheryl played along, ushering Nana up the stairs and down the hall.

She made sure the woman was secure in her room before she sank back into her own bed. She didn't know which was worse—watching Nana slip into a world of dementia or hearing Nana's point of view about her life.

Shutting her eyes, Cheryl commanded sleep to drape over her consciousness.

As the blackness slowly descended, a single tear slipped from the corner of her eye.

~*~

Cold.

So, so cold. Not the kind that touched her skin. The kind that sank into the marrow of her bones. Into the soul she tried to deny. Gooseflesh covered the whole surface of her body as she moved through the dark passage.

Don't go in...

The voice, always the same, whispered. The feathery breath of whoever was behind her rustled the stray hairs that fell against her neck. It sent a tremor down her spine.

She turned her head, but a hand, hard and insistent, pushed her forward.

Don't...

Despite the warning, her feet—naked, as were her legs—carried her forward anyway. A hand—hers—reached for the single knob on a gray steel door—the only thing she could see in the darkness.

Don't...

She shut her eyes against the voice and turned the knob. The heavy door opened. She opened her eyes, and a harsh, piercing light pushed her into a white blindness. She reached to cover her eyes, but the same hard hands grasped her wrists and held them firmly to her side. Pain ripped through her body. Pain like she'd never known before. Scalding, immeasurable agony seared through her core.

Screaming filled the room, vibrating her skin, filling her ears. Hers. Others. A chorus of agony, of souls being divided and flesh being torn. So loud. Awful and unforgettable.

Cheryl fought against the cruel hands that held her as she tried to cover her ears.

Make it stop. Make it stop. Make it stop...

With a jolt, she sat up. Unconstrained, she felt around her. The bed beneath her. The covers that had been thrown to the side. Her body, shivering and drenched with sweat, but free from anything that would cause pain. Blinking, she sat up and placed her feet on the floor, willing her heart rate to drop back to normal and banishing the wailing echoes that lingered in her ears.

Make it stop. Please make it stop.

She trembled as she reached for her phone. Four thirty a.m. Reasonable enough to get up. She could go for a run, take a long, hot shower, and start her day.

Still shivering, she reached for the bedside lamp and flipped it on. Gentle yellow light flooded the room. Her pulse slowed. Long breath in. Slow breath out. Repeat. She continued until her limbs stopped quivering.

Would this ever end?

She searched for her running clothes in her suitcase, tugged them over her slim frame, and applied tennis shoes to her feet. The run would help. She'd feel the freedom of her own strength and speed, neither of which she'd had in the dream. They would assure her of reality—the dreams were only that. Dreams.

Nightmares. That wouldn't leave her alone.

Run. She'd run. That was the only thing she could do.

You were always there for me. My hero.
But I couldn't face you anymore. If you knew...
I missed you. More than anyone else, I think. We aren't anything alike, you and I. You are the bounce-back kind. I am the shattering type. But we had each other. Even when we didn't have anything else, we had each other.
Over the years, I've wanted to tell you so many times; it wasn't you. The fracture between us was not your fault. I chose the divergent path, and now I can't find my way back.
But I want so desperately for you to know.
I miss you.

~7~

"You know it's not safe to run alone in the dark, right?"

Ethan's voice caught her before she set her foot on the first riser to go upstairs. She'd pulled the earbuds from her ears before she'd come into the house, but the static of music coming from her iPod still scratched near her throat. With one hand, she reached to the opposite arm and tapped the noise off.

"I often run in the early mornings."

"Right." Ethan leaned against the front door and crossed his arms. "Probably in the safety of the gym in your building. Yes?"

Cheryl ground her teeth. "I'm a big girl, E. I can take care of myself."

He stared, his expression hard until he looked away. "At least now I know." He looked back to her again. "Would it kill you to let others—me—care enough about you to worry?"

Five thirty was too early for an argument. "Fine. I run in the mornings. Now you know, so don't let your blood pressure spike." She crossed her arms as she faced him straight on. "What are you doing up?"

"Getting ready to head over to the bakery. Same as always. Nana will be down in a minute."

"About her." She took a step closer. "How long has the dementia thing been going on?"

"You saw that, did you?"

"You could have told me."

"When? You and I, we don't talk. We barely text. I wasn't sure if you'd even care."

Cheryl filled her lungs with air, as if that billow would protect her heart from his sharp words. "Of course I care. You should have told me. How long?"

Sighing, Ethan let his arms fall to his sides and began moving to the kitchen. "Signs have been coming on for over a year. Forgetting orders. Recipes that she's known by heart for years... Nothing really all that concerning until a few months back. Brock came in, and she didn't recognize him. I took her to the doctor the following week. Early stages of Alzheimer's."

Alarms went off in E's head because Nana didn't recognize Brock? Okay, so he'd been a fixture in their home growing up, but he'd also been on the road quite a bit since then. World competitors have a habit of not sticking around.

As she followed Ethan into the kitchen, Cheryl sorted through the oddity of that scenario and decided it didn't matter. "Why'd you decide to tell me now?"

"I told you. I need your help with her."

"Looks to me like you've got it handled."

Ethan crammed a hand through his shaggy hair and then leaned with both palms against the counter on the small kitchen island. "I'm getting married, Cheryl. Next week."

Motion seemed to stop. Married? Married! Ethan wasn't the kind of guy who got married. He'd barely had a relationship that lasted longer than two months. What made him think that he should get married?

He pushed up straight and crossed his arms. The defensive stance. "Look, I know what you're thinking, but you don't even know me. Not who I am now. I'm getting married, and I'm happy. Nana's happy for us too. But the deal is, Brandi is a social worker, and she works with Brock—she's his state liaison—and she has to be on site pretty much twenty-four seven. That means I either continue to live here *without* my wife—which is not even an option—or I take Nana out of the home she's known for the last fifty years, which doesn't seem like a good idea, considering her mental issues."

"Whoa, whoa, whoa. Wait. Are you implying that I *move* here? Live with Nana, *here*?"

Ethan's eyebrows hiked, as if that were the dumbest question ever.

"No." With her fists clenched, Cheryl crossed her arms. "No. No. No."

"That woman practically raised you."

"And she knows I love her, but—"

"Really? How does she know that, Sherbert? By the expensive fruit and wine baskets you send at Christmas? The happy birthday phone calls you managed to fit into your self-centered life? Grow up. There's more to life than the girl you look at in the mirror every morning."

His words pummeled against her like rapid-fire ammo out of an automatic weapon. She pulled up her shield of feigned indifference. "You must have been dying to say that to me."

"No." Shoulders slumped, Ethan leaned back against the sink behind him and looked to the floor. "It kills me that you need to hear it." Slowly, his eyes found hers, and the expression in them threatened to break through her ice. "Where are you, kid? Why'd you leave us?"

Stillness settled between them, and the silence worked with his sincerity, chipping away at her resolve. None of it had been his fault, and if he knew the truth...

No. If he knew the truth, he wouldn't care where she was.

"Look at this." Nana came through the door, smiling. "Both my kids, back home at last." She went first to Cheryl and then to Ethan, patting their arms and planting a kiss against each of their cheeks. "Bless it, today feels like a holiday. Let's go bake something special."

Off they went. One big happy. If only that were true.

If she'd known how much she was going to lose that day that had changed everything, she would have run. But regrets didn't matter when it came to reality. The only choice was to continue pushing forward.

Which left Cheryl with an impossible problem. Hayden was in her past. It couldn't be a part of her future, even if Nana needed her there.

~*~

"Thanks for helping me with this, Brandi." Brock stood from the round table in the lodge where they'd been working. "I'm sorry about all the extra paperwork this week."

"This week?" Brandi snorted, though her smile belied her attempt at irritation. "You have *irregularities* regularly. This is SOP at Kelly's Ranch."

True that. But those irregularities didn't always end up with a medical report to file, along with all of the redundant papers necessary to fill out for Medicaid and CDHS.

Brock finished sorting the papers according to the colorful tabs. Yellow for him, blue to mail to his lawyer—just in case—green for the CDHS office, and red for Medicaid. The small piles looked like a whole lot of pulp for one kid. His mind drifted back to her. So-J. She was one of those kids—the kind that could infuriate him and grip his heart all within two breaths. She had a mouth and a temper. She also had some wreckage in her heart—her eyes told him so. One week didn't do that kind of kid a whole lot of good.

"Can I ask you something?" Brock looked up to Brandi, who stood ready to head for the door.

"Yep."

"Do you ever get calloused?"

"No." She sighed, dropping back into the chair she'd abandoned. "It's tempting, and honestly, I may be more jaded about the world since I started. But when it comes to them, as individuals? No. They still break my heart, and I let them."

He nodded. He'd never felt so deeply about anything as a snowboarder. Nothing touched him the way these kids did—and sometimes he wished he could go back to the safety of ignorance.

"Anything in particular tugging on you?"

He wanted to laugh—the social worker in Brandi never really took a day off.

"Sonja. She was worried that she'd get kicked out of her foster home because she had to go to the doctor." Brock glanced to her. She sat mute, listening. That was what made her good at her job. She listened more than she spoke. "It burns me that she maybe has a real reason to worry, you know? I just wish I could know that these kids would be safe and loved when they leave this place. And if they weren't..."

"We do what we can. One child at a time, Brock."

Sometimes that didn't seem like enough. While one child was safe, loved in a home that was sane and caring, another kid would be subjected to a personal hell the child hadn't asked for and didn't deserve. Where was the justice?

Words wouldn't come. Ranting wouldn't help.

"I'll check up on her, okay?" Brandi reached over and squeezed his shoulder. "I've got a meeting next week anyway. I'll set up a conference with her case worker while I'm there."

"Yeah, about that..."

"I already told you. This is what E and I have decided. We have a lifetime."

Brock lifted an eyebrow. "Kind of seems like a honeymoon is a one-shot deal."

"Not your business." Brandi stood, nailed a look on him that said *discussion closed*, and moved toward the exit. "Ethan and I are fine, so don't worry about it. I'll check on Sonja and get back to you."

He couldn't *not* worry about her and Ethan. Granted, it *wasn't* his business, but Ethan was his best friend, and Brandi had become pretty important to his world as well. When it came to the idea of the two of them married, Brock was all for it. But this no-honeymoon thing? Something in the situation wasn't right.

And then there was the whole So-J deal. Brandi checking on Sonja wasn't really a fix. But it was all they could do. Like the paperwork they'd just finished, it was simply something they had to file.

He hated that part of this job.

"Ethan called." Brandi paused with her hand on the doorframe. "He and his sister are coming out late this afternoon. Are you hanging around?"

For the impending blizzard named Cheryl Thompson? Not if he could help it. "I don't know. Thought I'd go fishing."

Brandi bit her bottom lip and nodded.

No fishing then. Brandi didn't have any reason to feel intimidated, from Brock's perspective. Cheryl didn't scare him. Then again, he wasn't about to become her in-law.

Brock stood and crossed the room. "Cheryl's just a person, same as anyone else."

Her mouth twisted. "True in theory. Ethan worries about her though. More now than even two weeks ago." She looked up, and they connected with a glance. "Last night, when she got here... E hadn't seen her in so long, and when he did..."

"What?" He had doubts about the wedding? That couldn't be it.

"It was like looking at one of the kids." She sighed, and her hand fell to her side. "Did you see it?"

Yeah, he had. "So what does that mean for you and E?"

"I don't know. He didn't see it before, but he lived a different life, was a totally different person the last time they'd been together. Now he sees it, and it scares him. Throwing this little surprise—*hey, guess what? I'm getting married next week*—that might not be the best idea, you know? Not to mention Nana. He didn't tell Cheryl about the issues there, so that's going to be traumatic all by itself. I just don't know how much to push on her, especially at the first meeting."

Hardly seemed fair. It took years for Ethan to pull his life together, and now he was in a good place. And Brandi, she was a gem. Didn't deserve to be thrown into that kind of a mess.

"Look, I know I'm not really qualified on this, but it seems like Cheryl's a grown woman, and she's made her choices every bit as much as Ethan made his. You two are happy, and you shouldn't feel bad about that."

"Yeah. If only life were that simple."

It wasn't. Simple, fair, predictable—life wasn't any of those things.

What about Cheryl's life? Brock remembered the twelve-year-old version of the woman, specifically the day of her mother's funeral. That'd been the first day he'd seen grief look like a shear granite face on the north side of a mountain. He'd been a little shocked, standing next to Ethan, whose silent tears dripped against his face, and watching Cheryl's blue eyes grow cold and distant. The events after that...

Not fair, any of it. But did that mean that Cheryl had the right to rob Brandi's joy?

"You know, hot dogs over a bonfire sound good tonight. Don't you think?" Brock gave Brandi a sympathetic grin, certain she'd understand that his switch in topics really wasn't a turn at all.

"She doesn't strike me as the hot dog type."

He laughed and shrugged. "Her choice. Not our problem. Tell E that we'll have a spread down by the pond around six. Maybe the fire will thaw the ice this time around."

Brandi chuckled. It sounded more like *not likely* than *hope.* Probably because Brandi knew how hard it could be to reach a wounded heart.

So hard, in fact, that most didn't even try.

Cheryl leaned back against the passenger seat as Ethan killed the engine. She wasn't up for this.

"Please, Sherbert. You'll like Brandi. She's amazing."

Of course she was. "Stop calling me that."

"Look." Ethan moved so that he could face her. "I know I threw a ton of stuff on you today, and I probably should have told you before. But that's not Brandi's fault. It's mine. I just didn't know how to handle this...and I really want you there."

"Don't lie to me, Ethan. You called because you need me to step in with Nana. Wanting me at your wedding wasn't even a thought in your head."

His expression fell, as if her words hurt. "Cheryl, you're my sister— my only family besides Nana. How could you think that?"

"We could count ten years' worth of conversations on two hands, Ethan. Don't pretend like we're close."

"Are you okay with that?"

Cheryl looked away. Outside her window, Brock moved down by the pond. Stacking wood, getting ready to light a fire. At least she wouldn't be the third wheel.

To her left, the door to the lodge opened, catching Cheryl's attention. A woman with rich toffee-colored skin and thick brown hair carried a tray piled with hot dog fixings.

"Is that her?"

Ethan moved again, ducking to see out Cheryl's window.

"Yeah. That's Brandi." A love-sick smile carried through his voice.

Yuck. And so not fair. "Kind of young, don't you think?"

He snorted. "Twenty-five."

Cheryl raised an eyebrow on him. "That means that she would have been learning to read when you were learning to drive."

"Good grief, Cheryl." Ethan shook his head and opened his car door. "Is being difficult one of your life goals? Brandi's awesome, and I love her."

His car door slapped shut before she reached to unlatch her seat belt. She watched while he strode toward the perky girl who smiled all gooey at him. After taking the tray from her hands, he leaned to kiss her. A very *Leave It to Beaver* moment.

Loneliness suddenly seeped around her, cloaking her with its heavy chill. Cheryl wrapped her arms around herself and shut her eyes.

You're fine. You do fine on your own.

She inhaled, pushing down emotions that should've died years before, and opened her eyes. A glance toward the fire pit, where Ethan and Brandi had walked, told her that Brock was watching her.

Figure that one. After all these years, there was Brock the Jock, King of the Slopes, calculating the best way to score.

Like Ethan would stand for it. He never did. Such a double standard her brother had kept. He didn't think twice about playing the girls, but when it came to her and his friends... She'd made it through high school a virgin largely because none of the guys in their town wanted to face Ethan if they messed with his sister.

Every girl should have a big brother. If only he'd followed her to college.

Brock continued to stare. What was he thinking? Maybe he figured Ethan wouldn't care anymore.

Cheryl sat for a moment longer, doing some calculating of her own. Flings weren't out of her playbook anymore. As a girl, innocent and hoping for that Cleaver kind of life somewhere down the road, she'd been entirely opposed to the shallowness of a short-lived blaze. Now, as a woman with her eyes wide open, she'd stepped into a handful of fizzling romances with full understanding.

True, she'd felt used and worthless afterward. Every time. But still...being wanted, even just for a while, was something.

Some women just weren't the June Cleaver kind.

Flipping the visor down, Cheryl checked the mirror. Not stunning, not like she would be if she'd planned this. But pretty. At least she always had that. Men often couldn't care less about education or accomplishments, but beauty? That always mattered.

Ready or not...

Brock kept his distance, though he said hi. Like he was taking a backseat.

Ethan stepped forward, his arm anchored on the other woman's waist. "Cheryl, this is Brandi, my fiancée."

Most people would paint up a brilliant smile and gush. Cheryl was not most people. She pushed out a hand, as if this were a professional engagement. "How nice to meet you."

Brandi accepted the gesture, looked into Cheryl's eyes, paused, and then moved in for a hug. "I'm so delighted to meet you. Ethan has often talked about his successful younger sister. I can't wait for us to become friends."

Cheryl was pretty sure she'd just been professionally analyzed. With her back stiff, she patted the woman's shoulder and then stepped away.

A stinging sensation alerted her to a mosquito drilling into her neck. Cheryl smacked it. Things she didn't miss about this life...bugs, and the ever-present feeling that she was always on the fringe of everything.

She stood straighter. "Ethan failed to mention you until last night, so I know nothing about you."

A hacking sound disturbed the air behind her as Brock cleared his throat. "I think we've got a good bit of heat going here. We can start on the hot dogs."

Ethan jumped at the distraction, skewering dogs and distributing pretend meat on a stick. When he pushed one at Cheryl, she waved him off. "I'm not hungry."

"Not hungry? We haven't eaten since noon."

"I grabbed something before we left Nana's." A lie. But those things were not good for you, no matter how delicious they tasted.

"You love this."

Loved. Past tense. "Let it go, E. I don't want one." She swatted another mosquito attacking her shoulder.

Brandi took the roasting stick and set it down. "I have some salad fixings in my apartment, if you'd rather, Cheryl."

She'd rather the hot dog. "That's not necessary. I'm fine."

"It's no trouble. I live in the lodge, just below the dining hall there, so I'll be right back."

Ethan set his stick down on the rocked fire ring and followed Brandi. "I'll help. Sorry, Cheryl."

They took off, leaving Cheryl alone with Brock, who'd stood at a distance during the exchange. She glanced at him, and he shook his head.

"That wasn't exactly the introduction Brandi was hoping for."

"What does that mean?"

"She was really nervous about meeting you. Think you could thaw out for your brother's sake?"

Cheryl raised an eyebrow. This was his tactic? *Good luck, buddy.*

With a small shake of his head, he snorted. "So you went away to school, became some chip-on-her-shoulder lawyer, and now you can't find it in your heart to be nice for your brother. I'd say you moved backward in life, Sherbert."

"I told you not to call me that."

He smirked.

Another pesky sting jabbed her arm. She slapped it. Hard.

"Here." Brock leaned toward the ground near an Adirondack chair and stood up with a spray bottle in his hand. "Don't be stingy with it. We're by the water here."

Cheryl took the unlabeled spray and inspected it. "This stuff could kill you. I'm not putting it on my skin."

Brock laughed. "Know what could really kill you? A mosquito."

She pinned him with a glare.

"Not kidding. Take a guess at what the most deadly creature on the planet is."

Not going for it, pal.

"Hey, E," Brock called up the path, "name the creature responsible for more human deaths than any other on God's green earth."

Cheryl glanced up the road. Ethan and Brandi strode side by side, Ethan carrying a plastic container, and Brandi with two bottles of dressing in her fists.

"The mosquito," Ethan called back.

Cheryl crossed her arms. "Liars."

Brock lifted a shoulder. "Google it."

She looked from Ethan to Brock to Brandi.

The other woman reached Cheryl's side, holding out the bottles for Cheryl to choose. "They're not lying."

Cheryl looked at her options. Ranch and Thousand Island. Both loaded with fatty calories. She twisted her mouth and took the ranch.

"Just use the spray, Sherbert. I promise you'll thank me later."

Ugh. Brock hadn't changed at all. Pushy and relentless.

"What'd I tell you about my name?"

He laughed.

Not what she'd expected from Brock Kelly. Could be a long night.

~*~

She applied the repellent. Shocking.

Brock told himself not to smirk, but his expression didn't obey. What a little punk Cheryl had become. What happened to the shy girl he'd known back in high school?

"So, this wedding..." Cheryl lifted a condescending look to her brother.

Ethan didn't let her rankle him. He planted an arm around Brandi's waist, drew her close, and met Cheryl's stare dead on. "Here. Next weekend."

"Is there a reason you're so rushed?"

Brandi's skin turned crimson.

"Crimony, Sherbert." Brock crossed his arms. Yes. He just called her Sherbert. Again. "Did you lose all your people skills?"

Ethan rubbed his neck. "Look, this is my fault. I should have told you." He looked at Cheryl with a pleading expression. "We've been engaged for months. I just so badly wanted you to be here, and—"

"And you thought baiting me with Nana was better than telling me the truth?"

The air held with a frozen moment of tension.

"I don't know how to reach you anymore, Cheryl. I didn't know what else to do."

With a sad shake of his head, he moved away from the group. Brandi followed, glancing at Brock with a helpless expression.

What a disaster. Probably would have been better if Ethan had let Cheryl miss the big event.

So sad.

Ethan and Brandi wandered down the road. Brock watched as her arm slid around Ethan's waist and he tipped down to press a kiss into her hair. They didn't deserve this.

"Wow." Brock moved his attention from the couple to Cheryl. "You *are* something."

She turned ice daggers on him. "Forget this. I'm gone."

"Yeah? Plan on walking?"

After glancing up to the car Ethan had brought her in, she patted her jeans pockets. Couldn't get anywhere without keys. She looked back at Brock.

He shook his head. "Nope. You made your little ice castle—you can just sit here and wait until Ethan's ready to go home. Could be a while, since this is the first night off Brandi's had in a week. Might as well make yourself comfortable."

Cheryl glared, drew a long breath, and then plopped onto a chair. Like a twelve-year-old.

Brock went back to his hot dog, because what else was he supposed to do with an ice queen sitting at his fire? Man, she was some kind of bitter. Where'd that come from?

He glanced back at her and caught that look. The one he'd seen the night before, the one Brandi had also noticed. Hollowness shadowed her glassy eyes, and Brock's resentment crumbled.

"You really don't eat hot dogs anymore?" He forced a friendlier tone than he'd yet managed that night.

Cheryl shrugged.

"Come on. You used to put down just as many as we did." He moved to sit in the chair next to hers. "What happened?"

"They're not good for you. I won't pollute my body with something that isn't real food."

"Ah...do you not understand? Whatever enters the body from the outside is not what defiles a person. It goes into the stomach and out, into the sewer, not into the heart."

Cheryl tilted her face to him. "What?"

"Jesus's words. Not mine."

"What's that supposed to mean?"

"I think it means you should worry about what you allow into your heart and out of your mouth more than what you put into your stomach."

Her jaw worked as her expression turned cold again. "I don't remember you being a Bible quoter."

"True enough. I don't remember you being an ice princess." He tossed the roaster, minus his hot dog, toward the fire pit and scooted back into his chair. "Tell you what—I'll tell if you will."

"Tell what?"

"What happened. Why I'm not the same."

She snorted. "Not sure that's a fair deal."

So there was a story. Not that he doubted. "We'll see."

Her eyes lifted to him. "I guess I am curious. Shouldn't you be king of the slopes somewhere?"

Brock chuckled. "Well, it is May, you know."

"Off-season never stopped you from training."

"True." He sat so that he could lean against his knees. "I was for a while. Maybe you already knew that. Even made it to the Olympics. Then, a few years back, I took a trip on sort of a dare from my dad. Went to Mexico. It changed my life."

"A dare changed your life?"

"No—an orphanage."

Cheryl raised an eyebrow, a look that said she wasn't buying it. "You visited an orphanage, decided you liked kids, and opened a camp where people could dump their children for a week? Very noble."

Brock held her gaze, silently challenging her. She'd find out on her own, and in the meantime, she could think what she wanted.

"Well? Does that sum it up?"

"Your turn."

"What?"

Settling against the backrest, he propped his hands behind his neck. "I've shared part of my story. It's your turn."

"Your story wasn't that interesting."

He tilted his head. "Is yours?"

Her eyes darted away, and that shadow fell over her features again. Somehow that made Brock's heart squeeze.

Cheryl sat in silence, staring at the fire as the evening gathered in a soft gray around them. When she finally spoke, it was with a quiet tone.

"This isn't a tourist dump, is it?"

"No."

Her chin dipped toward her chest. "What is it?"

Brock examined her, wishing she was readable, but not knowing why. "We bring in foster kids—kids that need a place to go short term for whatever reason."

"How long do they stay?"

"Usually for a week—foster families take vacations and can't take the kids with them, so they come here. Respite care. Placement issues. Sometimes, though, kids have other things come up, so it depends on the situation."

She processed, picking at her nails. "That's...unexpected."

"Right? Never thought I'd get here, did you?"

Though her eyes held a smidge of guilt, she looked at him directly. "No. I didn't."

Brock held her gaze, letting a small grin tug on his lips. She didn't duck away, and her blunt honesty drew him.

"Your turn," he nearly whispered.

She looked away.

"That was the deal, kid." He reached over and shook her shoulder. "What happened to the nice, shy girl we used to know?"

"Life."

"That's not very telling." Actually, it was—it could be. Life could really hand out the blows.

She turned back to him, a pasted smile on her face. "You know what? I haven't had a hot dog in years."

She stood and moved for the roasting stick he'd pitched earlier and began to fumble with the package of Ball Parks. Her hands trembled, and Brock's heart dropped.

Whatever had happened, it had to have been awful.

~9~

Planting her fists on her hips, Cheryl scowled at Nana. "Why didn't Ethan take them with him?" She brushed the grainy moisture from her face. She'd forgotten how sweaty and gritty she'd become after a morning in the bakery. Didn't miss it either.

"They weren't done." Nana finished placing the last of the six-dozen rolls into a box.

"He could have waited."

Nana leaned against the counter and smiled at Cheryl. "But he didn't."

"Well, he can take them out to the ranch later. I don't need to run to Brock Kelly's just to deliver rolls."

"We always deliver to Brock, and he's got a group of kids to feed tonight." Nana straightened and patted Cheryl's cheek. "Off you go. Play nice."

"No, wait." The excuses were running thin, but this last one would be the winner. "What if you have another episode?"

Nana grinned. "Ethan heads out to the camp five days a week, and he leaves me here while he's gone. Don't worry, love. I've got people looking after me."

And so Cheryl's presence was...pointless. *Busted, E.* The charade was up.

"Go on, girl." Nana pushed the stack of bakery boxes into Cheryl's arms. "And I mean it about being nice. Brock's a good man."

Cheryl let the insinuation hang. Not worth arguing about. Growling under her breath, she held her gaze on Nana for longer than necessary and then spun toward the door. It took less than five minutes to pile the boxes of fresh-out-of-the-oven rolls into the backseat of her car. She moved to the driver's door, but an itch on her shoulder gave her pause.

She had at least fifteen welts covering her arms. Mosquito bites. Turns out Brock had been telling the truth—she'd Googled *deadliest animal on the planet.* Yep. The mosquito. Followed by man. Interesting, if not appalling, and apparently not a pair of useless facts. Shutting the door she'd held partially open, she crossed Main Street—which doubled as the highway—to the Outdoor Adventures shop. Surely they'd have a strong repellent.

Her side trip took ten minutes, because old Harvey recognized her and thought they should catch up. Keeping her answers vague and short, Cheryl let him think she was glad to be back and then made an exit with the excuse that "Nana really needs this errand done right away." Armed with the strongest bug spray Harvey stocked, she set her little rental toward Kelly's Ranch.

The grounds were quiet as Cheryl pulled in. Where were all these children who had apparently revamped Brock's priorities?

It took a bit of a circus act to arrange the six boxes first onto the hood of her car and then in her hands, which made her glad no one was around, no matter how mysterious the emptiness of the place was. Making her way into the lodge was a whole other show. She hooked a finger around the pull on the main doors, tugged until she could slide a foot into the passage, and then shimmied herself, plus boxes, through the passage that seemed eager to shut.

"Hello?" she called into the dining hall.

Nothing.

"Delivery here. Fresh bread." She continued moving toward the doors at the back of the large room. Surely they led to the kitchen. She paused at the swinging doors, taking another look around. Nobody home.

Whatever. She'd leave the bread and go back to town.

Using her backside, she pushed into the swinging doors.

The kitchen sat empty. Stainless steel counters stretched across the work area, spotless as they gleamed under the florescent lights. She moved to the closest end and unloaded her awkward delivery. Boxes secure on the counter, Cheryl paused to inhale the doughy goodness. So tempting...

"Whatcha got there?"

A scream escaped from Cheryl's throat before she could swallow it.

Brock laughed, moving toward her from the back door Cheryl hadn't noticed.

"Jumpy?"

"Brock, you jerk." Fists curled at her side, Cheryl silently told her pulse to calm down.

"Jerk?" He continued to chuckle. "I live here, remember? You're the one breaking and entering."

"Am not. No one answered, and Nana insisted that you needed these rolls now."

"That was quite a performance, getting that stack of boxes in here all on your own."

Punk. "Nice. Thanks for the help."

"And miss the show? Never." Brock stepped closer. Grinning, he gripped her shoulders and leaned around her to inhale. "Hot out of the oven? That's a nice changeup."

"Don't they always come fresh?"

He snorted. "No."

Nana. The little stinker. Cheryl ground her teeth. Heat crawled up her neck, which was irritating. "Okay, well this has been fun. Bye."

"Wait." He stopped her retreat with a hand on hers. "Where are you going?"

"Back."

"Why the hurry?"

Was he setting a play now? After he'd completely insulted her the night before? She stared at him.

"Come on. You need some fresh air." His hand still on hers, he tugged until she took a step toward him.

"Where is everyone?"

He led her out the back door he'd sneaked through, holding it until Cheryl hit the outdoors. "Ethan and Brandi have the kids out on a hike. It's my morning off."

Bet Nana knew that too. "What do you do with your morning off?"

"Fish."

Ew. "Uh, no thanks."

"You need to chill, girl." He paused, flashing a thoughtful look her way. "Actually, no. You need to warm up. Sunshine would help."

Did this seriously work for him? "Your version of humor isn't really funny."

He shrugged as they reached the corner of the lodge closest to Gramps's old cabin. His gear waited, a long pole leaning up against the building and a tackle vest lying on the ground.

"Come on. What's the worst that could happen? You'll get a tan from real rays, and I can tell Ethan that his pathetic attempt at a setup was tried and proved to be a sad failure."

"I think this was Nana's doing."

One corner of his mouth lifted. With raised brows, he tipped his head in the direction of the pond.

Cheryl sighed. "Fine. Let me grab my sunglasses." And bug spray.

Brock nodded and reached for his gear. Catching his smirk, Cheryl wondered if he'd been in on the scheme as well.

Fishing indeed.

~10~

Figure that. She said yes. And what was he thinking asking her, anyway? Fishing was supposed to be relaxing. Having Cheryl the winter-storm-of-the-century along would certainly be anything but.

Brock inhaled, long and deep. Nana was some kind of nuts, even without the dementia at work. Who in their right—or alternative mind—would pair him with Cheryl Thompson? Rubbing the back of his neck, he looked back up to the car she'd driven, where she was dousing herself with spray.

Ha. That was a quick one-eighty. Brock chuckled. Guess little miss know-it-all didn't know everything. He set his fishing gear down on the dock and walked over to the fire pit. She'd probably appreciate a chair. Not that he expected her to stay long. But maybe a little sit in the sunshine would do her some good. And then, when Ethan asked, because he was definitely in on this scheme, Brock could say, *She just sat there for ten minutes and then left. End of story.*

He lifted one of the Adirondacks and walked it over to the dock. Placing it on the back left, opposite side of his casting arm, he stood upright and watched Cheryl walk down the path toward him.

She *was* pretty. Dark hair hanging loose to dance in the mountain breeze. Eyes the color of the wild blue geraniums that grew along the hiking paths.

Pretty, yes. She knew it too. He'd seen her in E's car the other night, preening like a cat after she'd caught him looking at her. Like she knew exactly what he was thinking. He hadn't been thinking any of those lustful thoughts she'd obviously assumed were going through his head. He'd been wondering why she left and never looked back.

Cheryl stepped onto the dock, bringing with her a spray bottle and a heavy scent of Deet.

"So you believe me about the mosquitoes, do you?"

She dropped onto the chair. "They ate me alive the other night. Not fun."

"Tried to warn you. What did you use? You stink."

Her eyebrows lifted. "Just what you said: bug spray."

"Huh. Guess you mean to keep every insect away within a two-mile radius."

"Exactly."

Brock shrugged out of his hoodie, slid his vest over his T-shirt, and pulled his pole upright. After he selected a fly that hopefully matched the latest hatch, he tugged the end of the line loose.

"You want a go at this?" He spoke without looking at her.

"Fishing?"

He nodded.

"No. My dad took me once, when I was little. Said every fisherman had to bait their own hook. Not my thing."

"Let me guess—you used worms." He looked over his shoulder at her.

She wrinkled her nose. "Never again."

He turned back to the hook he was working on. "Well, if you change your mind, I use flies—the fake kind. I tie them myself."

Silence.

She wasn't really thinking about it, was she? *Me and my big mouth.*

Brock glanced back to her. She sat on the edge of her chair, rubbing both arms.

"You okay?"

Her attention snapped to him. "Yeah. These stupid bites are really annoying. I think the bug spray may have made it worse."

"Don't scratch them."

She dropped her hands and leaned back against the chair. "Okay, smart guy. I do know *some* things."

Clearly. He finished with the fly and shimmied the pole until he cradled the handle in his palm. "Sure you don't want a try?" *Why was he still offering?!*

"Definitely sure."

Good. Feeding the line, he began the rhythmic swings, casting like Gramps had taught him when he was a boy. He completed the first set and began jigging the line with a delicate touch, when Cheryl started fidgeting again.

He didn't even look. "Don't do it. It'll get worse."

She kept moving—he could hear her squirming against the wood of the chair.

"You'll scar."

"Oh my gosh!" Her howl punctured the air.

"Cheryl! You'll scare the fi—" Brock glanced back and froze.

Cheryl stood—no, danced on the dock in front of her chair, her arms flailing around as she moved to brush at every exposed part of her skin. She'd worn jeans, but her tank top left plenty of surface area to cover.

"Are you okay?"

She continued to wiggle, moving like she was desperate to get away from an invisible attack. "My skin is on fire!"

Brock set down his pole and moved toward her dance floor. The bottle of bug spray she'd used sat on the arm of her chair next to her phone. He grabbed it, reading the label.

"Good grief, kid. Where did you get this?"

"Harvey, at Outdoor Adventures."

"You might as well dump lighter fluid on your skin."

She locked her eyes on him, a mixture of anger and tears in her eyes. "You said to use bug spray."

"*My* bug spray. Not this." He looked her over again. Fiery red streaks smattered her arms like graffiti. "You're probably allergic."

Her hands continued to rub at her shoulders, neck, and arms. Though her lips pressed tight together, a throaty noise—something like a muffled scream—escaped.

The red on her skin kept darkening, spreading.

Brock glanced around, his eyes settling on the water gently lapping against the dock. He'd never hear the end of it, but maybe if he went in with her...

Did it even matter?

Decision made, he wrapped her in a bear hug, and though she fought against him for the two backward steps it took for him to reach the edge of the dock, he held tight and launched off of the wood landing.

The cold water hit like a jolt of ice, and he let go of her as soon as they were submerged. When he surfaced, she was already flailing at the top, gasping for air.

She remembered how to swim, right?

Two strong strokes and he was right next to her again.

"Don't touch me, you jerk." She shoved water at his face.

"Can you swim?"

She calmed her fight against the water. "Yes, I can swim," she snapped.

He kicked away from her. "Good. Get that junk off of your arms and neck before you get out."

After reaching the dock, he hooked both palms on the wood surface and launched upward, lifting himself out of the cold water.

Man, wet jeans were heavy. And his tackle vest? He'd have to empty it completely to make sure nothing rusted—which the tack probably would anyway—and it would take hours to dry it out.

He kicked his sopping shoes off by his pole and finished reeling in the line. Fishing. With Cheryl. Great idea.

Her hands appeared over the edge of the dock, and a feminine grunt accompanied the noise of splashing water. The top of her head bobbed up and then fell, followed by another telling splash.

Brock snorted.

She tried again. Small squeak of a grunt, glimpse of her dark hair, and then a splash.

He laughed.

"Shut up." Her voice darted from the surface of the water.

"Do you need help?"

No response.

With his wet pant legs rustling against themselves, Brock moved to the edge of the dock and squatted. Cheryl glared up at him. He couldn't help but smirk.

"We tell the kids that we say *help please* when we need something."

She continued to shoot flares of indignant hatred from her eyes.

"Okay. Well then, good luck." He began to stand.

"Get me out of here."

Eyebrows raised, he looked back at her. "What was that?"

Her lips trembled.

"Are you crying?"

"No. It's cold."

That was true. Mountain ponds never warmed up much, and it was only the end of May. They could still get snow.

"Would you like out?"

"Brock!"

"Ask nicely."

She looked away, swallowed, and looked back at him. "Please get me out." Every word was ground out like it was pure torture.

He moved to kneel on the dock and reached for her arms. With a secure grip, he lifted, coming to his feet as she emerged from the water. Once her feet were secure on the dock, he let go and turned away.

Interesting catch.

Probably his only catch of the day. Fish weren't going to be biting for a while, not after that ruckus.

He ran a hand through his hair, shaking out the water, before he began gathering his gear. A quick glance back told him Cheryl hadn't moved. He stood again, hands on his hips, ready to lecture her for being such a brat.

Her arms wrapped tight around her body, she stood dripping wet and shivering.

"Hey. You okay?"

She didn't answer.

"Cheryl, did you get hurt?"

She shook her head. "I hate being cold."

Something in her voice caught his heart. It was almost like a call for help—not just for that moment, but for something deeper. An ice princess who hated being cold. Maybe there was more to that...

Brock looked around, and his attention landed on the sweatshirt he'd shed before he'd put on his fishing vest. The zip-up hoodie wasn't much, but it was better than nothing. He snagged it, draped it over her shoulders, and began rubbing her arms.

She continued to shiver under his hands. Without thinking, he pulled her against his chest, wrapping his arms around her. Though she remained stiff, she didn't push away.

Suddenly he remembered how pretty she was. Those geranium-colored eyes. The wavy dark hair that now hung down her back, rivulets of water racing down the glossy strands. And if she smiled...

What a dumb thing to think about.

He stepped back, moving his hands to her shoulders. "Better?"

"Yes."

"And the stinging...did you get all the bug spray off?"

"Yes." She shivered again.

It was pretty chilly standing there dripping wet. Dry clothes would help.

"Come on. I've got some sweatpants that have a drawstring. Unless you'd rather stay in your soaked jeans?"

She shook her head and moved beside him.

He couldn't resist pulling her under one arm. Just to keep her warm.

~*~

Brock had given her a towel and led her to his spare bedroom. Cheryl stood in the middle near the bed, shivering while she waited for him to reappear with some dry clothes. So awkward.

She couldn't quell the trembling. Cold, yes. But the chill was more than physical. Brock saw her...into the deep places. She could feel it, and the sensation terrified her.

"So, you'll need to cinch them up tight." Brock's voice came from just outside the door before he reappeared in the bedroom. "They're bound to cause some embarrassment if you don't. Fall right off your malnourished little self."

Heat penetrated her cold cheeks. Brock grinned, letting her know that he could see her blush, and winked.

"I am not malnourished."

He scanned her body, head to toe, and raised his eyebrows. "You could definitely use some more hot dogs." That ornery smirk of his poked a dimple into his cheek.

"Why do you care what I eat?"

"Why are you so easily provoked?"

Cheryl glared and held out a hand, which quivered.

He didn't pass her the clothes. "You're really freezing, aren't you?"

"That pond isn't exactly a hot spring."

"No. It isn't. Why don't you hop in the shower? I've got to head over to the lodge, so feel free to take all the hot water you want."

Cheryl imagined the conversation with Nana later, starting with Nana asking why she came home in Brock's sweats. Add a hot shower at his place into that dialog. That'd be perfect. Of course, Nana had started this whole disastrous affair. Hot rolls indeed.

"I just need dry clothes."

Brock shrugged, tossing the sweats onto the bed. "Suit yourself, stubborn." He turned and moved out the door, talking as he went. "There's always hot coffee at the lodge when you're ready. Or not. Whatever, Sherbert."

"That's not my name."

His chuckle reached her hearing as he continued away from the room.

Infuriating man.

She ripped the towel from her shoulders, tossing it to the floor as she moved to smack the door shut. Her fingers found the button of her jeans, and she began peeling the wet denim from her soaked body. Hopping on one foot with the waistband wrapped around her knees, she tugged the skinny opening over her foot. The heavy fabric folded over on itself and stuck.

"Dang it," she mumbled. "Come off." She gave it another strong tug and thought the fabric gave. It was too late before she realized that she wasn't free of the wet captivity, and as she attempted to set her foot down, the rumpled legs of her pants caught on the waistband.

"No, no, no!" Her arms whipped the air like a pair of windmills, but she couldn't regain her balance. Crashing to the floor, she landed on her hip and groaned in pure irritation.

Tapping sounded on the bedroom door. "You okay in there?"

She looked up from her sprawled-out position on the floor and speared her side of the door with a look as if she could see the man on the other side. "I thought you went to the lodge."

"So you're good?"

"I'm fine."

"Okeydokey, Sherbert. I'm going now. Try not to destroy my house."

"Brock, you idiot."

His laughter came loud and clear through the door. "I'm not the one falling all over the place. Good luck, kid."

"You're so irritating!"

His chuckle moved away from the door and grew fainter as he left the house. Was it possible for this day to get worse?

She stayed on the floor to tug her legs free of the jeans. Gooseflesh rippled over her body, and she shivered again. The report of the front door opening and closing signaled Brock's departure. The house was hers alone. That hot shower sounded better and better with every passing moment. She snatched the towel lying limp on the floor, stood on her bare legs, and wrapped the damp terrycloth around herself. Cracking the door, she peeked through the opening, just to double-check. The hall stood empty. After another check both ways, Cheryl darted from the bedroom to the only bathroom in the house, through the door across from hers.

She secured the lock and spun to face the shower. Laid out on the vanity to her right was a fresh towel, a small bar of red-and-white striped soap, and a note.

Take your time, Sherbert.

Why did he insist on calling her that?

She flicked the note aside and grasped the small round soap, bringing it to her nose. The zesty aroma of cranberries filled her senses. With her eyes closed, she inhaled again.

Why did Brock have a girly bar of smelly soap in his house? Weird.

She'd ask him. Right after a long, hot shower.

~11~

Brock set the last of his fishing tackle on the picnic table, which was currently bathed in sunshine. Hopefully, it'd all dry quickly and he wouldn't have to be irritated with Cheryl about ruining his gear.

He wouldn't be irritated with her either way, and he knew it.

Man, though, that woman was one long run of bad mood. He'd never known her to be such a snippety grump when they were in high school. Actually, he remembered thinking she was kind of sweet...

He rubbed his forehead and turned toward the lodge. Cheryl had already occupied too much of his day. He didn't need to give her real estate in his mind on top of the messed-up morning they'd just shared. His one day off, and she showed up. *Thanks for that, Ethan.*

Stepping from his deck, Brock moved toward the lodge. His progress stalled when he came to Cheryl's car. It leaned at a telling lopsided angle. He wandered to the rear passenger side and looked down. Yep. Flat. He couldn't stop the growl that rumbled his chest.

Coffee first. And lunch. He rubbed his neck and blew out a breath. Changing a tire wasn't that big of a deal.

Cheryl would cross her arms and scowl. That'd be fun.

Maybe if he made her some lunch—something other than hot dogs—it would soften the inconvenience and she'd take it better.

With his mind set on a plan, he finished his trek to the kitchen. The scent of fresh rolls greeted him, and some of the tension in his shoulders drained. Bread, cheese, and oranges. Surely she'd be good with that menu. Maybe she'd even say thank you.

He wouldn't count on it.

He had two plates loaded with sliced cheddar-jack and rolls and was running a knife through a couple of oranges, when Cheryl pushed through the back kitchen door.

"How was the shower?" He grinned without looking at her.

"Hmm. Think you're pretty smart, don't you?"

He thought he'd been fairly nice, leaving her a clean towel and some soap one of the cabin leaders had left behind several weeks back. Guess she could take it for whatever she wanted.

"Thank you." Her soft voice came close behind him.

He stopped cutting and froze for a moment. A faint smell of sweet cranberries mingled with the aroma of the oranges he'd been cutting, and he couldn't resist a long breath. Glancing over his shoulder, he found she stood behind him, fidgeting with the cuff of the sweatshirt she wore and looking toward her feet.

Not what he'd expected. He set the knife onto the cutting board and turned.

"You're welcome."

Cheryl looked up and lifted a hand to push her damp hair off her face. It was there again, that vulnerable expression he'd seen at the bonfire the other night. The one that pulled on his heart. Without thinking, Brock took in her whole appearance. She looked tiny, swallowed up in his sweatpants and hoodie. Small, and completely adorable. With the almost timid expression in her pale-blue eyes, he could nearly imagine that she was the girl he faintly remembered—his best friend's little sister, whom he might have had a bit of a crush on.

No he hadn't. Had he? Couldn't remember, and it didn't matter anyway.

He cleared his throat and turned back to the counter. "Are you hungry? I'm starving, so I thought maybe you'd try eating today..."

"Please stop."

He looked over his shoulder at her. She'd folded her arms over her chest, and the softness that had been in her eyes hardened. They locked gazes for a breath, and then he dipped a small nod. No more picking at her food aversions. Maybe he should quit trying to irritate her all together. He couldn't define why he was doing it in the first place, and whatever the reason, it was bound to be a childish one.

"I'm almost done here, and we can eat." He picked up the knife and started back on the oranges.

"Did you say there was coffee somewhere?"

Brock nodded toward the sink opposite where he worked. She slipped around him to pour herself a mug.

"Do you want some?"

There was that unexpected soft voice again.

"Yeah, I'd take a cup." He divided the orange slices between the plates and then scooped them up.

She finished pouring him coffee, and they both moved to the swinging door that led into the large dining hall. Brock used his back to push the door open and held it while she passed in front of him. Again, a faint hint of sweet cranberries tickled his nose.

Cheryl stopped two feet into the room and scanned the smattering of tables dotting the large space. "Where to?"

"Did you get warm enough?"

She smiled—a real one, not a sarcastic, snotty version. "Mostly. Coffee should finish the job."

Brock tilted his head toward the large stone fireplace on the opposite wall. "I can build a fire, if you want."

Her attention left him as she examined the room, slowly taking in the log walls, wide picture windows, the fireplace, and finally settling on the piano. "Quite a place you've made here."

"Thank you." His chest expanded. Who knew Cheryl's mild approval would matter?

She continued to gaze at the piano.

It wasn't anything special—the instrument had been a hand-me-down from a place over in Steamboat. Brock brought it in because he thought the kids might enjoy plunking on it every now and then. Sometimes they did. Usually it was more like pounding on it, which he typically ended with a quick redirection outdoors. Once in a while, though, one of the kids would sit down and play. The beat-up old thing needed tuned badly, but when those young fingers could summon music from the keys, it didn't matter. He always heard the beauty in the music, not the flaws wrought from neglect and abuse.

Brock moved forward, stopping beside her. "I remember you playing."

Her attention flew up to him. "You do?"

"Yep." He grinned, heat tickling his cheeks. "I used to hang around, just to see if you would."

"You did not."

Actually, he had. Hadn't thought about it in years, but in that moment, his memory produced a vivid picture of Cheryl sitting at the upright piano in Nana's house. She'd looked happy, lost in the melodies as she slipped into the oblivion of song. He'd remembered wanting to sit next to her on the bench, to watch her fingers as they magically turned notes into music.

Strange memories to dwell on after he'd just thrown her into the pond. Especially since nothing—well, not much of anything—about the grown-up version of Cheryl Thompson was endearing. That was a puzzling contradiction...

Not really his concern. Brock led the way to the table nearest the fireplace, and they settled onto chairs opposite each other.

"Do you still play?" he asked.

"No." The single syllable came short and cold.

"But I thought Nana gave you the piano?"

"I sold it." She wouldn't look at him. Instead, her focus moved from the food on her plate to the window over his shoulder. "Life changed."

"Yes. I can see that."

Her gaze collided with his and held. The hollow sadness in her eyes reached into his chest and gripped his heart. He didn't know what to do with it, but he was certain that few saw what he'd just glimpsed.

Panic suddenly filled him, and he looked away. The last time God revealed something so plainly and powerfully like that, it had been a calling that upended his life.

No. And that was stupid anyway. Considering a parallel between Cheryl and that moment in Mexico was presumptuous. Ridiculous.

"Tell you what." Brock pushed against the tug of fear. "How about we pray, then I'll build that fire."

"Don't worry about it. I'll head back to town when we're done."

"Well...that could be a problem." He lifted his mug and sipped the hot coffee. "You've got a flat."

"What?"

"The rear passenger tire on your car. It's completely flat."

She pushed up from her seat and marched to the window. As predicted, she crossed her arms and scowled. "That's awesome."

"Well don't get all frosty about it." Brock thunked his mug back onto the table. See? Clearly no parallel between God's clear redirection in Mexico and whatever kept nudging him about this woman. She was simply a pain. The end. "I'll fix it. Just let me eat first."

Her mouth twisted to one side. "Fine."

Fine? How about *thanks?*

Brock choked down a growl. Cheryl could handle her own life. His was completely full—didn't have room in it for a spoiled woman who'd apparently forgotten all of the manners he knew she'd been raised with. That whole calling thing? He'd imagined it—probably because of the work he did with the kids. Work that he was certain about, because these kids needed an advocate, someone to be their voice. Cheryl was different—she had a voice of her own and was clearly more than capable of using it. She wasn't powerless.

She certainly didn't need him.

~12~

Humiliation never ceased on this little ranch. First a dunk in the pond, then a fall in Brock's spare bedroom, and now she was stuck. Nana was going to hear about this. An earful complete with "You'd better not ever pull something like that again."

Brock shoveled his food into his mouth like he was a starved man. He hadn't been that rushed two minutes before. More than likely had something to do with her little temper tantrum.

Why was she always so horrible?

She tried to cut the thought short before it formed. Guilt, when she allowed it to penetrate, made it hard to wall up her emotions.

"Is there a spare in the trunk?" Brock asked.

She lifted her attention from her plate to him. "Excuse me?"

"A spare tire? In the trunk?"

"I don't know. It's a rental."

"That explains some things."

She scowled. "Such as..."

He snorted. "What's a born-and-raised mountain girl doing driving a little squirrel-mobile like that around these parts? How'd you even get it over the passes? And why'd you pick *that* color?"

"You don't like the orange?"

His silent smirk served as an answer.

"Well, I didn't pick any of it. So now you know."

"One mystery solved."

"Were there more?" Oh no. The words were out of her mouth before she could filter them.

Brock lifted his eyebrows and waited, as if he expected her to retract the question. She should—that was quite an opening for heaven knew what—but she didn't. What would he want to know about her?

No one really cared enough to dig into her personal life. Ever. So how curious was he?

She remembered the way he eyed her the other night—she'd known that look well. Interest. Interested how? That was the question. It usually had the same answer. She also remembered how he'd questioned her later that evening. She'd avoided him, and he'd let her.

Why the questions now?

"Okay." Brock brushed the crumbs off his fingers onto his plate and leaned back against his chair. "Since you asked...let's start with, where have you been all these years?"

Cheryl tipped her head to one side and studied him. He didn't shrink away. There was always a point, however, when men knew enough. Backstory wasn't that interesting to them, which usually kept her relationships...uncomplicated. They would ask just enough to be polite. She would give just enough to make them feel successful in their charade.

"Not a big mystery. I've been in California."

"Yes, that's what your brother said. Some big-time lawyer. He's pretty proud."

Ethan proud of her? Probably not. "I'm not a big-time lawyer. I'm an assistant to the LA district attorney. The deputy DA. It's not really that glamorous."

"Must be pretty important. You haven't been back in years."

"Says the famous world traveler." She lifted an eyebrow. "How long have you been back?"

"Five years." He reached for his mug and took a sip.

She waited for him to fill the silence. He simply set his mug down and looked at her.

Not the sultry look that she'd come to expect from men. Brock's inspection dug deep, beyond the carefully maintained exterior that made her the object of many lustful eyes. His intensity was electrifying, making her heart quiver. What did he see when he studied her like that?

Time to redirect his attention. "A camp for foster kids...that doesn't sound very Brock King-of-the-Slopes Kelly to me."

"We already talked about that." He leaned back, crossing his arms. "Why didn't you come home? Even just for a visit?"

She looked away, wishing that he'd stop probing her with his eyes, sifting her with his questions.

"Ethan says something happened, but he doesn't know what."

Her wall of indifference didn't raise fast enough, and she flinched. Quickly, while staring out the window, she cut off the emotion that threatened to strangle. The stoic mask she kept at the ready hardened her face. She didn't have to answer his questions.

"He's right, isn't he? Something happened."

She pushed off the chair. "I'm going to get started on that tire."

Brock continued to watch her. "Do you know what you're doing?"

No. She didn't. Dad hadn't been around to show her, and no one else had bothered to teach her things like car maintenance.

"I told you I'd take care of it."

"I don't want to be stuck here longer than I have to," she snapped.

He drew a long breath and slowly pushed off his chair. "Okay. I'm on it, after you answer one question."

"You're blackmailing me?"

"More like a ransom for your car."

"No."

He crossed his arms.

"I don't owe you anything, Brock Kelly."

"You haven't even heard the question."

Hadn't he already asked it? What happened?—that was what he wanted to know. She settled her coldest glare on his face. He didn't back off, nor did he lose his calm composure.

"Do you miss playing?"

She took the tiniest step back. "What?"

"That's the one question. Do you miss playing the piano?"

She glanced over at the instrument and then looked back at him. He grinned, but not the ornery kind. It reached past the circle of ice she maintained around her heart and began to thaw a tiny corner.

Dangerous. She crossed her arms over her chest and took a step back as he nodded toward the piano.

"It's out of tune, but you're welcome to play it." He finally stopped looking at her and stacked one plate on the other before taking them back to the kitchen.

Cheryl stood with her heart throbbing. Alone in the dining hall, she stared after the door Brock had passed through. He didn't reappear, and she heard the back kitchen door slap closed less than a minute later.

Why would he ask that?

~*~

Brock had the tire iron set out and was lifting the spare from Cheryl's trunk, when he finally heard the twangy notes from the piano inside. So. She did want to play—he hadn't just imagined the glimpse of longing in her eyes when she'd looked at the beat-up old thing.

She'd sold her piano? That just didn't make any sense. She'd played it every day. Every. Day. Why would she sell something that clearly had been important to her?

The broken chords and stuttering notes slowly morphed into fluid music. That it'd been a while since her fingers had touched the keys carried through the songs she stumbled through at first, but by the time Brock had the car jacked up, the spare tire on, and was ready to crank down the lug nuts, she had found her rhythm.

Maybe he should have worked slower.

He reversed the pump on the floor jack and slowly lowered the car body until he could slide the lift out from under the frame. It took ten more minutes to replace the jack, fit the flat tire into the rental's trunk, give each of the lug nuts one last turn, and put the tire iron away. Wiping his hands on an old dish towel he'd kept in the garage, Brock checked his watch. One o'clock. His day off was quickly trickling away. Fishing had been a bust, and he hadn't started on any of the chores he would have liked to check off. Mowing the lawn around his cabin. Rehanging the front door that had begun to sag, making it stick and difficult to open. And changing the oil in his truck.

He'd have to pick one and call it good. Oddly, though, when he pictured Cheryl sitting across the table from him, drowning in his old sweats, irritation wasn't what he felt.

Intrigue. And compassion. Not irritation. Strange, since she was about as approachable as a mountain lion and as warm as a January night.

He left the garage and walked toward the lodge. Music continued to drift from the dining hall. Brock paused, his hand on the door, and listened while the familiar tune floated on the cool mountain air.

It had been one of her favorites—he knew because she'd played it often. She didn't play it as well now—the movement came clumsily, and the chords were often wrong. But she was playing from memory. It made him smile.

Careful not to disturb her, he slipped inside and wandered toward her spot at the piano. Lost in her effort, she didn't notice him until he sat on the bench next to her.

Her fingers stalled, and the music silenced. She looked up, and his breath nearly hitched. Soft-blue eyes. Eyes that he recognized from years gone by.

He swallowed back the startle and forced a grin. "From *Forest Gump*, right?"

Her far-off gaze cast down to her hands, which still rested on the keys. "Yes. The 'Feather Theme.'"

"I remember."

A pause settled between them, and then she breathed out a tiny laugh. "I haven't even heard it for years, let alone played it. That was terrible—and I can't remember the rest."

"It wasn't terrible."

She glanced at him again, and her smile faded. He felt her body stiffen, and she pulled her hands away from the piano. Retreating again. Coming back to the present, because whatever was between now and way back then hurt.

Brock wrestled against the urge to ask what had happened. He'd tried that already. Thing was, people who buried their pain usually didn't heal. But they didn't appreciate being poked either.

Maybe she just needed a friend.

"I wasn't lying, you know." He leaned down and nudged her with his shoulder.

She looked up again. "About what?"

"Hanging around to hear you play. I really did that."

Her eyebrows pushed together, as if she didn't believe him.

"I wouldn't lie to you. Promise."

She studied him for another breath and then nodded.

What did she see when she looked at him? The cocky King-of-the-Slopes guy who'd somehow decided that the world crumbled at his feet? Surely she knew there was more. Just as he knew—*felt*—there was more to her than Arctic winds and a strict diet.

Urgency clawed in his chest, which spiraled confusion in his brain. He couldn't define why it was suddenly so important that she know he wasn't the shallow, self-obsessed man he'd been in front of all of the crowds all those years ago. Or worse, why he needed to know what lay underneath her blustery facade.

But not knowing why didn't deter the need.

Brock elbowed her, tipping his head as if they were two teenagers whispering in study hall. "Your turn."

"My turn for what?"

"A secret. I told you one. Now it's your turn."

Tossing her hair, which had dried, over her shoulder, she snorted. "You're cute."

"Thanks. But I wasn't kidding." He held her car keys up and away, dangling them as if they were bait. "Come on...just one. It can be anything, like you secretly love hot dogs. Or you knew what that can of bug spray would do to your skin, but you really wanted to go swimming..."

She rolled her eyes and laughed. A real laugh.

Brock leaned down and brushed her shoulder with his again. "Come on..."

With her palm, she pushed him away, and their gazes locked. The playfulness in her eyes faded, and she shrank into herself as she looked away. She didn't want him to see, which only fed the longing to peel back the layers.

He nearly gave up that she'd give him an answer at all, but she didn't bolt from the bench they shared. He waited, still and silent.

"I hate my job." Her throaty voice quivered.

Whoa. That was way more serious than he was expecting. "That's kind of big."

She pushed her fingers through her hair. "Yeah, well..."

"Did you ever like it?"

After a deep breath, she pulled her posture straight. "One secret. That's all you get." Palm up, she held out her hand.

Let it go. Shouldn't be that hard...shouldn't have been so interested in the first place.

"Fair enough." He fisted the keys he'd kept out of her reach and transferred them to her hand.

She slid from the bench and stood. "I'll get your sweats back to you as soon as possible."

"No rush. I know where you live."

Pink touched her cheeks, but she tipped a polite nod as if to say, *Good day, sir,* which actually didn't mean good day at all, but rather, *I can't stand to be here with you for another second.* With a toss of her hair, she turned for the door.

Such a moody woman. Not the kind he should have any interest in at all. She'd be demanding. And exhausting. He totally wasn't interested.

"Sherbert." But teasing her *was* kind of fun.

Her retreat stopped short, but she didn't face him.

"You're welcome to come play the piano anytime." He could make himself scarce when she did. Not that he expected that she would. But *if* she did...he could find a quiet corner to listen. That wasn't stalker-ish or anything.

She peeked over her shoulder at him, the blush still very much on her pretty face. He waited for it...

Nothing. Just another nod, but not a word about her nickname.

Brock swallowed a chuckle. He'd just uncovered another secret.

And maybe a slight problem.

I remember family.

We had been one once.

A collage of outings—hiking and skiing and horseback riding. Days near the river with picnics. Evenings near the fire playing Taboo. Hot cocoa. Lasagna night.

Mom died, and so did everything else. We didn't see you much after that. You started traveling. For work, that's what you said. That didn't seem like the truth. I don't know what it was that took you away, because you didn't travel before her accident. Whatever it was, it became more important than us.

And then one day you came home with her. Engaged. How could you be engaged? We'd never even heard of this woman, and you were going to marry her?

I guess you started a new family. A new life.

Eventually I started my own version of a new life too. I wonder if yours has worked out better than mine.

~13~

Cheryl drew a breath and began rifling through the rack of dresses. She hadn't packed for a wedding—*thanks for that, Ethan*—and she didn't really know what to wear to this one anyway. Truth was, she'd only been to a handful of weddings in her life, and none of them had been exactly fun. She'd avoided them if she could, especially after her dad's. That had been a long, crappy day for a fourteen-year-old. The whole deal had gone down something like, "Cheryl, meet your new stepmother...she's the one in the white dress. Oh and by the way, I'm moving to Cheyenne. You and your brother can stay with Nana while we get settled, and we'll figure out something permanent later."

Later had a long expiration date.

Why was she thinking about that now? Irrelevant. She was shopping for something acceptable to wear to Ethan's wedding, not taking a drive down the deeply rutted road of bad memories.

Her hand landed on a lavender sundress. The delicate floral print seemed a little whimsical for her norm, but for a wedding... She had a semidressy gray cardigan with her. It'd do just fine for E's outdoor, spur-of-the-moment nuptial arrangement. Glad to have found something acceptable, she paid the girl at the small boutique's counter and made her way out the door.

Tourist season had stepped up in Steamboat. Not to full-capacity level, but definitely more traffic than there had been the previous week. Her cowgirl boots, which she'd found at the back of her closet at Nana's, smacked the concrete sidewalk as she strode toward the little car she still hadn't traded in. Wasn't worth the effort now. She'd stay for Ethan's wedding and catch a flight out of the valley the following Monday or Tuesday, depending on how long it would take to find full-time help for Nana.

She kept the rhythm of her steps at a fast clip—a habit developed from her all-business lifestyle. As she approached her car, parallel parked at the end of the main part of old town, she opened her purse and dug for her keys. Suddenly a hand cupped her elbow, large and clearly masculine. Immediately she stiffened, flexing the arm that had been touched and curling her fist on the opposite hand. With one motion, she shoved at the intruder with her shoulder and stomped on the large foot nearest her own.

"Ow!" A familiar voice yelped near her ear. "Sheesh, Sherbert. I'm not a thug."

Pulling in a breath, Cheryl looked up to Brock's bug-eyed expression. A moment of minor remorse came and fled before she could draw a second breath, and then she turned to face him straight on, her posture stiff with anger. "What the heck are you doing, Brock Kelly! You can't sneak up behind a woman and not expect her to react."

"Holy moly, girl. Do you always assume someone's after you?"

She held his look with defiance and then blew out a lungful of air. "Sorry."

"Wait, what?" The dimple on his right cheek poked out when he grinned. "Say that again."

Twisting her mouth, she eyed him and then turned to finish her walk to the car.

"Come on," he coaxed, his hand taking her elbow again.

"Watch it."

"Say it. Sssss..." He drew out the sound like a snake, helping her sound it out.

So lame. "Shut up, Brock. You deserved it."

They reached her car, and she stepped off the sidewalk, moving to the driver's-side door. Brock jumped in front of it, blocking her way.

"Get out of the way."

"Naw-uh. You owe me coffee, I think."

"Not a chance."

He leaned back against the car, kicking one foot over the other. "Okay, dinner, if you insist."

Cheryl jabbed her fists onto her hips. "Move. Now."

His shoulders moved while he chuckled. "Does that work in court?"

She squinted, pursing her lips.

"Guess what, Sherbert?"

She continued to glare, and he leaned down until his nose nearly touched hers.

"I'm not scared of you." His minty breath danced over her upper lip.

She leaned back a little, but caught the look in his eye and stalled her retreat. Teasing laughter danced there, but something sincere lurked beneath the fun.

Brock straightened, unfolding his legs, and pushed off the car. "Okay, you win, kid." His hand once again cupped her arm. "I'll buy."

"Dinner?"

"Are you hungry?"

"No."

"Good. Coffee's cheaper. A little." Somehow, through that little exchange he had escorted her back to the sidewalk and away from her car. "Have you tried the new little bakery on the edge of town?"

"When would I have done that?"

He laughed as if she were joking. "Right now. But it's not really within decent walking distance, so hop in." Two steps later, he stopped at his Bronco.

"Has anyone ever told you that you're presumptuous?"

"Naw. Charming, yes. Determined, absolutely. Never presumptuous."

"I'm pretty sure you're lying."

He reached to open the passenger door. "I told you I wouldn't lie to you. I wasn't kidding." Standing there with his hand still on the door, he waited. "Anytime now, Sherbert. It's good coffee."

"One secret." She took a step closer, one hand on her hip.

One eyebrow pushed into his forehead. "Excuse me?"

"That's the price. Tell me one secret."

That dimple indented his cheek again. "I'm not sure this is a fair deal. You stomped on my foot, remember?"

"You snuck up on me."

He studied her, the teasing never leaving his expression, and yet somehow his stare grew more serious. "Okay. Here it is." He leaned again, this time tipping his head toward her ear. His breath tickled the skin on her cheek as he whispered. "Ethan told me you were coming into Steamboat today."

She watched him as he stood straight. "And?"

"It's not my day off." One knuckle tapped on her nose, and then he turned to walk around the front of the car.

An avalanche of heat crashed over her. What was his game? She knew players, and Brock Kelly didn't fit the profile—at least not this version. She'd known desperate men too. He certainly wasn't one of those either.

This kind of situation called for direct confrontation. Cheryl steeled her resolve and climbed into the truck. She barely had her seat belt secured before she asked, "What are you after?"

"Told you. Coffee."

"Skip the games, Brock." She looked at him, and he paused before starting the engine. "Say it straight."

All fun left his eyes, and that feeling returned again—the one that said he saw things in her no one else bothered to look for. A shiver spread over her arms, and she huddled closer to the door.

Brock cleared his throat and turned the key to start the engine. "Will you be my date tomorrow?"

"Date?" It sounded so...juvenile. And sweet. Not a come-on line. Not a suggestive euphemism. Just an honest, straight-up request. That had never happened before.

"Yeah. Will you be my plus-one at Ethan and Brandi's wedding tomorrow night?"

She couldn't help but stare. He didn't fidget. Just sat, looking back at her with an open expression, and waited.

Not even an ice queen could say no to that.

"Okay."

His mouth broke into a smile, and he nodded as he shifted into drive. "Good."

Cheryl wiggled to face the dashboard. "You can't call me Sherbert all night though."

Brock chuckled again. "Too late to negotiate. You already agreed."

"It's never too late to negotiate."

He smirked. "You're not going to win this one."

"Wanna bet?"

"Cup of coffee. And I've already won." He reached over and tugged on a small clump of hair. "I happen to know that secretly you like it."

She pulled away and shoved at his hand. "That is *not* true."

He glanced at her with a raised eyebrow. "No lies. That's the deal."

Her arguments died in her throat.

~*~

She really is stunning.

Brock rubbed the back of his neck, reminding himself that constantly watching Cheryl qualified as staring.

But she'd agreed to join him.

Almost as astounding as the fact that he'd asked.

God, what am I thinking?

He'd felt bad, lying in bed the night before, thinking over his encounters with Cheryl. Ethan had put her in a bad spot—hadn't been completely honest with her and then expected her to be something she clearly wasn't when he'd thrust his fiancée in her face. She could have been more civil, but still...

Brock could have been a whole lot more compassionate.

Enter the date question. He hadn't planned on a date—didn't need a plus-one at a wedding. But maybe it would make her feel a little more comfortable. That was the extent of it.

Except he couldn't stop staring at her. And wondering... *Not good, and not his business.*

Cheryl was not a woman to be messed with. Not because she was coldhearted, but because he knew, without knowing any details at all, that the chill in her heart hadn't happened without a reason. He'd thought long and hard about it over the four days since their fishing fiasco. The old Sherbert he'd remembered from their high school years wasn't dead. She was trapped. Somehow Brock felt commissioned to strike out on a search and rescue.

Her secret wounds whispered to him, crying for a warm wave of compassion, which could be a serious problem, because the physical attraction he felt when she was near would make this complicated. He'd already confused the honest desire to help his best friend's little sister with the fact that Cheryl Thompson was a very beautiful woman. Especially when she smiled. Which she had, several times in fact, since he'd "bumped" into her an hour before.

"So...Brandi." Cheryl took another sip of her refilled mug and let the statement-cloaked question hang in the air.

"Yes. Brandi, your brother's fiancée." Brock leaned his elbows on the table. "Was there a real question in there?"

"You seem to be a fan."

He shrugged, almost flattered by her guarded jealously. Well, not almost. "She's good for E."

"How do you know?"

"She's just a good person, and Ethan has really stepped forward as a man since he met her. He's not as...self-oriented. I mean, come on—did you ever in a million years picture your brother leading groups of prepubescent kids on hikes and out for canoe trips on a regular basis?"

"I never pictured either of you doing such things."

"Yeah, well..." Heat touched his face.

Cheryl set her mug on the table, challenge written on her face. "Did it take a woman to transform you?"

"No." Was it getting warmer? Brock drummed his fingers against the table. *No lies.* That'd been the deal. "I lost a woman in the process, actually."

Questions passed over her expression.

Might as well tell all. Everyone else knew anyway.

"Kayla. That was her name. We were engaged. No wedding date set or anything...just, well, we lived together—traveled together—you know. I guess I thought a diamond made everything okay. She was an agent, eventually became my agent while I was touring. We met at an event somewhere along the road. To make a long story short, I jumped in when I probably should have been more cautious, and then when

God got ahold of my heart and changed my priorities, she wasn't game."

"She left you because you didn't want to compete anymore?"

Anger pressed into his chest. Why'd it still bother him? "Yeah, more or less. She said we wanted different things in life and we just weren't going to work."

Cheryl didn't answer. She sat, her silent gaze prickling insecurities that he'd long thought he'd left behind.

It didn't—shouldn't—matter what a woman thought of him, of his life choices. He was done with them.

Which explained why he'd come after Cheryl that afternoon, didn't it?

"Did you love her?"

Brock's attention darted back to her eyes. Clear and soft, blue like the color of a Colorado sky on an early spring morning. His breath caught while his heart jumped.

He focused on the question, pushing away the physical reaction she'd provoked. Had he loved Kayla?

No lies.

"I don't know, really. Probably not like I should have. But I'd made a commitment, and that mattered to me. I guess it hurt that it didn't matter all that much to her."

Her probing eyes finally slid away, but somehow there was no relief. In fact, he missed the connection almost as soon as she severed it.

"Your turn," he whispered, rebuking the intimacy of his tone. Clearing his throat, he settled back in his chair, putting a little more distance between them.

A small smile tugged on the corner of her mouth. "This is quite a game you've invented."

Not a game... Was it? He didn't know what it was.

Cheryl drained what was left of her coffee and then toyed with her empty mug. "What do you want to know?"

What happened... Not that. She wasn't ready, and for some reason, he was pretty sure he wasn't either. Strange that. Not like her secrets really had any bearing on his life.

Cheryl waited.

Brock drew a breath and sorted through the questions he had about her...surprised by how many there were. Way more than a man ought to have for a casual friendship.

Skip that.

He picked a mystery and laid it out for her to solve. "Why did you go to law school?"

She breathed a little laugh, like she expected something tougher. "Why not?"

"You didn't strike me the lawyer type back in the day."

"I'm surprised I struck you as anything back in your slope-junkie days."

"Are you saying I was self-consumed?"

One of her shoulders lifted.

"Okay, maybe you're right. But it wasn't like I never noticed anyone else." He risked eye contact again. "Not like I never noticed you."

She ducked away, looking toward the windows on her right. A few silent heartbeats skipped by before she spoke again. "What do you think I should have done?"

"Honestly? Music. You always seemed happiest at the piano. I don't understand why you stopped playing."

Her jaw moved tightly, and Brock could see her swallow. "That's a different question entirely. You only get one right now."

He waited, wondering if he got to choose which secret she would tell.

"My dad." Her voice turned hard. "He said he'd pay for law school. That was pretty much the only option. So that's what I did."

Bizarre. Why did her dad care if she went to law school or studied music? Or, better question, why'd she care what her dad wanted?

"Would you change it, if you could go back?"

Her eyes collided with his again. She looked like she was drowning.

"I can't even begin to tell you all of the things I wish I could go back and do different. But that's not part of this game, is it?" Cheryl stood, clearly done with their conversation and with this...date?

No. Whatever.

Brock watched as she transformed back into the ice princess that had stormed her way onto his dock almost a week before. Pain stuck in his chest as his heart squeezed. Why did she do that? He followed her lead, pushing in both of their chairs and taking the mugs up to the counter before he traced her steps out the door. She'd nearly reached his truck when he caught up to her.

"Sherbert."

She halted, turning to face him with that phony irritated mask.

"Everyone has regrets."

The mask began to slip. A little.

Brock reached for her hand, and she didn't move away. His thumb slid over her knuckles, and he watched the hardness melt from her posture. With a small tug, he pulled her close and tucked her head under his chin.

"Don't let the things you wish you could take back keep you from the life God wants to give you."

She snickered, even though she didn't push away. "What's that from, some class you took for helping foster kids?"

Ouch. She sure could fling a sharp dart of sarcasm. "No."

Stepping away from his embrace, she looked up with expectation.

"Gramps." Brock let his hands fall away from her shoulders. "He said it in a letter he left for me with his will. I read it a few weeks after Kayla left."

Color washed over her face, and she turned toward his truck. "I'm sorry."

With his index finger under her chin, he lifted her face back to his. "I told you. Everyone has regrets."

~14~

Brock moved his feet to the rhythm of some country love song. Didn't know the name. Wasn't a country kind of guy. But this was a wedding, after all. Why not throw a little "When I Said I Do" something or another in for good measure?

Ethan and Brandi swayed together to his left, wrapped up in each other's gazes like a pair of teenagers crushing. They were...cute. If a couple could be such a thing. A straight-shot love story right there. Neither one had a single doubt from their first date—which happened to be around the fire pit just off in the distance—that they were headed for a happily ever after.

He hoped. Uncomplicated was something to be envied. And loyalty...something most missed. He'd have to remember to wish them both in his toast later.

Continuing to sway, his attention drifted to the deck stretched above the makeshift dance floor. Nothing uncomplicated there. Total mystery, that other Thompson kid. And yet, like a child to a cornstalk maze in October, he was drawn to her.

"She sure has you distracted." Laughter lay under his mother's voice.

He redirected his gaze, focusing on Lydia Kelly, who happened to be his dance partner and who also deserved a better portion of his attention, since she and his dad had been gone for the last three weeks on a riverboat cruise in Europe. Happy fortieth anniversary to them.

"Sorry, Mom. What was that?"

She patted the arm he held loosely around her and grinned. "Oh, my boy. The Thompson girl. Can't keep your eyes focused from her for more than five seconds."

Suppressing a smirk, Brock banished the heat prickling his ears.

"Gone a long while, that one," Mom probed.

"Yeah. First time home in years."

She nodded, her eyes lit with a knowing smile. "All grown up and quite beautiful."

Brock snorted. "I noticed, Mom."

Her smile bordered on the mocking type, and then she turned serious. "She was a quiet one, wasn't she?"

"Yeah." This was getting a little too uncomfortable. And if his mother knew Cheryl all grown up, she might not be encouraging his budding interest.

"And now..."

No avoiding the topic. Oh well. If there was anyone in the world he could trust to push him in the right direction, it was his parents. Even in tough places where lines had to be drawn, they'd proven themselves both wise and faithful.

"She's..." Sharp? Bitter? Cold? "She's not the same."

Mom's mirth faded, and she tilted her head. "Perhaps the stones life threw at her when she was younger finally found their mark."

"Maybe." Seemed like more. But how was he to know?

The song ended, and another picked up. Same basic beat, so they continued on the floor.

"And...her wounds call to my son?"

Brock glanced back up at Cheryl just in time to see Mr. Thompson hold his hand out to her. That should go well. He looked away but caught her scowl before he refocused on his mother.

"I don't know, Mom. She kind of terrifies me."

Mom breathed a small laugh. "Ah. King of the Slopes, the daredevil himself has finally met a woman who didn't faint at his smile."

With a long breath, Brock rolled his eyes. "It's not like that. She is my date tonight, if you didn't notice."

"Oh good. I wouldn't want your head to deflate too much." She cackled good naturedly and then leaned in to give him a Mom hug.

"Thanks."

She opened the space between them again and squeezed his hand. "Here to keep you grounded."

Somebody probably should. That was what went wrong before. Too much ego, not enough lead.

They paced off a few measures in silence. Then Mom tipped her chin up to look at him.

"Remember back in maybe third grade or so, you got suspended for fighting?"

Great, she was serious about the *keeping him humble* part. "Yeah. You were some kind of mad."

"I was." She nodded. "Until I found out the whole story. That you'd stood up for the little Fulton boy and wound up with a fat lip and a bruised rib because of it."

Brock looked away, remembering Tagg Fulton. Everyone thought he was weird. Small for his age, he barely spoke, and he always wore a long-sleeved Superman shirt. It was filthy, and the cuffs had holes worn through. Nobody understood why he refused to wear anything else.

The other boys called him "duperman." Tagg would turtle into his shoulders and look to the ground, but he'd never say a word. Brock had always felt a little sorry for him, but he never said anything. Then one day Brock missed his bus and had to walk home. He happened to follow Tagg. With carefully measured steps, he'd kept at a distance, because no one walked with the weirdo, and Brock didn't want a label just when his popularity was starting to boom.

Tagg talked to himself as he walked, and sometimes he played out some sort of fight scene he must have had going in his head, throwing punches into the air, dodging invisible fists aimed for his face, and occasionally rocking a side kick. Fairly normal ten-year-old-boy stuff. But then Tagg stopped, and Brock ducked behind a nearby trash can to spy. The boy in the Superman shirt kicked at the ground, and his voice came loud enough for Brock to make out the words.

"Don't ever touch her again."

Shivers crawled over Brock's neck, and he held the sides of the trash bin as he leaned around to see better. Tagg's face went toward the sky, and he reached a single, flat palm toward the air.

"Someday, Mom. I'll be your Superman. Just wait."

Even at ten years old, Brock had known he'd just witnessed something dark and heart shattering. His stomach had rolled as he crouched behind that bin, and he swore the next time someone dared to call Tagg "duperman," he'd step between the two.

He did. Wound up out of school for three days, and after that, he never saw Tagg again.

The same shivers that had prickled his neck that day so long ago crept over his skin again as the memory closed. So many *if onlys...*

"I wish I knew what happened to him."

Mom's eyes had gone soft and misty. "I know. I don't know if I ever told you—even though we disciplined you for fighting, we were proud of you. And almost...sort of thankful for the whole thing because we were able to glimpse your compassionate heart. You're gifted with it, you know?"

Brock swallowed, trying to follow his mom's line of thought. "Fighting?"

She chuckled. "Well, maybe in a way. Fighting for grace. God has given you such a tender heart toward those who ache."

Ah. So this did relate to Cheryl. But pity and compassion, they weren't the same thing, no matter what a thesaurus said. Pity had a way of crippling people, making them codependent and unstable. Compassion was more like love—it grew strength and courage. Right now, with Cheryl, he wasn't sure he had the two in their proper place. And then there was that whole attraction thing...which made everything pretty much a mess.

"Son, there's nothing wrong with wanting to be the knight." Mom stopped moving and stepped back, placing her right palm over his heart. "You are a warrior here, and what you do is amazing. Just don't forget whose armor you wear, and ultimately, who will truly win in the end."

Words wouldn't form in his mind. She was talking about Cheryl, right? Her statement seemed...almost prophetic. And scary.

And massively humbling. Because this warrior for grace had called the very woman his mother was championing an ice princess. Not so valiant. Or gracious.

He pressed his lips together and searched his mother's face for answers. She gave him a teary smile and moved to kiss his cheek. "You'll do the right thing."

"What if I don't know what that is?" The question rushed from his lips.

"He'll show you. Day by day." She patted his cheek and stepped away. "Just keep listening."

Swallowing, Brock stood at the edge of the dance floor and watched his mother walk away, until his attention was stolen by Cheryl stalking down the dirt drive.

He'd put money on it: the encounter with her dad hadn't gone as her foolish father had hoped.

Okay, God. I'm trying to listen. Now what do I do?

~*~

He actually did it. Cheryl tried to wrap her mind around Ethan's marriage. Her brother, a husband? She hoped he'd grown up. The Ethan she remembered was hardly steady-boyfriend material, let alone the kind of guy a girl would want to marry.

Still, it'd been a pretty service. Guess they'd always have that.

Brock's little kids' camp had been lit up with tiny white lights strung along the deck of the lodge and the dock at his pond. The road and pathways were illuminated by the yellow glow of paper lanterns. Not bad. For a wedding.

Fighting the urge to rub at the sore muscles in her cheekbones from her painted-on smile, Cheryl let her gaze cast over the people swaying below. Brock danced with his mom, smiling with ease as the pair conversed. Possibly talking about her. Being reintroduced to Lydia and Jim Kelly had felt a little bit like being the new kid at a big school. They were nice, all smiles and gentle touches on the arm, as they doled out the expected "It's so good to see you again," and "Tell us how you've been," and "Brock, you must bring her out to the house sometime soon where we can catch up properly." Ready to meet the new girl—for the moment.

Cheryl didn't plan to stick around to see how they'd react if they got to know her. Thus, they'd be left with the illusion of who Brock thought she was. It was nice, actually, to think that someone would perhaps hold her in high esteem in his memory.

As Cheryl stood at the edge of the deck, taking in the semidark view, a masculine voice touched her hearing, giving her chills.

"Can I dance with my little girl?"

Steel locked hard in her chest. She couldn't believe it. Why had Ethan invited him? He hadn't had anything more to do with either of them than a monthly check in the mail and a full guilty-parent scholarship to the school of his choosing. He didn't deserve to be there, and he had no business asking her to dance.

Cheryl turned to face the man who had abandoned them almost twenty years before. "You don't have a little girl here."

Mitchell Thompson took a small step back. "I'm looking at her, aren't I?"

With a cool gaze locked on eyes shaded remarkably similar to her own, Cheryl crossed her arms. "What are you doing, Dad?"

"Asking my daughter to dance."

She snorted. "You're a little late for that."

"I know." He nodded, glancing to his feet. "But we still have today."

"No. We don't."

"Look, Cher-bear—"

What was with these people and their cutesy nicknames? "Don't ever call me that again." Leveling a look of pure loathing on him, Cheryl drew in a steady breath. "I have your last name because I'm stuck with it. That's all you and I have in common. Don't think that you can show up and we'll just start right off where you walked out."

Hurt passed through his eyes, but he tipped his head. "That's not true. You have my eyes. We're both lawyers. Lot's in common..."

"No."

"Come on, hon. Ethan and I, we've worked on some things. Can't you and I try?"

"Absolutely not. I don't know what E was thinking, but I'm not game. You left us, and you can't undo that."

"I thought at the time I was doing what you'd want. What teenage kid wants to move from the only home they'd ever known? And with a new stepmother? It made sense to leave you with Grace."

Cheryl stared at him, dumbfounded by his idiotic logic, even after all the years. "You know what, Dad? Just keep saying that. Over and over and over. It almost sounds like you believe it." With a quick pivot on her booted foot, Cheryl stalked away, heading toward the darkness beyond the small cabins.

Gravel crunched beneath her boots as she continued down the road. Parking had been assigned at the elbow in Brock's long drive so that the area nearest the lodge was clear for the wedding. That gave her a half mile of cool mountain air to steady her shaking hands before she'd reach her car.

Nana. Her escape cut short. She was supposed to take Nana home. Exhaling, she let her shoulders sag as her chin fell forward.

"Can't be as bad as all that." Brock's voice drifted from a few feet behind her.

She lifted her head and turned. "Are you stalking me?"

"Nah." He closed the few feet between them, stopping close enough she could smell the crispness of his cologne. He'd jammed his hands into the pockets of his good jeans and leaned to nudge her shoulder.

He was always showing up.

"You are, aren't you?"

He chuckled. "Honestly, I'm not. I saw you talking to your dad. Was worried about my date, is all."

He paused, letting the breeze dance in the small space between them, and then reached for her arm. "You okay?"

"Fine."

"That a standard deflection answer?"

She scowled. "You're a pest. Do you always pry like this?"

He shrugged. "Depends."

"On what?"

"If I think the question needs answering."

She sensed a circular conversation in the near future. Better to just drop it. "I'm fine, Brock."

His hand still rested just above her elbow, and he gently squeezed the spot. She liked the warmth, but it provoked a shiver. He didn't miss it.

"You're cold."

The least of her problems. She tugged on the hem of her lightweight cardigan. "Maybe. I forgot how quickly it cools up here."

"But that's not why you were leaving."

Mashing her lips together, she looked back over the enchanted scene behind Brock. It suddenly struck her how odd her inability to enjoy beauty was. She could see it, but to soak it in... let it fill her being? She couldn't. Had she always been that way?

She shivered again.

"You need something hot to drink." Brock tugged her toward him and then wrapped his arm around her. He began rubbing her other arm as if she were in danger of hypothermia. "And a warmer jacket. Come on."

He moved, and she followed. Back to the wedding scene they went, keeping to the dark edge of the road as they strolled.

"Cheryl, I really do want to know if you're okay. A real answer."

Fine sat on the tip of her tongue. It *was* the standard answer. She had no idea if she was okay. She only felt...cold. "I can't believe my dad showed up."

"Ethan invited him."

"Why?"

Brock pulled in a long breath and let it go slowly. "He's been working through some stuff. I think reconciling with your dad was important to him, and having him here was a big step in that process."

"So twenty years of neglect is wiped away, just like that?"

He stopped moving and turned to face her. "You know it isn't."

She held his gaze in the semidarkness for a few breaths and then looked away. "I wish E had warned me."

"He probably should have. I'm sorry."

"Does Ethan know what he's getting himself into with this marriage?" Cheryl paused, rubbing her arms as the chill sank deeper. "No, I mean does Brandi know? People like Ethan and me..."

He waited for her to finish. She couldn't. Didn't really know where she was going with that. The silence extended, and her shivering returned. After a long, intense look, Brock closed the small space between them and wrapped her in his arms. He said nothing as he held her.

The steady rhythm of his heart tapped against her cheek as his warmth enveloped her, seeping into her skin and bringing a foreign sense of comfort. Cheryl let her eyes slide shut as she snuggled into the safety of his embrace. For a moment she could pretend that this place of safety would last, that this wasn't what it always was...a preliminary negotiation for a trade agreement: his limited-time offer of care in exchange for the satisfaction of her body in the not-very-distant future. They'd play the exchange out until it was no longer new and thrilling, and then the deal would be off.

But that inevitable end wasn't in this moment. She pushed the looming ache away.

For now, she felt warm.

~*~

Brock tried to talk himself out of it, leveraging logic against attraction.

Honestly, he wasn't very well practiced in that area. So when Cheryl snuggled against his chest, his hands wove into her hair, and on instinct he cradled her head. She slipped her arms around him, and the moment the pads of her fingers began grazing over the muscles in his back, he knew he was in trouble. His pulse began to throb, and he felt his mind slip from clear thinking into the enticing fog of sensual command.

He was holding a beautiful woman...how was it that he'd expected not to physically respond?

"Cheryl..." He began to untangle the soft locks of her hair from his grip. She ran her hands over his shoulders to his chest and looked up. Heat surged as his gaze locked with hers, and when her lips parted, he moved to accept the silent invitation.

Hunger seemed to fuel her kisses, and she tucked her body next to his. Brock lost himself in a moment of visceral passion before logic broke through again. This wasn't supposed to happen.

He pulled away, working to ignore the longing she'd awakened. She moved to follow him, to reclaim his mouth and pull him back into the fog, but he caught her face in both palms.

"I didn't mean to do that," he whispered, working to tame his breathing.

He studied her as she slowly pulled away, her fingers uncurling the grip she'd wrung on his shirt. His hands still framed her face, and he traced her jawline with his thumb. Emotions he wasn't sure he could read passed through her eyes...mostly confusion. Maybe some hurt.

"What did you mean to do?"

He meant to...what? What had he wanted? This beautiful woman who had just ignited a blaze inside of his chest had an iceberg in her heart. Did he really want to mess with that?

"I want to know you." The words came out strong, with conviction. He hadn't thought them through, but once they were out, he was certain they were the truth.

"I'm right here." She leaned in close, the moist warmth of her whisper brushing his chin. "You're the one pulling away."

"That's not what I mean, Sherbert, and you know it."

She pulled back. "No, I don't. I know how you looked at me when Ethan first brought me out here. I know what that kiss was a minute ago. What else am I to think?"

She was utterly serious. In that instant, he knew exactly how every other man had treated her. How she expected men to be.

"That's not me, not what I'm about."

"Well, maybe that's true—I don't know—but maybe it's me, what I'm about."

"I don't think so."

"Why? Guys can be forward and physical, and it's all good. Expected. But a woman? Not a chance, right?"

"Are you a player, Cheryl?"

She stepped away, forcing him to drop his hands. "You don't want to know me, Brock." She made a move in the direction where she'd parked her car.

With one long stride, he stepped into her path.

"Yes I do."

"Brock." Her voice cracked, and she looked away.

He'd touched on something tender in her heart, and she wanted none of it. He wanted all of it. The conviction surged. They'd both landed back in Hayden on purpose. For many purposes actually. And this thing blooming between them? Part of that purpose.

Crazy. Maybe he'd taken one too many slams to the head on his many snowboarding crashes. Cheryl Thompson, the ice queen, had planted deep in his heart within a week's time. Hadn't he been done with women? Not to mention, she'd be one of the most difficult creatures he'd ever encountered. He worked with some pretty difficult kids, so that was saying something.

Maybe he should listen to her; maybe she was right. The things she had locked up felt ominous. Maybe he didn't want to know.

With that thought, a noose locked around his heart and pulled tight. Strangling tight.

One hand reached for her face, and his fingers brushed her cheek. The coolness of her skin seeped through the pads of his fingers, and every other thought scattered. She needed warmth, and for some unexplainable reason, he longed to give it to her.

"Yes," he whispered, bringing her eyes back to meet his, "I do."

She stood still as he once again closed the space between them. With the hand that still touched her face, he tucked her close again, and the other arm he wrapped around her shoulders.

She shivered against him. Brock was certain her physical reaction wasn't just because of the chilly mountain air. She wasn't alone in that one.

This hadn't been his plan. He was terrified too.

~15~

Cheryl finger-combed her hair and piled it into a ponytail. She wasn't a ponytail kind of girl. She wasn't a kayaking kind of girl either. But standing with the warmth of Brock's body against hers, his arms anchoring her close to his chest, she couldn't say no to his invitation. That had been at E's wedding, two days before, and in the forty-eight hours since the delusion that she could somehow step back into the shell of the young woman she'd left behind had fizzled into a filmy, wispy notion. She couldn't be that girl without stepping into places in her heart that were forbidden.

Today she would tell him. This had to end.

It was time to get back on track. She would spend tomorrow calling around, making inquiries about help for Nana. Still without a clue as to what she would do with her life back in LA, she was certain she couldn't stay in Hayden. If Ethan and Brandi were only a ten-minute drive down the road, surely it would be fine to hire someone to look in on Nana. The woman still ran the bakery, for goodness' sake. She was doing fine, and Cheryl hadn't seen any other signs of dementia.

Just that one.

She shivered, remembering the woman's total departure from reality. And her words.

No. It was just the trauma of having Cheryl step back into her life that had rocked Nana. In fact, it would probably be best for Nana if Cheryl left. Her life would go back to normal, and she wouldn't have the stress of having Cheryl back in her home. It was best to leave next week.

And that was exactly how she'd explain her decision to Brock.

Brushing her bare arms, which still were sandpapery with goose bumps, Cheryl glanced at herself in the mirror. Her lightweight hiking pants weren't the latest cut, but what could she expect? They were over a decade past their day. Jeans wouldn't work for a day on the water, and the morning still hadn't warmed up enough to convince her to wear shorts. In fact, she needed a sweatshirt. She pivoted on one foot and began rummaging through her suitcase, knowing full well she wasn't going to find what she was looking for. Besides the jersey pants and tank she slept in, why hadn't she packed at least one casual piece of clothing? She'd come back to Hayden, after all. Cashmere was a little overdone in these parts. Unless she planned to frequent the upper-class hits dotting the tourist favorites in Steamboat, this was wrangler and quilted-flannel country.

Ugh. She hated quilted flannel. Had even before Hayden ceased to be home.

Come on. She just needed a sweatshirt.

She'd pillage E's room.

Solution found. After shoving her feet into her no-lace Converse tennies, she left her room and bounced down the stairs. She barely hit the landing and swung a left turn, habits from childhood coming back as though she'd never left. Ethan's room had often been her destination. He had all the good music. Had all the good ideas of what to do with a free and clear summer day. Had the fun friends.

Like Brock.

A small smile pulled on her lips. What little sister hadn't had a crush on one of her older brother's friends? But now Brock noticed her...wanted to know her.

He was strange. The way she'd kissed him at the wedding said *whatever you want, I'm game.* Men typically took that kind of move and ran with it. Brock had pulled away. They'd walked back to the reception. He'd danced with her a few times and held her hand for the rest. Didn't leave her side, which kept her dad at a distance, and when the evening settled, Brock walked her and Nana to her car, brushed a kiss across her forehead, and then brought her into his arms. He asked her if she'd go out on the water with him, and now here she was, looking for a sweatshirt in Ethan's room.

Full circle. If only life were that simple.

A few boxes were stacked on the floor against the wall opposite the door, but otherwise Ethan's room sat bare. Cheryl's steps slowed as she entered the space. The walls had been stripped of life. The pale-blue paint seemed to groan a hollow tune against her memories of posters, tacked-up sports jerseys, and Ethan's medals and ribbons from races he'd done well in. His bed had been stripped, and the naked mattress and plain wood headboard looked forlorn.

Ethan had moved out. His life had moved on. Permanently.

Cheryl wrapped her arms over her chest, her hands anchoring on her shoulders. Her breath hitched as she stood alone in a room where the memories continued to collide with the new reality.

Why was she reacting like this? She'd moved on. Her life wasn't here. At all. Ethan had every right to move on, and in fact, that step was long overdue. And yet, here she stood feeling strangled by a loss that had long since passed.

"Cheryl?" Brock's voice called from down the hall.

She startled. Had she missed his knock?

"Just a minute." Rubbing her arms, she stepped toward Ethan's closet. It was probably empty, but since she was already here...

"What are you doing?"

Her hand on the knob to the closet, she turned as Brock leaned against the doorframe. He'd shoved his hands into the pockets of his cargo pants, and his blue plaid flannel hung loose over a gray T-shirt. At least it wasn't quilted. And he looked...

Heat flared up her chest as she realized she was staring. A smirk lifted his mouth, poking at the dimple that lay just under his whisker-shadowed cheek. Those hazel-green eyes danced with laughter as they held hers.

"Good morning to you too."

"Ugh." She turned back to the closet, scolding the blush that kept giving her away. "See, you *are* presumptuous."

He chuckled, the sound moving toward her, telling her he was nearing. "No. Charming."

The hangers remaining in Ethan's closet hung empty. Mission failed. She shut the door and turned back to Brock, who had stopped only a step behind her. She tipped her chin up and raised an eyebrow. "Guess what I know about charming men?"

His smile faltered, but he held eye contact. After two breaths, the warmth of his hand enclosed around hers, and his thumb brushed over her knuckles. "Would you believe that I outgrew that stereotype?"

Yes. Clearly he had. Maybe. "We'll see."

He took a small step back, keeping her hand in his, and surveyed the room. "Wow. Kind of depressing in here."

Cheryl sighed. At least she wasn't the only one. But she wasn't going to open that door. "I was looking for a sweatshirt."

"Cold?" He gave her a once-over. "Why are you wearing a tank if you're cold?"

"That's why I was looking for a sweatshirt."

"Here." He started unbuttoning the few closures that held his warmer outer layer together.

She held up a hand. "I do *not* wear flannel."

He paused, gave her a look that said *You're acting like a twelve-year-old*, and then snorted. "Okay, fashion princess. Although I really doubt the wildlife are going to care. I have a hoodie in my truck. Will that fall within your clothing guidelines?"

"Yes."

"Well then, let's go. We're burning daylight."

He tugged her hand and kept it in his grasp all the way out to his vehicle. When he opened the passenger's-side door, he leaned in, snagged the hoodie, and then wrapped it around her. His hands landed on her arms, rubbing up and down. "There. Better?"

Cheryl nodded and then couldn't help but dip her nose toward the oversized sweatshirt. It smelled like him—like outdoors and woodsmoke and man. Warmth enveloped her and penetrated below her skin.

For a moment she wondered what it would be like to stay.

The water rippled under the polyethylene plastic of Brock's kayak. The strong undercurrent created small swirls in the gentle flow, just to remind the wise that its hidden power lay beneath the placid surface. He glanced over his shoulder at Cheryl, who paddled her smaller boat just a little behind his.

What were the undercurrents in her life?

"You ready for lunch?" He dipped one side of his paddle into the water on his right, creating a drag that both fought against his forward progress and turned him so he could face her.

She looked over the fields that waved a fruity-green texture toward the purple-mountain rises on all sides. Brock followed her gaze, his heart singing in the beauty that swallowed them. Life here...he wasn't sure why he'd ever searched for a life beyond this valley.

Then again, sometimes you had to lose something before you understood how amazing it really was. Thank God He'd led Brock back home.

"Brock?"

Water spattered his arm and the side of his face. His attention jerked back to Cheryl, whose devilish grin matched the ornery glint in her eyes.

"Did you just splash me?"

With a sassy smirk, she shrugged. "Could be. Whatcha gonna do about it?"

"Someone wants to go swimming again."

Her paddle dipped with fury first on one side and then the other as she moved to the bank on her right to port. She glided through the water with ease, reminding him that she was no rookie when it came to a kayak. Growing up, they'd all spent plenty of time on Gramps's ranch: in the water, with the horses, or on the dirt bikes.

Fun days that at the time seemed like they'd last forever.

Today was a good day to remember.

Brock's boat slid against the muddy bank three seconds after Cheryl's did. She wiggled free from the skirting, tucked her paddle into the clips, and tugged her boat securely out of the water before she took off across the long, grassed pasture. Brock hurried to follow, double-checking that both boats would remain out of the current's reach and ditching the life vest he had zipped over his chest. He sprinted to catch her.

She glanced over her shoulder at him as he began to close the gap between them, and a giggle rippled over the grasses. The sound seeped through his chest and soaked into his heart. Music he didn't know he'd missed.

Within one hundred yards of the river, he caught her, snagging her around the waist with one arm. He shifted his momentum back, and they both tumbled to the ground.

"Brock!" she laughed, wiggling against his hold.

He pinned her on the ground. "Did you splash me?"

She buttoned down her lips and mocked him with her laughing eyes.

"That's it." With one hand he locked both of her wrists together, and the other found the spot just below her life vest.

"No!" she squealed. "No tickling. I hate being tickled!"

"Maybe you'll think next time..."

His fingers continued their relentless attack, and she continued to laugh and scream, wiggling against him. Laughter bubbled from deep inside as he pinned her against his chest.

"Please," she panted. "I can't breathe."

"You're talking, which means you're breathing." He tested the spot above her knees, and she jerked away from his touch.

"No! Uncle." Her arms broke free of his hold, and she snatched his hand away from her leg. "I say uncle."

"Nah. That's not going to work."

Their hands wrestled as she tried to contain him and he continued to reach for her knee.

"What then?" She arched back against him.

He fell backward and wrapped her up with both arms and legs. "You want free?"

"Yes." She breathed, still winded and giggling.

"It's gonna cost you."

She relaxed, her head dropping back against his chest. "Let me guess. A secret?"

"Yep."

"And then we get to eat?"

"Only if you like hot dogs."

"You're such a pain."

He tightened his hold and brushed her waist again. "Watch it, princess."

She strained against him again, dancing away from his touch. "Okay, okay. One secret."

Anchoring her against him with one arm, he pushed up on an elbow. "All right. Let's hear it."

She twisted, tipping her chin up to his face, and grinned. "Here it is: I actually love hot dogs."

Brock rolled to his side and let the arm that held her captive against him fall slack, but he fisted the bottom of her life vest. "That doesn't count. I already knew that."

Her nose wrinkled up at him. "Okay. Fine, Mr. Clever. What do you want to know?"

He studied her. The faded smattering of freckles across her nose and cheeks suddenly struck him as adorable as he realized she wasn't made up for their day on the river. Raw, authentic, this Cheryl sprawled out in the middle of a thick green pasture was the Cheryl trapped underneath the cold layers she usually maintained. He wanted to keep her just like this.

If he asked, would she tell him why she wasn't always this way? Why she armored herself, and what had happened in her life that had made the shield seem necessary?

He released his hold on her life vest and reached for a wisp of hair that had fanned across her cheeks. His fingers grazed the skin of her face, warm in the unobstructed summer sun. Her eyes closed, and her mouth relaxed into a soft smile.

He wouldn't ask for history today. Today, she could smile in the warmth. In the light of the beautiful summer day, she could be herself without digging into the past, without trying to beat away the hurt of whatever had happened.

Today was a day for laughter.

"Must be thinking awful hard." One blue eye opened, squinting up at him.

So beautiful. He grinned as his chest tightened. "Tell me one thing you wished someone would have done or said for you in your lifetime."

Both eyes opened to examine him. "That's weird. And not really a secret."

He propped up on one elbow, his head leaning against his hand, and ran the fingers of his other hand over her hair again. "Is it something you've told other people?"

"Well...no."

She bit her bottom lip, drawing his attention to it. The tightness in his chest cinched harder, and his mouth began to tingle. Their kiss at the wedding seeped into his memory, and heat spilled through his veins. How easy it would be to lean down, to draw her beautiful face close, to taste those sweet lips...

That was what she expected from men.

He withdrew his hand and rolled to his back again. "So tell me. One thing you wish."

"Roses."

He turned his head to look at her. "Roses?"

"Yeah. I wish someone would give me a bouquet of red roses."

Was she being serious? Or just dropping hints? "Roses?" His voice hiked with suspicion.

"Okay, forget it, buddy. You asked. I answered. Let it go."

"No, wait. Are you serious?"

She looked at him, long and steady. She was serious, and he'd just made her feel stupid.

Wrong move.

"No one's ever given you roses?" That seemed farfetched. The woman commanded men's attention. No doubt she could snag a date whenever she wanted. Men would fall all over themselves to gain her notice. Flowers were pretty cliché in that scenario.

"No."

"No?" *Relax, dude.* This was getting stupid.

She rolled her eyes and turned to look back up at the endless blue sky. Brock turned his attention heavenward too, still dumbfounded. How was that even possible? Giving a girl flowers, that was standard dating practice, wasn't it? Maybe not for him, but for most guys.

Huh.

"Why red?" he asked, still mulling over the fact that he'd never given a woman flowers. That was an interesting twist.

She shifted again, and he felt her eyes on him for the space of a breath before she plucked a blade of grass near her hip. Bringing it up to her line of sight, she began peeling the long stem into curly, thin strips.

"Red roses say *I love you.*"

Her voice had hushed over the last three words, barely touching them as if they were fragile and rare.

She wanted to be loved.

Brock lifted his hand and reached for hers, brushing her fingertips until she let what remained of the shredded blade of grass fall to her chest. He wove his fingers loosely with hers. Together their hands floated to the space in between them, and they stayed there, soaking in the warm rays and the peace of the valley.

She wanted to be loved.

Love her.

The thought seemed to come from outside of himself, and it carried the weight of a divine command. Love Cheryl? He wasn't there yet. These things took time. Cultivation. And Cheryl was...complicated. Not that he didn't want to get to know her, and maybe they'd fall in love and then...

Love her.

He swallowed, squinting at the sky overhead. Was he nuts? Imagining things? He couldn't just force love. Look what happened the last time he'd tried...

The last time had been different. Very different. He'd done his own thing, as he had been doing for several years, in all aspects of his life, and he'd just expected to be blessed because he was Brock Kelly, King of the Slopes.

Love Cheryl? Could a guy really love when he was commanded to love?

God, are You really telling me...

Love her.

Thoughts swirled with emotions as Brock shut his eyes against the confusion and budding fear. If he was supposed to love her, how would that look? Did he start right now? Tell her he heard a "voice" and that she needed to start rearranging her life?

Wait. That was not how love worked.

Here they'd been having an awesome day, and it had gone and gotten all complicated.

Beside him, Cheryl drew in a long breath and released it slowly. Brock opened his eyes and tilted his head to see her. She lay still against the blanket of cool green, her face tipped toward the source of warmth and light, and a small smile rested on her lips.

Complications rolled away as he studied her content expression, and a strong surge of tender warmth settled over him, like a gentle hand had just wrapped around his being.

He tipped his head closer to hers and whispered, "Want to know a secret?"

Her eyes didn't flutter open, but her smile grew. "That'd only be fair."

The hand he still held twisted in his, and he brushed her knuckles as if to whisper *stay with me* in the silence. Her fingers relaxed and then threaded with his again. She turned her face toward his and blinked twice. Those soft-blue blossoms settled on him, and his chest seemed to cave.

"Are you going to tell me?"

That I might could love you? That I think I'm supposed to? No. That wasn't the secret.

"I've never given a woman roses."

Her small body moved with a gentle quake of laughter. "Not true. I saw you give your mom one at your last home basketball game your senior year."

"Doesn't count."

"Why not?"

"It wasn't my idea, and I didn't buy the rose."

Her gaze rested on him for two more heartbeats, and then her lids slid shut. The soft smile, the countenance of peace, however, didn't lift from her face.

Maybe someday he'd tell her the other secret. Maybe it'd be sooner than he'd ever imagined.

You held my hand as we lay quiet in the summer sun.

No one had done that before. I drifted into that surreal place between sleep and awake, floating, it seemed, on a memory of something that never was.

I ached in the beauty of that rest, yearning for it to last. If only I hadn't... Maybe this would have been. The years since that day I have wrestled, writhed, pushed away, and cut off...and all the while this had been in the waiting, in the future.

If I'd only known.

I wanted to stay in that place of pretend magic and imagine it could last. Behind the golden glow of my closed lids, I could see your eyes as you took me in...and you saw beneath the presentation I carefully maintained. You knew I loved hot dogs without me telling you. You also knew why I didn't eat them, or cinnamon knots, or drink full-calorie lattes. Why, until that day, I never wore my hair in a scraped-up, messy, untamed ponytail. Why my face was always touched to perfection. These are the things I can control.

You saw me, and you knew.

It made my soul tremble. I can't control you—what you see, the layers you peel away. I've worked too hard to bury what I did not want to remember, but you, with every brush of our skin, every moment of eye contact, every seemingly innocent exchange between us, you were excavating, even if you didn't know what or why.

I didn't want you to know.

~16~

"Something came for you today."

Brock's deep voice smiled to Cheryl over the phone.

"Came for me? To the ranch?"

She was supposed to be making other phone calls—ones about Nana and about her leaving. But the morning slipped away while she relived their kayaking trip yesterday, and she'd dozed off while she lay flat on the floor, imagining the cool earth at her back and the soft-blue blanket of sky overhead.

"Yep."

"Why?"

"Because I ordered it for you. Now it's here."

She was there again, lying in the grass beside him, her fingers in a feathery dance with his. It had been the closest to a perfect day that she could remember. And every time she summoned the memory of Brock's fingers capturing hers, her stomach fluttered and her heart gave a pain-pleasure-filled squeeze.

She didn't want to face reality. One more day of pretending...

Couldn't hurt, could it?

"Hello, Sherbert?"

She breathed a soft laugh. "You're quite proud of yourself that you can get away with calling me that, aren't you?"

"Shouldn't I be?"

Her heart began that odd little compression, and he wasn't even in the room.

Brock spoke again before she could dissect the implications of her reaction. "Are you coming out, or do I have to come get you?"

"I thought you had kids arriving tonight."

"We do. I can take a small break though."

She swallowed. She hadn't been pursued like this since college. Brock's relentlessness filled her heart with delight and her head with confusion. Where was he going with all of it?

"Okay, fine," Brock said. "I'll come get you, drag your stubborn bones out here, and then you can figure out your own way home tonight."

"What?"

See, this was what was off with this man. That kind of proposition was the perfect setup for the intimacy all men aimed for, and yet Brock added that last clause—that she'd go home tonight. Cheryl was pretty certain that was *very* intentional. Should have maybe struck her as sweet, except she knew he wasn't "saving himself for marriage." He'd already flushed that one, if it had ever been his intention in the first place.

So why'd he continue to pursue her and yet keep the bedroom door closed? Men, as she knew them, didn't function that way.

"I'm getting in the truck, so you'd better be ready, but I'm telling you, Sherbert, it's a long hike back."

"Okay, okay." She laughed, in spite of her whirling thoughts. "Stay put. I'll head out in a few minutes."

The smack of a car door shutting popped in her ear. Huh. He'd been serious. Which begged the question...if she'd let that one play out, would he have sent her home?

Maybe she should have let that scene roll. The sooner he brought this arrangement to the inevitable conclusion, the sooner they'd go their separate ways, and her life could move on.

Not really what she wanted. But the deeper he forged into her heart, the harder it was going to be when it was over.

And the one thing she'd learned for certain about men was that these things always ended.

Always.

~*~

Brock rubbed his hands together, glancing from his spot at the large picture window to the piano on the opposite wall.

It was like Christmas morning when he was ten. Except there was a piano instead of a tree, and the present wasn't wrapped, and it wasn't for him. But she would smile. That'd be for him. He couldn't wait.

Crazy how it had taken him less than twenty-four hours to completely embrace the words he'd felt pressed into his heart the day before. *Love Cheryl.*

Done. Now what?

Could it really be that easy? He felt ridiculously giddy, like he had when he realized he'd won his first race at age seven. But he'd felt this way before. A couple times with Kayla, but mostly on a mountain, after a killer ride. Adrenaline. That was all it was—chemistry gone crazy that made his heart pound and his head float.

That was a rush, a high. It wasn't love. But for today, it was there, and he'd ride it.

The crunch of rocks under the weight of tires drew his attention down the driveway. Sherbert cometh. Hallelujah. He toyed with the idea of asking her to stay, to see the kids and to witness what this ranch was about. Because then maybe she'd be impressed—proud of him and the man that he was becoming. And the high would just keep on soaring.

She climbed out of her Hot Wheels car and moved toward his house across the way. He'd intercept her, pull her back to the dining hall. As he passed the tables, already set for the twelve kids who were coming that week, he conjured an image of her at his side, working with him. Loving these kids, advocating for them long after they'd left the ranch. Cheryl was a lawyer—she could be a massive asset to Kelly's Ranch.

Picture perfect.

He pushed through the door and stepped onto the lodge's deck. "Sherbert."

She paused and turned, her loose hair fanning around her shoulders. Man, what a bonus that God pushed him to such a beautiful woman. Although, she could definitely stand to eat some more hot dogs. The winters up here would freeze her bones within three seconds. No wonder she was cold all the time.

"What's this all about, Brock Kelly?" She grinned even as her hands came to her hips. "I have things to do, you know."

"Did you bring me some cinnamon knots?"

"No. Nana sold out by nine this morning." She moved up the small hill toward the lodge.

Brock waited for her, admiring the view while he leaned against the railing. Cheryl bounced up the three steps to the deck and walked toward him. Smiling.

She was happy. Air filled his lungs and threatened to burst his chest.

"So, where is it?"

"Where is what?"

"Whatever you called me out here for."

"Maybe I just wanted to see you."

Pink brushed across her cheeks, and Brock reached for her hand. He didn't have to tug very hard for her to lean against his chest. That heady-floating feeling filled him as he wrapped both arms around her. Breathing deep, he inhaled the scent of cranberries.

"Did you steal my soap?"

He felt her chuckle against him. "You don't use it."

"How do you know?"

She buried her nose into him and inhaled, then tipped her chin up and looked at him with a raised brow. "What are you doing with girly soap in your home anyway?"

"A counselor left it in the women's washroom a few weeks back. Finders keepers."

One perfectly arched brow lifted higher. She believed him, didn't she? She didn't think...

Moving against him, she raised up on her toes and brushed her mouth against his. His thoughts tipped sideways as warmth rushed over him. Her lips lingered, and he moved one hand to cradle her head and the other to the small of her back, pulling her against him.

He hadn't kissed her yesterday. Not out in the field. Not on the water. Not when they'd come back to the ranch and he'd told her how much he liked having her along. She'd looked at him before she left—*the look*—the one that said she'd expected him to. That she was waiting for it. But he'd needed to think straight, so he hadn't.

Thinking had just blurred. This feeling...it could be love, right? Falling, floating, giving, wanting. It could be...

Or it could just be chemistry. Not the same thing.

Leaning his head against her forehead, he broke the kiss and drew in a cleansing breath. With her eyes closed and her heart strumming against his, he soaked in the moment. She looked happy.

His heart soared.

"So..." She didn't open her eyes as she spoke. "You just wanted to see me?"

"Oh, I wanted to see you." He moved for one more short kiss and then leaned away. "Because something came for you."

"That's what you said the first time. Which is it?"

"Not which. Where. And it's this way." He turned her toward the door and took her hand. Together they swept through the entry and past the tables to the piano. With a flourish of one hand, Brock indicated a small package waiting on the music shelf above the keys. "Ta-da."

"Mail? You're giving me your mail? This isn't a trick to get me to look at a lawsuit or something, is it?"

"You're so cute."

"No I'm not."

Really, she was. "Just open it."

"It's addressed to you. That's a federal offense."

"Not when I told you to do it, smarty pants."

She stuck out her tongue. Bet no one else had seen her do that. Ever. Brock loved it.

~*~

The manila envelope floated away as Cheryl stared at the soft, thin book. It'd been years since she'd held one, looked at one. She traced the image of a feather floating against a faded-blue background.

She knew every song inside. Once upon a time, she'd known them by heart and hadn't needed the music to play them.

"What do you think?" Brock brushed her elbow with one knuckle. "I know it's likely not the one you used to use...but maybe—"

"It's the exact book I played from."

That was amazing. How did he do it? Did he actually remember the book? Maybe he'd done more than listen to her play all those years before.

"I thought I remembered you playing most of those songs, so I hoped it was the one."

"Very impressive, Brock Kelly."

She looked up at him, and he grinned. There was power in his look, like he thought something about her was precious. It made her insides uncurl like a blossom that had been balled up against the chilly night and had just been grazed by the warm morning sun. A battle cracked that beautiful moment. This couldn't last, and she'd been bound to tell him that she was leaving. He was only infatuated with the girl he remembered anyway. He really didn't want the woman she'd become.

"Sit." The weight of his hands rested on her shoulders and squeezed. "Play."

She opened the music book and let her eyes filter over the titles. "All of Me," "Somewhere in Time," "Neverland," the "Feather Theme"... Her attention drifted down the list and landed on the last song. "Theme from *Sabrina*." The blossom inside shriveled, and she trembled.

"You okay?"

With a quick intake of breath, Cheryl pushed down the darkness clawing its way up and over her being and glanced at him. "Fine."

"Cold?"

Didn't even begin to describe...

He stepped behind her and secured both arms around her frame. "You should own a sweatshirt, Sherbert. You're always cold."

Sweatshirts, wool sweaters, heavy blankets—none ever warmed the frosty night in her heart. But there was no way to explain that. Cheryl leaned against the solid chest at her back and drew in two deep breaths. Here there was warmth, and it was so tempting to stay. She could play the charade, and maybe if she filled the role long enough, they would both believe it was the truth. He would never have to know. And maybe finally, finally the claws of the past would turn her loose.

With him, maybe she would be free.

His hands brushed over her arms, and he pressed a kiss to her hair. "Warm yet?"

"Better."

"Good. I'm dying to hear music from this old beat-up relic." He nudged her back. "Play."

But the *Sabrina* song...

She didn't have to play a single note of it. Stuck way back there at the end, she wouldn't have to turn to the final melody. *Block it out. Ignore it.*

Like it wasn't even there.

The narrow spine cracked as she opened the book to the "Feather Theme" and folded the binding back so the pages would stay put. With a single motion, she set the music on the piano and slid onto the bench, her fingers then finding the smooth, cool keys. Most were smooth. No, a few were smooth. Most had been roughed up by time and wear and abuse. But when she pressed three fingers down to form a simple G chord, the notes melted together pure and true.

She looked up at Brock, who stood a step back and behind her. "You fixed it."

"Just needed a little internal work." He winked. "I had a guy come out and tune it."

She looked back at the piano. A beat-up version of its former beauty. But it could still make beautiful music.

Drawing a breath, Cheryl looked over the first six measures of the "Feather Theme." It was like opening a forgotten file on her hard drive. Though she hadn't looked at the music in ages, it was familiar, and it pulled her in. Her fingers followed, stumbling a bit at the beginning, but as the movement of the music settled over her, the muscle memory began to awaken and take over.

Suddenly there wasn't a then and now with a slash separating the two. There was only the song, the music that had managed to survive in her heart. She was no longer Cheryl the hard and cold lawyer. Cheryl the beauty without a soul. Cheryl the used and then abandoned. She was Cheryl the song. Her own melody somehow sang beneath the notes that she played, harmonizing in a way that only her heart could hear. There was beauty in it. Real beauty—not the kind that she maintained with strict discipline. One that was her own, but not really from herself at all.

Inherent, not achieved.

Please...

Her eyes slid closed as she tried to grasp the intangible. Whatever it was that sang to her and for her, she wanted it to stay. The music hovered, its glow of warmth radiating over her and fueling the song that traveled from her heart to her fingers. No longer did she play what was written, but a song that her memory couldn't immediately identify, yet was certain she knew.

"Be still my soul..." Brock's baritone voice behind her shattered the isolation, but the music continued flowing through her heart and out her fingers. "...the Lord is on thy side."

Breathing became labored. A hymn. She'd been playing a hymn, one that she'd learned about a year after her mother's death. A shiver ran down her spine, and her arms trembled. Yet the music continued, and Brock continued to sing.

"Thy best, thy heavenly Friend through thorny ways leads to a joyful end."

The final chord sounded, and then she curled her fingers into her palm. She bit her bottom lip, drawing a shuddering breath. What had just happened?

Brock's warm palm lay on her shoulder. "I don't remember hearing you play that."

"I didn't, not when we were older."

"When did you?"

"I learned it when I was fourteen. I'd forgotten..." She pushed her hands, now folded together, into her lap. "I don't know why I played it just now."

He slid onto the bench next to her, his hand moving beneath her hair to cup her neck. "Maybe you needed to hear it."

The song—the lyrics made her soul quake. That couldn't be good. She and God, that heavenly "friend," were strangers. They'd long since practiced a cold silence, and there wasn't any possible way He would want to lead her to "a joyful end."

Brock's hand squeezed against her neck. "You okay?"

"Yeah." The word came rushed and punchy. Like a door slamming closed.

"You can talk to me, you know?" His hand slid down her spine. "I've learned to be a decent listener."

While still staring at her hands, Cheryl forced a smile on her lips. It felt like those waxy versions they used to use at Halloween. Or maybe more like the kind the morgue would shape to the face of a corpse.

Brock didn't need a corpse in his life.

She pushed her shoulders back and looked at him. "Listen, Brock. This has been fun. The kayak trip, and the piano...it's all sweet. But I'm leaving soon, and I don't see you following me, so maybe whatever this is needs to end here."

He studied her, and the look in his eyes said he didn't believe a word of it. "You hate your job."

"It is what it is."

"Doesn't have to be."

"Look, I have a life in LA. I never intended to stay here."

"What do you have in LA?"

Her chest seemed to lock down hard as irritation took hold. "I don't have to answer to you."

"What about Nana?"

She growled. "I'm taking care of it. And it's not your business."

He continued to search her, his jaw clenching. "I think you're running."

"Think what you want." She couldn't look him in the eye. Mashing her lips together, she slid away from him to get up.

His hand locked on her elbow, and she looked down at his grip before meeting his stare.

Her heart stalled.

No man had ever looked at her with that depth. Her soul felt naked, and the thought that he could see, that he *knew*...

Shame crashed like ice shards over her heart.

No joyful end. Not for her. She'd made her choices long before this moment, and she would have to live with it long after it passed. Brock didn't need to be a part of that nightmare.

She tugged her arm, but he maintained a firm, but not tight, hold. "One secret."

Her chest tightened harder. "No."

"Just one, and I'll let you go."

Her lips trembled as she pressed them together. Surely she could think of one dumb thing to tell him. Something insignificant. Something that wouldn't tie up her heart any further.

"How about I go first?" He stood, moving so he was in front of her. That look...

Oh, stop. I can't do this...

One rough finger snugged under her chin, forcing her gaze to his.

"Brock, don't." She swallowed, cleared her throat, and pushed forward. "Okay, my secret...I can't stay here. Not because I don't want to. I just can't."

"That's a mystery, not a secret."

"That's all I can give you."

Truly. She'd never been that deep or honest with anyone, and she couldn't offer any more. She stepped away from the halo of his body heat, and his fingers slowly uncurled.

Blinking, she looked away. "Good-bye, Brock."

The music and the man who, for a moment, had warmed her soul. She left them both. They couldn't be a part of her life.

~17~

Brock watched Cheryl as she passed through the doors leading outside, his heart in a jumbled knot.

She was leaving. Was he supposed to stop her?

It'd been stupid to think that they'd fall in love over the weekend. That wasn't how it worked. He hadn't wanted anything to do with women—love—in the first place.

Man, what was this squeeze in his chest about? Made it hard to breathe.

He followed her outside but turned to the deck rail rather than taking the steps down toward the driveway. Leaning on the railing, he traced her path with his gaze as Cheryl continued her retreat and ducked into her car. After a quick turn of the engine, she reversed and accelerated toward the highway.

Gone. She hadn't even looked back.

That was what he got for listening to his imagination.

Love Cheryl? Sounded so...storybook while they were lying in the grass with her hand in his. What was God thinking?

Love her.

Seriously? She just left. Clearly his head was wrong.

The words branded themselves in his mind—he could visualize them in capped, boldface type. And that tightness in his chest? He ran a hand across his sternum. Could be indigestion. Severe indigestion.

Or not.

God, You're going to have to bring her back. Or maybe I'm supposed to go after her?

The music that Cheryl had played five minutes before drifted through his mind. *Be still my soul, the Lord is on thy side...*

He wasn't good at waiting. And trusting? Kayla had killed that.

I didn't want a woman, remember?

The melody kept playing against his arguments, and he could still see those two words embedded in his thoughts.

Love her.

This was going to be much harder than he had thought.

~*~

She'd left the music on the piano. Intentionally. But the melodies, long locked away, collided into a medley of songs deep into the night.

All the more reason to leave. She couldn't think here. She couldn't capture control and keep her thoughts within the tracks that she'd determined acceptable. That moment of surreal...love? Wasn't real. She needed to stick with real and manageable.

Brock was not manageable.

He'd been about to say something deep before she left. Something that was going to undo her, make her tidy, well-managed life explode with all sorts of messy details from the past. How ignorant it had been for her to imagine that she could maintain a charade—be with him and pretend the past didn't exist. He tugged on her timeline, dragging her history forward as if compelled to unpack it, to examine each little horrible detail. Lawyers did that. They practiced until they became proficient at it, using the details to nail a conviction.

It never worked out well for the one whose baggage was being examined.

She couldn't go there. She didn't have to.

In the morning she'd pack the little bit of clothing that she'd pulled out of her carry-on and take her ugly rental to the Yampa Valley Regional Airport. The first flight west would be carrying her and her luggage. This time for keeps. The only thing separating her and escape was six hours, more or less, of sleep.

She squeezed her eyes shut. Sleep.

Practiced her relaxation routine. Sleep.

Slowly, the feeling of drifting began to carry her consciousness.

Please don't let me dream...

⁓*⁓

Cheryl was certain she was the last person he expected to find on his front deck the following morning. Brock met her at the door, the shadow of his unshaven whiskers darker than usual. He looked into her eyes as he leaned against the doorframe.

"Thought you were catching a plane."

"Me too."

He lifted an eyebrow.

"I don't have an answer, so don't ask."

His eyes asked, but silence stayed on his lips. He leaned back, sweeping his hand toward the inside of his house as an invitation. Cheryl stepped over the threshold and then followed him as he moved toward the kitchen. The only sound that filled the air was the gurgling of Mr. Coffee as it spit out the last of its steaming brew.

"You look tired, Sherbert."

Cheryl ducked away so he couldn't examine her so closely. "I didn't sleep well last night."

"I was just making coffee. You want some?"

She nodded. He turned to the cabinet to grab another clean mug. His continued silence pricked her tongue into action.

"I was at the airport, and the flight was delayed because of the storms out west. Then I couldn't find my ID to check my luggage. I swear I looked in every fold and zipper in my wallet and purse. In the middle of my search, Nana called and said she just had a feeling I shouldn't be on that plane. And I..."

She'd known even before she settled in her little car that morning that she shouldn't be leaving. But saying that...it would lead to talking about her dreams. She'd die if she had to do that.

The dream the night before had been altered. The voice behind her, telling her not to go through the door, had been Brock's gentle tenor, and he was nearly begging her not to do it. And the music—there hadn't ever been music in that awful dream. Last night, however, the faint chords of the *Sabrina* song drifted from behind a different door, a door that hadn't been there before. Remembering all of it made breathing a challenge.

Brock stood motionless in her pause and then set the mug down on the counter, his intense look seizing her heart. Men didn't look at her like that. Lust, yes. But this yearning in his gentle eyes, it was soul deep. He snagged a place deep inside, tugging on it like a lost treasure sunk deep into a murky bog. The pull was painful and terrifying. She'd been safe in that capsule of loneliness. Not happy, but safe.

But what would it be like to breathe? To touch the fresh air, to expand her lungs? To feel? The thought made her want to curl into a ball and hide in a dark place.

She moved to push a clump of hair that had fallen over her eyes. He beat her to it, and their fingers brushed as he tucked it behind her ear. His large, rough hand enclosed over hers and brought it to brush her knuckles against his lips.

"You had the same feeling." He finished the sentence she'd left hanging.

Cheryl studied him as she slowly pulled her hand away from his. Most men would make that statement with a clip of arrogance, as if they were the magnetic force holding her whole world in place. Brock didn't. Matter of fact, a tinge of wonder mixed in his tone.

"It's been a long time since I've had a feeling like that...or at least, since I've followed it. Especially when it runs counter to what I want."

He stepped away to pour her coffee. "Do you know what you want?"

A small, defeated laugh left her chest as she accepted the cup of coffee. He was always probing...

"No."

Raw honesty. He'd said from the beginning *no lies.* Did that mean exposing everything? Brock seemed to want it all—everything she had locked in her heart.

But really, he didn't. She was certain he really, really didn't want to know.

Her stomach rolled, and she slouched as she wrapped her arms over her middle. Another quiver rattled her insides. What was she doing here? She should have been on a plane.

"Did you find your ID?"

Cheryl looked up to find him studying her, still with that depth that made her cower, but also with a hint of lightness that said if she wasn't ready, it was okay.

She sipped her coffee and nodded. "It was in my wallet. I found it when I was going through my purse at Nana's. After my flight left. It'd been there the whole time. I don't know how I missed it."

Brock leaned against the counter, his jean-covered legs stretched out and one ankle propped over the other. His blue flannel shirt hung only half buttoned—he'd probably shed it before noon as the warm summer sun pushed the temperatures upward, and he'd finish the day out with his trademark gray V-neck T-shirt. Everything about him said casual, easygoing. Everything about her was anything but.

He shouldn't want her.

Pushing away from the counter, Brock stood straight and covered the three steps between them. Without pause, he reached for her coffee with one hand, and with the other he threaded her hair and moved to cradle her against his chest. Also trademark Brock.

The sound of the mug thunking against the counter was followed by the feel of his other arm tucking her close. She closed her eyes, breathing in the fresh musk of his scent, and savored the warmth of his arms. When she raised her arms and wrapped them around him, he strengthened his hold.

"Maybe it's time to stop running, Sherbert." A ripple of his breath passed over her hair as he whispered against her.

Life with this man...it'd be worth coming home for. Except she couldn't stop running.

He wouldn't be able to understand that. Not unless she told him.

But if she did that, this beautiful thing with him would be gone. And this time she'd feel the rejection more deeply than with any other man because he'd melted her indifference.

She'd be alone again. She was certain she couldn't endure that.

~18~

"How's Nana holding up?" Brock rounded the table to Cheryl's left, setting plates as he talked.

Earlier in his kitchen, he'd held her in silence for she couldn't think how long. Willing to simply be, he hadn't pushed her to talk about the day before, her leaving, or for promises for the future. When she was ready, she stepped away, and together they headed over to the lodge. Brock had let her hand go when they reached the piano, and she accepted his silent urging to play.

She'd heard his heart in his wordless embrace. Every beat against her cheek had felt like a tattoo embedding on hers. What was she to do? She'd meant what she'd told him before; she couldn't stay. She really couldn't fathom a life in Hayden when the memories, and with them, the suffocating sense of guilt, surfaced so easily. But with every moment spent with him, trying to imagine going back to her cold, lonely existence became harder. After this taste of life with Brock...how could she accept the emptiness of life before?

Stuck. So, so stuck.

But that didn't have any bearing on what Brock had just asked her.

Cheryl spun on the piano bench to face him. "She's fine. Honestly, I think Ethan's overly concerned."

"Oh, she's had some interesting moments." His mouth twisted to the side. "Did E tell you about her little trip up to Rabbit Ears?"

"No." Unease twisted in her gut. They didn't talk about Rabbit Ears Peak. Taboo for the Thompson family, and anyone connected to them. "When was that?"

"Couple months back. He'd been out here working, and when he got back into town, he found the bakery abandoned—and a couple of pans of bad-smelling rolls turning to charcoal in the oven."

"What?"

"Yep. She'd left them and headed up the pass."

"Why?"

Brock set the last of the plates on the table and looked up at her. The seriousness in his eyes said it all.

A lump grew in her throat. "She was looking for my mom?"

He nodded.

Mom had been gone for almost twenty years. What had Nana been thinking?

"E said it was hard to get her home. She kept insisting she had to find Janie. He was pretty ripped up about it."

So Nana's slips from reality weren't harmless. The bakery could have burned to the ground—even taking the little shops on either side of its location with it. Nana could have been lost—how did E even know to go looking for her by the peak? Neither of them had left a boot imprint on a trail anywhere near Rabbit Ears in decades.

"You okay, Sherbert?"

"Yeah." She sighed, slumping until her elbows rested on her knees. "I'm just trying to piece it together. I don't understand why she'd do that."

"The mind is pretty powerful."

"Why would she slip back there though? It was so long ago."

Brock shrugged and settled beside her. "I don't know. They say memories have a way of surfacing...songs, smells, someone who looks like the person from the past. Maybe it was the time of year. I don't remember—when did your mom die?"

"Late summer, right after the tourist season." Cheryl twisted her fingers, focusing her energy on holding on to indifference. This long passed, it shouldn't balloon her emotions to talk about her mom's death. It happened, they got through it, and there'd been a long stretch of time since. "It was really weird—freak accident. She wasn't even climbing one of the more difficult routes."

Brock's hand brushed along her spine. "What happened?"

Cheryl sat straighter. His gesture was sweet, but she was a big girl. She didn't need to lean on his shoulder for this. "She was going for one of the trickier transition holds, and the volcanic rock chose that moment to crumble. Her harness failed, and she dropped. Impact crushed her ribs and punctured her lungs. Her climbing partner scurried down to help her, but by the time the emergency responders got to them, Mom was gone."

Brock moved to hold her hand, but Cheryl stood, stepping out of his reach.

"I'm sorry, Sherbert."

Not looking at him, she shrugged as she sealed off the nudging emotions deep in her heart. "She lived on the edge and loved climbing. I guess we're happy she died doing something so important to her. What do you do?"

He didn't move, but she could feel his stare. Maybe the question really was, what would he do with her? She hated counseling sessions and didn't want to start one with him. Her dad had forced her into them for months after Mom died. Cheryl didn't see a point. Mom was dead. Talking about it wasn't going to bring her back. Exploring her feelings about it wasn't going to put her life back on the path she'd been on before. It happened, it was over, and life moved on. The end.

But Brock, he was the probing kind. Maybe that's what this whole thing with him was about. He saw her hardness, thought she was wounded and needed some fixing, and he had a Fix-It-Felix syndrome going on.

She didn't need that. Didn't want it either. Crossing her arms, Cheryl turned to look at him, intending to say good-bye and mentally making plans to catch the early flight tomorrow morning. This time, she wouldn't let a few hiccups keep her on the ground.

Brock's eyes met hers. "She misses you."

"What?" Her dead mother missed her? He was crazy.

"Nana Grace. She misses you. More this year—at least she shows it more this year—than ever. I don't know why, what triggered it. But she talks about you often. Her sweet girl—says she'll come home soon and everything will be okay. That you'll find your way back."

Cheryl clenched her jaw. That was exactly what Nana had said in her delusional slip the other night.

"Maybe she's talking about my mother, not me. She's a little nuts, you know."

"She's a little heartbroken." His eyebrows hiked. "And when she describes her girl, it's her little raven-haired sweetie. That wasn't your mom, was it?"

Mom had light-brown hair and amber eyes. Cheryl favored her dad, who in his younger years had looked like Tom Selleck. Mom had always said that Cheryl had been twice blessed from her father—Hollywood good looks and an Einstein IQ. Both were wildly exaggerated, and sometimes Cheryl got the feeling that her mother wished just a little bit that her daughter had inherited her crazy thirst for adventure, and maybe at least her hair color.

"Nana's not stable. She could have easily gotten us confused." Because she and her mother were so much alike.

"Don't think so."

"Why?"

"Because when she went to look for Janie, she was specific about it. When she talks about you, there's no confusion about who she's thinking of, just about where she actually is physically."

And he was such an expert. "I think you should stick to things you know. Riding the slopes—you were good at that. Psychology? You're not really qualified."

He folded his hands and leaned against his knees. For a moment he held her look, and then his attention moved toward the floor.

Man, she was a razor sometimes.

"I'm going." Her arms fell to her sides, and she shimmied around the table as she moved toward the exit.

Brock, still sitting, straightened, and when she came near enough, he reached to grasp her arm. "Stop running, Sherbert."

She stopped but held herself stiffly. "This is dumb. I don't even know why I'm here. And stop calling me Sherbert."

"Will you stay if I stop?"

"No."

His thumb brushed the inside of her forearm, and the tension drained from her muscles. Her traitorous body. Certainly he felt her relax, because his hand slid down her arm until their palms kissed and his fingers clasped around hers. With a gentle tug, he pulled her toward his lap, and she couldn't fight the gravity that set her on his thigh.

But she didn't have to look at him.

"Cheryl."

No. Not going to meet those deep, beckoning eyes. She was leaving. He wasn't going to change her mind. "What do you want from me, Brock? I told you already—I can't stay. I can't fix Nana, and you and I aren't going to work."

"Why?"

Why...to all three things? Cheryl sighed and pressed her lips together.

Brock didn't wait for her to answer. "I saw you the other day, in the grass, under the sun. You smiled. The kind of smile that people have when they go home."

"So? Lots of people smile in the sun."

"Do you?"

She rolled her head to the side to look at him. "Stop this. I'm not a project. I don't need you to fix me."

"I didn't think you needed fixed."

"Then what are you doing?"

His mouth closed, but he held her look.

"Why would you want to be with me? What did you call me that first night at the bonfire? An ice princess? Why would you want that in your life?"

"That's what you were acting like. That's not who you are."

He knew this how...because he saw her smile the other day? That was ridiculous. But her heart scrambled after his claim, longing for it to be so. Couldn't it be true, if Brock Kelly saw something other than a stone-cold woman in her, couldn't it be so?

Probably not. Because she'd worked too hard at indifference to let anything else be a part of who she was.

"I think you want me to be the girl you remember. But I'm not. Brock, trust me. You don't want this."

"I think you're scared."

"Of what?"

"That you're wrong. About all of it. I think you've got that woman—the one I know is in you—locked up for some reason, and you're afraid to let her out because she might get hurt." He leaned his forehead against the spot just above her ear, and his voice dropped to a whisper that danced across her cheek. "And I think you're terrified of this."

Cheryl swallowed as the hair on her arms prickled against her skin.

"Am I right?"

Why was she still sitting there? She pushed away, determined to leave, but one arm snugged around her waist, and with his other hand, Brock grazed her chin and turned her to look at him.

"No lies, Cheryl. Are you scared?"

Did anyone ever lie to this man? It didn't seem possible as she suddenly felt hypnotized in his steady gaze.

"Yes." The hushed word left her mouth before her discipline could stop it. She squeezed her eyes shut, too cowardly to see his reaction.

He shifted her so that she curled against him and then cradled her head into the curve of his neck. "Me too, Sherbert. I promise, though— I'm not going to hurt you."

Tension pulled on the base of her skull. Threads of pain began to stitch their way into her brain. She knew he was sincere. Brock wouldn't hurt her—not on purpose.

She wished desperately that she could give him the same promise.

~*~

Preteen kids filed off the bus, one after another, their initial responses to the ranch almost universally the same. They'd drop down off the final rise of the bus, take one or two tentative steps forward, and then stall. Adjusting their backpacks, they'd survey the scene—the pond, the cabins, the lodge, Brock's cabin, and finally the sky. Before they moved off toward the lodge with the others who'd gone before, they'd look back at the bus as if they were leaving one world and entering another and were unsure if that was a good thing.

As often as he'd seen this patterned reaction, Brock couldn't guess the thoughts running through those little minds. He wished he could know...were they excited to be here? Or maybe indifferent. It was one more place they had to try because home didn't really exist. Had they been coerced into coming? Probably—they didn't exactly have a choice in the matter. Did that make them mad? Had they ever been in the heart of the mountains before? Had they ever seen anything so wide and big? Did it thrill them? Scare them?

He couldn't tell. They kept an emotionless mask firmly in place. A skill acquired by necessity.

He stood on the deck, watching the unloading scene, and his thoughts drifted back to Cheryl. Music floated softly from the dining hall behind him—he'd managed to talk Cheryl into staying, into playing while he finished his preparations for the week. He'd been shocked when she did.

Her thoughts were about as evasive as those kids'. Crazy, he could predict the pattern of her actions, but the thoughts behind them? That was the key. He'd never be able to understand her unless she stopped closing up.

The accusation she'd thrown earlier continued to chase through his mind. She wasn't a project, and she didn't need him to fix her. Fixing wasn't his business anyhow, so that seemed irrelevant. But did he see her as a project? Did he see these kids as projects?

He saw them as his calling—both the kids that came to the ranch and now Cheryl. That wasn't the same thing as a project, was it?

The sound of two car doors shutting one right after the other cracked through the thin air, drawing Brock's attention from the growing circle of kids and the four counselors who'd arrived on the bus with them. Brandi circled the familiar Isuzu Trooper that had just parked near his cabin and moved to the passenger's side, where Ethan waited, his hand stretched out to her as she came near.

Lovebirds. Brock grinned, even as his stomach twisted a bit. A weekend trip to Denver was hardly a honeymoon—and he knew for a fact that Brandi had squeezed in a meeting with the overseeing office while she was there. What a way to begin their marriage. He wished he could have changed it. When she told him about the wedding, he'd told her that he'd call the office and cancel the group that week and ask them to reschedule her mandatory check-in. She'd insisted that he didn't.

"Ethan and I have our whole lives together," she'd said.

Brock had tossed that one back and forth in his head for about a week, and then he'd gone to Ethan about it. It was true they were committing to a lifetime together, but still...

If it were him, he'd want a little bit of time alone with his bride. More than a weekend littered with business meetings.

Ethan hadn't seemed as confident in his answer when Brock finally brought it up. But he didn't contradict Brandi either. "She'll feel guilty about letting the kids down," he said, and then he changed the subject, asking about which flies Brock was tying in his limited spare time.

Guilt swirled as those conversations replayed. Brock watched as the newlyweds moved hand in hand toward the lodge. When they neared the group, Ethan kissed Brandi's forehead, released her hand, and continued toward the deck. She stayed, shaking hands with the counselors—two of which had been up before—and then began introducing herself to the kids, one by one.

Ethan climbed the hill and took the steps to the deck. Brock stuck out his fist when E came near, and after a bump, he moved for a man hug.

"How's the groom?"

E grinned. "Married."

"Yeah. Is that good?"

"So far, can't complain."

Brock chuckled.

"Dude, is that my sister playing in there?" Ethan tipped his head backward, indicating the lodge.

"Yep."

"How'd you swing that?"

Brock didn't answer, and he bit back his smile.

"Hmm..." Ethan rocked back on his heels and crossed his arms. "Been taking up a different kind of fishing while I was gone, eh?"

"Like you didn't set that whole deal up. Fresh-baked rolls. You're such a dog."

"I expect gratitude, man, not insults." He faked a jab-hook combo and then bumped Brock's arm. "And she'd be as good for you as you'd be for her."

Brock lifted an eyebrow. "What does that mean?"

"You'll get her. See past the box of steel she lives in. And she'll keep your head from ballooning."

"My head from ballooning?"

"Yeah. You know, because you think every woman that comes up here has some ulterior motive that has to do with the great and powerful Brock Kelly."

"What?"

"Bro." Ethan turned to face him, his eyebrows shoved up into his forehead. "Don't deny truth. That's exactly what you think. You stare down your nose at these women, who, for the most part, are just here to do their job. Don't think for a minute my sister won't call you out on it.

I haven't seen her much over the past decade, but I can tell you right now, she knows arrogance like she knows the C scale, and she'll drill you on it."

This was turning out to be a great day. "Maybe you should go back to your wife."

Ethan laughed. "She is awesome, right?"

Brock eyed him and a grin poked out.

Ethan clapped him on the shoulder. "My wife has work to do, and so do you. So I'm going to see my sister."

He did have work to do—and apparently a bad image to overcome. Time to meet the help and not assume the worst of them. Moving to the steps behind Ethan, he stalled and caught E before he went into the dining hall.

"Don't let her leave."

E gave him a suspicious look. "That doesn't sound good."

He didn't know the half of it. "Just, seriously. I don't care if you have to hide her keys. Don't let her take off."

I knew in my gut the truth. I ignored it. Buried it.

You called to me—beckoned me back. I refused to listen.

But I didn't know what else to do. Threatened with humiliation, with loneliness, and with a task I was certain I could not do, I felt trapped. Not like stuck in traffic, but like a doe caught in the iron teeth of a bear trap. The sacrifice would lead to life, even if it meant I left part of me behind.

Life. That's what I thought I was walking toward. It seemed my only real option. So though it was dark ahead and I was terrified, I moved forward.

In my innocence, I had no idea how dead someone could feel.

I am a cold tomb, a walking cube of lifeless existence. Breathing but frozen.

Trapped in a life that is everyday death.

~19~

"Ethan, my head is screaming obscenities at me." Her palms covered her eyes as she tried to focus on controlled breathing exercises. That dull ache from before flashed hard and fast into a full-on migraine. "Just let me go home."

"Can't. I promised Brock. I don't think you should drive like this anyway."

She felt his weight compress the cushions beneath her on the small, cheap vinyl sofa she'd curled up on. Ethan's hand settled on her shoulder and squeezed.

"What's with the headaches, Sherbert?" he spoke softly. "This is the third migraine that I know about since you got here. Have you seen a doctor?"

"Stop," she moaned. "I can't talk about this right now. I'm gonna be sick."

He moved again, and she felt something like cold plastic pushed against one hand.

"Here."

She peeked through the small shaft of light made by her squinting lids. He'd given her a large empty yogurt container.

"I'll dump it if you do get sick. Just stay here. Can you take an Advil?"

Like one little tablet would touch this. "Or four."

"What do you want to drink?"

Stop talking. Stop making her think. "I don't care. I just want my bed. And quiet. And darkness."

Quiet. That would have prevented the explosion of pain in the first place. If she'd known a passel of kids was going to burst through the lodge doors while she was playing the piano, she wouldn't have let Brock talk her into staying. She'd thought they were coming in the evening, not at two o'clock in the afternoon.

Why hadn't he said anything?

"Okay. I'll go find some meds and see if I can track down Brock." He squeezed her arm again. "Stay put. I mean it, Sherbert. You're not going anywhere right now, so don't move."

The cushions shifted again as Ethan moved away. She could hear the faint sounds of Brock's cook—Cammy?—stirring around in the kitchen. She'd apparently been off visiting her daughter during the small break after the wedding, but now, as the kids would be hungry for supper in a few hours, she worked by herself in the next room. That noise blended with the chorus of shouts outside. The kids were playing some sort of game organized by Brock and Brandi. Something to do with a flag and running and screaming.

Brock was out there in the whole mix. She'd watched for a time. He came alive, very much like her memory of him on race days. All energy, full-blown smiles, and fun. The kids breathed in his enthusiasm, and somehow it seemed their marionette strings, which had pulled them half alive from the bus, fell away, and they became real. Vivid. And loud.

No more screaming.

She moaned, pressing one ear into the vinyl beneath her head and covering her face with her free hand. No more noise. Please, let a black blanket of silence overtake her. Please...please...

"Hey, Sherbert." Brock's soft voice drifted from above her head. "What's going on? E says you're not feeling well."

She pulled her hand away from her face and forced her eyelids open. Light pierced through her skull like jagged blazes of lightning, and she could make out the features of his face as he hovered over the back side of the sofa. "Headache. Need to go home." She squeezed her eyes shut again.

"Pretty bad, huh?" His fingers brushed over her cheek. "Don't think you'd better drive if you can't even open your eyes."

"Please, Brock. Just tell Ethan to give me my keys."

"No. I'll take you."

"Brock, the kids...they love you. You need to stay."

"E and Brandi have got it. No worries, kid." He came around to the front of her temporary bed and lifted her shoulders up. Squatting, he slid an arm under her legs as if to lift her.

"I can walk."

"Can you see?"

"If you pick me up, I'll puke on you. Let me walk."

Brock chuckled. "Even sick, you sure have bite, you know that, Sherbert?"

She couldn't even raise her eyes to him to give him a proper scowl. "Just take me home."

"All right. Here we go." He guided her to her feet, and though he'd just insulted her, his arm came around her waist with a gentle touch.

Her stomach rolled as a painful dizzy spell washed over her. A high-pitched squeal rang through her ears, and the world became a harsh collage of sharp, blazing white shapes. Though irritated that she was in the middle of this migraine because of Brock's failure to communicate, she tucked her face against his gray T-shirt, covering her exposed ear with one hand.

"You gonna be sick?"

She moaned.

"I'm pretty sure that's yes. You want to puke here, or can you wait until we get to the cabin?"

What cabin? "Home," she mumbled against his shirt.

"Okay. Here we go." He held her tight against him as they moved forward. He directed her blind steps out the door and down the stairs. Something felt off as they continued, but she couldn't bring herself to look at the blinding light beyond her shut eyes. The sense of disorientation grew as the ground didn't dip beneath her feet as it should have, and when Brock paused, he didn't bend to open a car door. He reached forward, and the click of a latch didn't sound right.

He moved her forward again, and the light beyond her closed eyes lessened.

"Brock." She stopped moving and pushed against his chest, forcing herself to look. His cabin. She wanted to crumble, and tears stung the base of her eyelids. "I want to go home. Please, you said you'd take me home."

His hand cupped the back of her head, and he pulled her against him again. "No one's there to check on you."

"So?" She'd done this drill a million times. She didn't need anyone to check on her.

"I'll worry."

"I'm a big girl."

"You could just sleep it off in my guest bed. Clean sheets and everything. I promise."

She leaned against him, his mild scent filling her nose as she worked on those unsuccessful breathing rituals. Deep breath in. Focus on the strong rhythm of his heart against her cheek. Long breath out. The pads of his fingers gently massaged the base of her neck. In. He held her up. She didn't have to be alone. Out.

A shout cracked the air outside, jarring her brain and sending a mushroom cloud of pain into her skull. Her entire body coiled, fighting against the roll of nausea building from the deep.

There was no winning against it. With a jerk, she pulled out of his hold and jammed her face into the yogurt container she still gripped in one hand. The convulsion sent her to her knees, and Brock gathered her hair in both his fists while her stomach emptied.

A cold sweat covered her skin, and all her strength drained. She moved to lie against the floor but found herself being pulled into Brock's lap. Had he gone down on the floor with her? The container she'd just filled with putrid fluid was removed from her hands, and a soft kiss brushed her forehead.

"That was fun," he whispered.

Horrible. Not fun. Crazy man.

"Please take me home, Brock."

He pressed another kiss to her head. "Okay. Stay put for a minute, and I'll get the truck."

She was moved and gently laid against the cool wood floor, and then he shuffled away.

God, please... she moaned, wanting to cry but knowing it would do no good. *Please make these stop...*

She was somewhere between fitful sleep and painfully awake when Brock lifted her again. This time she didn't argue. As long as she was going home. There was no way she could stay at his cabin. Even if she had loved seeing Brock be the fun those kids needed.

The nightmare was coming. It was usually the most vivid right after a migraine, and there had been nights when she'd woken herself up with her own sobs.

No one needed to know anything about that. Especially not Brock.

~*~

"I'm going to stay a little longer." Brock clutched the phone against his ear. "She's puked three times, and she doesn't seem coherent anymore. Nana Grace is already asleep, and she seemed a little...distant tonight. I just want to make sure they'll be okay."

Ethan sighed. "I can come stay with them if you think I should."

"No, dude." Brock brushed his chin. "You're still on your honeymoon, sort of. Everything's okay with the kids, right?"

"Yep. Dinner was good, and they're all settled. Nothing to worry about. Brandi needs to chat with you about some stuff from her meetings, but that'll keep for the morning."

"Okay. I think I'll just give it another hour or so, and then I'll head back."

"'Kay." Ethan snickered. "So you kind of like my sister, eh, bro?"

Brock rolled his eyes.

"Only took you like fifteen years to admit it," Ethan said.

"You would have killed me back in the day."

"Nah. Not you. I would have thought you were weird, because, dude, she's my little sister. But I trust you. I have to say, though, good luck with that one. She's no damsel in distress, if you know what I mean."

Maybe completely untrue. Distress didn't always look like a cry for help. Sometimes it looked like a well-trained blade of steel.

"She's definitely not boring."

Ethan laughed. "Always the thrill seeker, right?"

Yeah, something like that. "Hang up and go find your wife."

"Done. Later."

The call ended, and the space around him grew still. Brock glanced up the stairway, hoping by then Cheryl was lost in a black cloak of nothingness. Poor woman. Ethan had said this had happened before since she'd come home. That was a little concerning. Maybe she needed to visit a doctor or something.

Obviously not tonight. There was nothing else he could do. He'd catch a *Burn Notice* rerun or something, check on Sherbert after, and then go home. He should be in his own bed by midnight, and they'd start again tomorrow.

Michael and Fiona were about to blow a hole in some warehouse on the television screen, when a cry sounded from the space above the couch, where Brock had stretched out. He looked at the ceiling, as if he could see through it, and waited.

It came again, stronger. Then another, still louder.

"Stop!" Terror trembled through Cheryl's scream.

In a breath, Brock was on his feet and taking the steps two at a time.

"Stop." This time she pleaded, tears in her voice.

He didn't pause at her bedroom door, but clawed at the knob, pushing with his shoulder as if he needed to break through. The door gave, and he found Cheryl huddled against her headboard, rocking back and forth, her hands clutching her hair, arms pressed against her ears. Spasms of sobs quaked over her body.

He'd never heard a cry come from so deep, as if her very soul were ripping apart.

Three long strides carried him to her bed. She didn't fight him when he touched her shoulders—strange, because he would have sworn she was being attacked in her dream—so he gathered her close and held her tight as she continued to cry.

"Shhh, Sherbert. You're safe. I've got you, and you're safe."

Her hands dug into his shirtfront, and she turned her face into his chest. She continued to tremble with sobs.

"Cheryl, wake up. You're safe."

"Make them stop."

"Make who stop what?"

"Stop crying. Please, please stop crying," she pleaded desperately.

Brock moved so that he could take her head in his hands and look at her. "Cheryl, you have to wake up. Who is crying?"

She hid her face, trying to tuck it into her shoulder. He wouldn't let her.

"Baby, wake up!" His fingers pressing into her head, he gave her a small shake.

Cheryl's hands covered his and initially tried to push him away, but then she looked at him and stilled. Completely. She blinked twice, sniffed, and then took in a long, shaky breath.

"I'm sorry." Her voice hitched.

He loosened his hold as he exhaled, suddenly aware of how his heart throbbed against his ribs. "Are you okay?"

"Yes."

Her hands slid from his, and he combed through her hair with one hand. She turned away, removing herself from his lap.

"Cheryl?"

"I'm fine."

He caught her hand. It still shook. Not at all fine. "Tell me what happened. In your dream."

After slipping her hand from his, she shuffled until she could slide between the sheets. Brock moved off the mattress, landing on his knees next to her bed.

"Talk to me."

"It was nothing." She reached for the heavy top quilt.

Brock beat her to it and brought the covers over her shoulder and tucked them under her chin. "That was not nothing."

She shut her eyes. "Go home, Brock."

He cupped her head with one hand, and with his thumb, he traced her dark eyebrow. "Cheryl..." His voice cracked.

Turning into the pillow beneath her head, she burrowed away from him.

What should he do? With a light touch, he fingered the wisps of hair that had escaped from beneath the quilt. Cheryl didn't move. The silences grew heavy and felt as if it were pushing between them, building a barrier he couldn't see or understand.

What was she keeping from him? Why would she refuse to tell him what had terrified her so violently?

Someone along the way had done something to her. Rape? Yes. That was likely it. His stomach twisted. Surely she would know that she needn't be ashamed of something out of her control. Surely she would know that he wouldn't reject her because of it.

Apparently she didn't know. The bondage of fear wasn't always rational. He'd learned as he worked with trauma kids that their behaviors didn't always come from rational places—they were often rooted in fear. Fear that the worst would happen all over again.

No. Cheryl didn't know she was safe with him. He'd simply have to show her...and maybe, over time, she'd begin to trust.

~*~

Brock finally left.

Cheryl rolled to her back, horrified. And yet she secretly wished that he'd stayed. Maybe even pushed a little more. That he hadn't let her retreat into her lonely, cold existence, maintaining a death grip on a secret she wished desperately she didn't have to keep.

No, that wasn't what she really wished. If he'd pushed, eventually he'd find out. All of those loving looks, those tender touches...they'd be gone. Irrevocably removed.

Irrevocable. That was the word, wasn't it? Some things were irrevocable. Nothing fixes them. You can't take them back.

You simply live with them. Or die. Sometimes the two were the same—a living death.

A door unlatched beyond her bedroom, and the sound of shuffling feet whispered from the hall.

"Brock?" Nana's hushed voice drifted to Cheryl's hearing.

He was still there?

"Hi, Nana Grace. This...I...uh..."

Cheryl imagined Brock looking to his hands, his ears bright red.

"She has them quite a lot," Nana said softly.

"The nightmares?"

"Yes. I hear her whimpering. They've never been that...violent before though."

A pause settled. Then, "I was downstairs, and I heard her scream. I promise, Nana—"

"I know. I heard you run up the stairs." Another gap of silence. "Is she okay now?"

"I don't know. She woke up, so that's good, I guess."

"What happened in her dream?"

Brock sighed. "She wouldn't say."

"Hmm. Maybe she can't really remember."

Yes. She could play that one. It'd work.

"Seemed pretty vivid."

Brock and his stupid logic.

"Did she have nightmares before?" he asked. "Like when she was a kid?"

Nana must have had to think on that one. She answered after an extended pause. "Maybe once or twice. After her mom died. But not like this."

"What about headaches? Has she always struggled with them?"

"No."

Cheryl sank deeper into her covers, squeezing her eyes shut. *Stop asking questions. No more hunting.*

He needed a distraction—something that would make him believe she was fine, the woman he wanted. If he'd stop digging, maybe she'd stop trying to bury things deeper, and the dust would settle. They could play that everything was picture perfect.

She knew of only one way to begin that charade. And maybe this time it would last.

~20~

Brock leaned his elbows against his desk, letting his forehead rest in his hands. So tired. Blame it on no sleep. And a whirlwind of anxiety. Cheryl—

Brandi cut off the thoughts before they could form as she swept into the office.

"They ran another investigation on Sonja's living situation."

"And..." Brock knew the answer before he even asked. If it was all good, Brandi would have led with that.

"She's been moved to an emergency location until new long-term arrangements can be made."

"Why?"

Brandi's mouth twisted to one side. "You know better than to ask, Brock."

He did, but that didn't remove the desire to know. Hundreds of good people offered their love and protection within their homes for foster children. Why did So-J have to be the one to find her way into the rare situation of system abuse?

Man, that kid had really snagged his heart. He could still picture her rich brown eyes, slightly slanted and oh so mischievous, when they weren't completely hard and cold. A sense of possession and protectiveness locked in his chest—not really unusual, but unusually strong this time.

"How long until they find a new home for her?"

Brandi sighed, dropping into the chair across from his. "I don't know for sure...there are some complications. Her track record..."

Another detail Brandi really wasn't supposed to make known.

"Let's just say she's more of a challenge than most."

That could be saying a lot. Brock's hand drifted over his hair and anchored on the back of his neck. Why'd he feel so responsible? So tangled up with this girl he'd known for all of one week?

The image of So-J suddenly collided with his mental picture of Cheryl, curled up at the head of her bed, sobbing. Two traumatized souls he felt bound to.

God, what are you doing to me?

Nothing about his life in that moment reflected his plans from years past. Not one single image. He'd been on track to set some amazing records—had actually landed a few of them—in the sport of snowboard cross racing. He was a man who loved thrills and speed, and if he was being honest, all of the attention that came with being good at both.

Now? Now his heart was so tangled up he couldn't sleep. Cheryl's bondage. A gut-deep concern for a ten-year-old girl named So-J who was bound to compel him into action. He didn't have a map for these things. No plotting web to untangle this story line God seemed to be thrusting upon him.

But it was his story line. Their stories—Cheryl's and So-J's—were now a part of his, intertwined, with all the frayed edges and convoluted knots he was certain to *not* understand. God's will launched him into the middle of it all.

It terrified him with a level of fear equal in proportion to the conviction that moved him forward. While maybe physically a strong man, made solid by days spent weight training, running, and taking ride after ride after ride on the slopes... Emotionally? Spiritually?

He wasn't Superman in those departments. Realistically, he was barely average.

"What are you thinking?" Brandi tilted her head and lifted a brow.

"Who says I'm thinking anything?"

"Your face."

Brock twirled a pen he'd snagged from the mug resting on the corner of his work space. "So-J..."

"You want her here."

He met her eyes. "Yeah. There's something about her."

"Good." Brandi dipped a single nod. "Because I've requested a home visit for Ethan and me."

"Wait, what?" That wasn't what he had in mind. Close, but not exactly. "You just got married. Is that going to be an issue?"

"We're stable. I'm already a familiar face in the system. I don't think that'll be the issue. The issue would probably be location. Over the mountain range is quite a long distance from the Fort Collins area."

He hadn't even thought of that hurdle. "That's where she's from?"

"Yeah, and her mom's still there. Not anywhere near ready for reunification, but she is still there."

Brock nodded, his heart dropping. Not a chance. This wasn't going to happen, and suddenly his chest hurt.

"I'm going for it anyway." Brandi stood, crossing her arms. "I just needed you on board. I can make arrangements for visits, go the extra mile. I travel that way often anyway."

"What about Ethan?"

Brandi's eyebrows pulled in. "What?"

"Your husband? Is he on board?"

"Oh." She smiled, though a blush spread across her face. "Of course. All that stuff—I meant we. We're trying to have her placed here—Ethan and me. Together."

That was a little overstated. Brock examined her while a tiny wisp of concern drifted in his mind. Maybe the honeymoon was already over...

Maybe it wasn't any of his business and he should stop trying to read into things. And if they were going to bring So-J up the mountain to stay on a little more permanent basis, he wasn't about to set up a road block.

"Good. Well, I'm on board, for sure. And we can have you guys move into a cabin—or you could move into Gramps's house, and I can take the apartment downstairs, if you think that would help."

Brandi's grin—the much more normal expression on her face—resurfaced. "Shouldn't matter. We have two bedrooms and, obviously, the run of the ranch. If we can get past the location issue, I think everything else should fall into place."

She reached across the desk with her hand. Another common move—she was personal and business all in one setting. Ethan's total opposite, as he was not at all business, and sometimes not really that personal either. On the surface level, yeah, he was a people guy. But only the few and the privileged got beneath that layer.

Brock was glad Brandi had been one of the special few. Ethan needed her in his life. And maybe, so did So-J.

~*~

"My piano is lonely."

Cheryl pressed her phone to her ear and grinned at Brock's puppy voice. "Just your piano?"

"Well..." He chuckled. "Now that you mention it, it's been a couple of days since I've seen your smile."

Or decades. She hadn't smiled so much in her adult life as she had recently with him. But, and there was always going to be a *but*, she wasn't ready to face him after the nightmare. Two days had gone by, and she still shuddered when she imagined him asking her to explain. So she'd stayed with Nana. And he'd stayed at the ranch. Avoiding her too?

"Hmm...you know, the road goes both ways."

"I know. And trust me—I would have significantly less tread on my tires right now if not for the fact that I need to be here this week."

Man, when he decided to come on, he came on strong. Clearly he hadn't been pushing her away. Pleasure and fear made a sweet-n-sour concoction in her stomach. How to hold him close and keep him at a distance?

Oh, she knew how. But that plan required a little bit of privacy, not a handful of cabins full of kids.

"But"—his tone changed, becoming more serious—"really, Sherbert, you need to come out. There's someone here that I'd love to introduce you to."

That was a weird left turn. Who could she possibly want to meet at Kelly Ranch, outreach for messed-up kids?

"Will you come?"

She grinned into the phone. "You'll have to wait. I'm helping Nana."

"I know. Later? You could bring her. She loves the ranch."

That was true. Nana spoke about Kelly Ranch as if it were God's gift to Hayden, which was a little strange since the woman never, to Cheryl's knowledge, spent much time out there before Brock turned it into a kids' retreat.

"I'll ask her."

"Not good enough."

"What?"

"I'm going to keep calling you until I get a positive answer. So go on and be a baker. Just count on your phone pestering you every thirty minutes or so."

Over-the-top persistence. Maybe she should be flattered. Or freaked out. "What are you after, Brock Kelly?"

"You."

Again with the all-out charm.

"Hmm..."

"*Yes.* See, that's not hard. A simple yes will do, and then I'll leave you alone. For now."

His determination coaxed a laugh. "Okay. Yes. I'll be out later. Now go be a superhero."

"Good." He paused, and she felt his smile in the breath of silence. "You think I'm a superhero?"

Shaking her head, she pulled the phone away from her ear. "Goodbye, Brock."

"No, wait—"

Grinning, she cut him off. A little game of cat and mouse was always good. After all, she wasn't new to the art of...

Seduction?

Ouch. That wasn't a very nice thought. *Be gone...*

Still, the word left an imprint in her mind. It didn't feel good.

~*~

Cheryl finished washing the final pan, her hands drippy with lemon-smelling soap as she turned to Nana.

"Brock wondered if you wanted to go to the ranch tonight."

Nana's soft smile settled on her mouth, and a look of hope and joy filled her eyes. "No, child. I'm not up for it tonight. These old bones are calling for some time off my feet. Thank you though."

Cheryl dried her hands on the white towel, a touch of concern making her anxious. Nana had moved a bit slower today, and twice Cheryl had caught her doing some deep-breathing exercises. "Would you like me to stay with you?"

"Oh no, dearie." Nana moved to give Cheryl a side hug. "You go enjoy that kind man. He's a good one, you know."

He was that. But Cheryl didn't want to encourage Nana's hints. Not when she knew it'd all come crashing down eventually.

Nana looked up, her shaky, work-worn hand coming up to cup Cheryl's cheek. "You'll find your way."

With an uneasy pause, Cheryl examined the woman. She still seemed there, not gone into whatever mental trip she sometimes took, but Cheryl wasn't sure what she was getting at.

"I'm glad I got to see it," Nana said.

"See what?"

"You. Coming home." She moved up to her toes, pulling Cheryl's face down toward her, and planted a soft kiss on her cheek. "It's time, child, and you're almost there."

Cheryl's heart began to throb. "Nana..."

Nana moved out of reach and headed out the bakery door.

Cheryl didn't know what to make of her. What was more, it was becoming harder to fight against the invitation.

Come home.

If only it were that easy.

~*~

Brock could barely stay in his chair. Where was she, already? So-J would be off with the others before long, and he wanted to have Cheryl meet her before lights out. So-J would stay in a cabin with the girls for the rest of the week, but come Friday, they'd transfer her to the apartment with E and Brandi.

God answered that one fast. Almost whiplash fast. Which strangely sent up a red flag. That, and the fact that So-J was displaying a distinct disdain for Brandi. Troubled waters lay ahead for the newlywed couple, and it might be partly Brock's fault.

He hadn't asked them to foster her though. He'd intended to apply himself. Granted, a single guy paired with a ten-year-old girl was about as likely to happen as a ninety-degree day in January in Steamboat. But...

It'd all be okay. Things would work out—Brandi was really good with kids, and Ethan seemed to be bridging the gap in the meantime. There was bound to be difficulty, but they'd be all right.

"Sonja, you didn't clear your dishes." Brandi's soft but clear, commanding voice dragged Brock's attention from the window.

"So what? I don't *do* child labor."

"Well, *we* don't *do* feudal service here. So take care of your stuff. Starting with your dishes."

Yikes.

"The state pays you well enough to take care of us. Don't start with me."

"Okay, kiddo." Ethan stood next to her. "Why don't we try being grown up about this, shall we? Let's start with a promise. We won't ask you to do anything we're not willing to do ourselves. Okay?"

So-J folded her arms over her chest and cocked her head with a silent *yeah, right.* Brock's attention moved to Brandi, who flung a scowl at Ethan.

Unexpected.

Brock stood, stacking his used dishes onto his plate and then taking them toward the kitchen. He stopped beside So-J and leaned down as if to share a secret.

"It's not a bad deal, kid. Dish duty includes first dibs on dessert. How do you think I always get the biggest piece?"

Her eyes slid his direction, and he winked before he moved on toward the kitchen. Brock heard the clinking of ceramic against ceramic behind him, and he had to fight the temptation to look back.

Why'd Brandi start in on So-J right off like that?

Clear expectations. Yes. That was protocol. But the girl had just been moved. Who knew how many placements she'd had before this. A handful of grace...

Who was he to judge? Parenting wasn't part of his résumé, so he'd do best to keep his nose on his face.

Brock was loading his plate on a tray for the industrial dishwasher, when Ethan came through the door. E paused, his foot holding the door open, and So-J came through with her own little stack.

She still didn't look very happy, but she was doing it. Good step.

Brandi followed her, pinning another glare on Ethan as she passed. What was that about?

So-J slid her pile onto the countertop, none too gentle. "So what do I get?"

"How about the satisfaction of knowing you did something useful?" Brandi's dry answer seemed to tie tension between them all.

Ethan sighed. Loudly.

So-J crossed her arms again. "That wasn't the deal."

"You going to help me with these?" Brock asked.

"*All* of them?" She spread her hands wide toward the piles of dishes spread on the counter.

"You don't have to. You did your share, just like everyone else." Brock grinned at her. "But that dessert deal..."

"What is it? Because it better be good if I'm going to slave after everyone else. Otherwise you can forget it."

Brandi stepped forward. "Sonja, you can't talk to Mr. Brock with disrespect like that."

"Look, I've been in this game for a while. I know how it works. I may have to tell people that you're my foster mom, but let's just keep it real here. You're *not* my mom. Period."

Ethan came up behind Brandi, touching her elbow before she could respond. "Right. We're clear about that, kiddo. We're not your parents. But we'd like you to be a part of our family, for however long you can be. Families, they do stuff together. Fun stuff. Sometimes work stuff. And they respect each other. I told you, Brandi and I won't ask you to do anything we're not willing to do."

Brock held his breath while So-J's glare bounced between Brandi and Ethan. Slowly, almost imperceptibly, her shoulders relaxed.

Ethan must have caught it. With a slight nod, he picked up a dirty plate. "I think Cammy made scotcheroos, which happen to be my favorite. Double dibs for the kitchen help, so I'll be staying."

Brandi loaded her dishes, washed her hands, and left the kitchen. So-J stood in the middle, watching Ethan and Brock work for a few minutes before she began loading cups.

A win for Ethan. And maybe a loss.

Brandi wasn't acting anything like Brock would have expected. Something wasn't right.

~*~

Cheryl breathed in with a long, purposeful breath. They were just kids. She didn't need to cower because a group of ten-year-olds had just passed her on the driveway. Surely they'd go into their cabins soon, and she could have Brock to herself.

Right. Nothing to get upset about.

Her shoulders cramped with tension. Rolling her head from left to right, she told herself to ignore it and then moved for the back kitchen door to the lodge.

Brock's laughter made her pause, and a small smile tickled her mouth. Almost as good as music. She pushed through the door and found him dodging around the center island with Ethan hot on his trail.

"Quick, So-J! Catch!"

Something small and square left his hand. A little dark-haired girl snatched it out of the air and ran for the door into the dining room. Ethan spun around and darted after her, and she squealed as the door shut behind her.

Cheryl stopped near the sink. "What are you doing?"

Brock paused, his hand ready to push on the other door to go after the other two. "Sherbert!"

With a quick switch in direction, he made his way to her, his hands falling to his side. Without touching her, he came into her space, his smile transforming from goofy to...intimate?

"Where..." His lips brushed her forehead.

Cheryl shut her eyes.

"Have..." He kissed the tip of her nose.

She lifted her face.

"You..." He grazed her jawline with his mouth.

"Been?" Finally, finally, his kiss found her lips.

She smiled against his mouth, wrapped up in the delightful sense of being missed...wanted. He didn't draw out the kiss, leaving her longing for more, but when she moved into his chest, he wrapped his arms around her.

"I missed you," he said, a smile in his voice.

As she leaned into the embrace, she waited for the questions to tumble from his mouth. What happened in her dream? Why was she so afraid? Why wouldn't she tell him about it?

She wouldn't answer. Instead, she'd capture his mouth again, run her hand over his chest, up around to the back of his neck until she'd push her fingers into his hair. He'd shift, forget, and they'd move into the land of make-believe. Well, she'd move into the land of make-believe.

He'd be pushed into the land of physical response without mental calculation. Men were easy like that.

Heat swirled in her chest as she laid out the plan. A sour kind of heat. If he followed her lead, what would that do to her esteem for him? Keeping this man meant everything in that moment, but in the long run...

There was only one kind of run in this game—not long runs, just sprints. It was better kept that way. And so she waited...

He only held her, his fingers occasionally toying with the ends of her hair.

A screaming laugh shattered their hanging reprieve, and suddenly the dark-haired girl burst through the door.

"No!" she shouted, still giggling. "You're too slow, old man! You can't get my piece!" Still running, she darted around Brock and Cheryl, hiding behind Brock.

"Old?" Ethan stomped through the door, a very fake frown on his face. "I am not old! I still ride with sixteen-year-olds. I am definitely not among the aged."

Cheryl stared at her brother. What was with them? All of them? Their lives revolved around these kids, transforming them into silly, but somehow still cool, adults, the likes of which she'd not met.

The girl moved, stepping from behind Brock. Her smaller body brushed against Cheryl's arm, provoking an involuntary cardboard response. Every muscle contracted, and breathing became difficult. She glanced down, and the girl looked up at the same moment. Their eyes collided, and Cheryl found herself imprisoned by the connection.

Ten years old. She was ten. When was her birthday?

Stop it. Now.

Brock's hand moved against Cheryl's shoulder as he stepped back enough to also touch the child.

"Cheryl. This is who I wanted you to meet. Sonja—So-J to those of us who are cool enough to know her."

Cheryl finally pried her eyes from the kid's and looked at Brock. He grinned as if presenting the most famous, coolest kid in all of Colorado. Why did he want them to meet?

Oh no. He figured it out. He had to know, and he was...

Panic clawed in her chest, climbing to her throat as a wave of dizziness passed through her head.

"Sherbert? You okay."

No. What was he doing? No.

"Ew." The girl—So-J?—stepped back. "Dude, she looks like she's gonna hurl. Don't spew on me, lady. I only have two other shirts, so..."

Ethan came behind So-J, his hand covering her shoulder. "You're right. Cheryl, you don't look so good. Another headache?"

How about a full-body spasm? "I don't know. I'd better go home."

Ethan shot a quick look to Brock, one that said *you'd better figure this out—and good luck*, and then guided So-J out of the room.

"What was that about?" Brock spoke as soon as they were alone.

"I don't know." *Liar.* "I just suddenly didn't feel well. Nana stayed home, so I'll just head back."

"Hold up." He gripped her hand, stopping her retreat. He waited, his gaze traveling over her face with tender concern. "Not yet. I wanted to talk to you, and Ethan and Brandi have the activity tonight, so I thought we could spend some time together. Maybe whatever hit you will pass?"

Not if his topic of conversation was what she suspected. Then again, if they were alone, maybe she could forget that there were a dozen kids running around nearby who provoked haunting emotions, and she'd proceed with her clench-the-man plan.

"Maybe. Let's not stay here though. Okay?"

His eyebrows dropped. "Why not? I'd love to hear you play again, if you're up for it."

Stubborn man. Cooperate, already. Her way would be better for both of them.

He tugged her back toward himself until her shoulder brushed his chest, and leaned his head against hers to whisper near her ear. "Come on, Sherbert. You love music. I just want to see you smile again."

Seemed he had his own game plan for her. As the stiffness in her body drained, replaced with a warm rush, she wondered who was playing whom in this exchange. She knew what she wanted. What was his aim?

You.

A quiver shook in her middle. He couldn't know what he was saying. He definitely did not want her, not in the tender, loyal, intimate way he implied.

He brushed a kiss against her temple and moved away, taking her hand as he went. Unable to resist, she followed him into the dining hall toward the piano, though her steps drug against the floor.

The music waited, perched on the ledge and opened to the "Feather Theme." Unbidden, the melody began in her mind, and her fingers wiggled without her permission.

It wasn't fair that he should know her weakness and she shouldn't know his.

No. That was stupid. He was a man, and all men had the same weakness.

He pulled out the bench, and she slid onto it, her fingers brushing the keys. She played the first few chords lightly, tentative, because she was still very much out of practice, but the keys soon became familiar again, and each passing measure led her deeper and deeper into the escape.

It happened again. *Cheryl...* The song came back, loosed the chains that bound her soul, and called...

Come home.

Ache spread warm and yet almost beautiful in her heart. Home. How much she longed for it. She hadn't realized how badly she'd thirsted for home. If she could, without going through the agony of that moment all over again, she would go back.

Eyes closed, she bit the bottom of her lip as two paths parted in her imagination. She could stay on the one she'd been walking for ten years. It stretched long and lonely in a steel gray backdrop. Bleak. The second wound away, curving so that she could not see what was beyond. Narrow and lit only enough to see a few steps ahead, it seemed to dip downward as the curve arced around, but the edges were filled with living color, and the background, though dim, seemed softer.

She didn't take chances in life. Not anymore. She maintained control over every aspect of her existence, as much as she could. She wanted to see what was ahead. Except, what was ahead didn't look very lifelike.

What if she took a step into the unknown?

Yeah, she'd done that once. Didn't go well.

But there was life on that path...

In her mind, she nudged a toe onto that imaginary trail. Music played. Sweet, familiar, and warm. Another foot. The music remained. What if...

Brock sat beside her, pulling her away from the illusion, although the music continued to play.

"There it is." He leaned against her, his thumb trailing down her spine. "I knew you'd find it."

Find what? She opened her eyes to find his gentle smile and loving gaze fixed on her.

"We need to figure out how to keep you there."

She let her hands drop from the keys. "Where?"

"In that place where the real you is waiting. The place you just found."

He could see through her. *Oh God, no.* Not all the way through. She couldn't stand for him to see everything.

After another trek up and down her back, his hand drifted to her hip and he tugged her closer. "Listen, I've had an idea I wanted to run past you."

Did it involve fairy tales? Those things weren't real, and someday they'd both have to deal with that.

"So, So-J..."

She stiffened, and the music became discorded. The fairy tale faded.

If he noticed her reaction, he ignored it. "She's staying with your brother and Brandi as their foster charge, and last time she was up here she showed a small interest in the piano."

"No." Absolutely not negotiable. Not a chance. Ever.

"What?"

"No. I'm not a piano teacher."

"You're not really a lawyer either. Remember? You hate it. But you love music, and it heals. That little girl could really use something that—"

"So this was your angle." She stood, grabbing the book as she moved and slammed it onto the top of the piano. "Not me at all, was it?" She pushed out a derisive laugh. "Man, I've met some manipulators, but you—"

"Hold up. Manipulating? Who's manipulating?"

She spun on her heel and started for the door. Three steps was all she managed before his hand caught her arm and pulled her back.

"I told you to stop running. Are you completely unable to maintain a real conversation?"

"Are you still talking? I said no. I'm not doing it, so forget it."

He swallowed, his eyes wide and bewildered. After working his jaw a few times, he blinked, straightening so that he wasn't leaning in her space. "I'm not trying to manipulate you. I want to help." With one hand on his hip, he pushed the other through his hair. "I'm sorry. I don't know what to do."

She pushed out a harsh laugh. "I thought you said I didn't need fixing."

"Yeah, well, I can't figure out who you are. I see the joy and the peace bloom in you when you play. I thought it'd be something you could enjoy and share with a kid whose life has pretty much sucked up until now. But maybe you're just really all about you."

Regret began to billow in her chest, but she pushed it away. He didn't know what he was asking, and he had no business messing with her life. "Just stop, okay? Stop looking for a woman who isn't here." Cheryl stepped forward, looking up at him until his eyes connected with hers. "She's. Not. Here."

Oh, that look. Like she'd just killed his hopes and dreams, broke his heart.

She stepped away before it could undo her.

That was what she got for trying to go home.

Brock stood with his gaze locked on the vacant door Cheryl had just stormed through. What on earth had just happened? It had seemed perfect. Cheryl loved to play, and she was so good at it. And So-J...she'd need something to really ground her here, something of her own. He'd seen her plunk out chopsticks, which didn't say all that much, because kids did that all the time, but lessons seemed like something worth exploring. Especially since So-J and Brandi were not bonding well.

The last thing he'd expected was Cheryl's fury over the simple request.

And why'd she keep accusing him of trying to fix her? He just wanted her to be happy, to come back from whatever dark hole she'd been stuck in for the past ten years. It wasn't wrong to want to see her come back to life.

Sighing, he turned back to the piano, tipping his face toward the ceiling. "You're going to have to move here, you know. I don't have a clue what to do, and I keep messing this up."

Silence drifted from the rafters. Perfect. He dropped back onto the piano bench, still warm where Cheryl had sat. With his fists pushed together, he leaned his forehead against his knuckles.

"God, please help. This is too hard."

~21~

The theme music to *Dr. Quinn* greeted Cheryl as she passed through the front door. Ten thirty. Nana should have been in bed. She certainly would have known not to wait up for her. Unless Brock had called...

Great. He probably had, and Nana was probably up pacing, wondering what Cheryl had done with the two hours between when she'd left the ranch and finally made it back to Nana's.

Just a drive. That was all. She needed the speed, the cold night wind slapping her in the face as she wove through the abandoned mountain roads to the west. Nothing to be upset about.

Still, she should have called to let Nana know. Now the woman would be exhausted in the morning. Maybe Cheryl could convince her to close the bakery. On a Friday. For the first time ever.

Not likely.

Sighing, Cheryl dropped her floppy purse onto the table beside the door and moved for the front room. "Nana, what are—"

Her heart stopped.

Oh God, please...

"Nana!" Cheryl darted to the couch where her grandmother lay in an awkward position, her face tilted up as if she were gasping for air.

Except there was no gasping. Or breathing.

"No!" She fumbled with the cold, limp arm nearest her, searching for a pulse. "No! Nana! Wake up!"

Yanking on the unresponsive arm, Cheryl continued to shout. *God, how could you let this happen?*

What was she thinking, going off and leaving Nana alone? She shouldn't have gone...

Cheryl found herself on her knees, trembling, pleading with Nana to wake up.

Maybe it wasn't too late. An ambulance... Yes, that was what she needed to do. She almost fell over the coffee table as she scrambled across the floor toward her purse. Paramedics. They'd come. They'd bring those heart-shocker panel things—what were those called again? Who cared? They'd get here in time. They had to get here in time...

The emergency operator answered, set the EMTs in motion, and talked Cheryl through what to do while she waited.

And then she had to wait. She crawled, tears rolling over her cheeks, back toward her grandmother.

What would she do without Nana? She couldn't lose her now.

God, I can't find my way back without her. Please, God...

It was too late though. Nana continued to stare through lifeless eyes. Despair crashed over Cheryl.

She'd never be able to come home.

~*~

Brock clenched his jaw as he scanned the group. The cemetery seemed overcrowded. Not a resident in Hayden hadn't known Nana Grace, and most of them called her exactly that. Most would have welcomed that kind of tribute to their loved one, but he doubted Cheryl did.

Standing on the green hillside with the sun hovering over the peaks in the background, the moment had a flavor of déjà vu. Especially when he glanced to the woman standing at a distance to his right. She stood stiffly, eyes focused on nothing in particular, lifeless and dry.

This was how Sherbert handled grief. Locked down, stone cold, and cut off. Years ago, her reaction pushed him away as much as it made him sorry for her. Now...

He squeezed his mother's elbow on his left, glanced to his dad, who spoke to the crowd, and then quietly left his spot near his parents. She needed a touch of compassion, even if she wasn't willing to admit it. Maybe she didn't even know it. But this time, Sherbert wasn't going to go through the death of a loved one alone.

Standing on his sister's other side, Ethan peeked toward Brock as he stepped beside Cheryl. Emotion sheened his eyes, but a small lift of one side of his mouth told Brock that he approved; he was grateful. In the next moment, he looked away, back toward the coffin waiting for its final rest, and Brandi snugged her arms around his waist.

Brock looked down at the raven-haired woman at his side. Her chin dipped downward, and she tilted her face away as if she wished he hadn't noticed her. His heart split, and he thought back to Mother's suggestion of knighthood. How he longed to have a shield to cover her with. He'd tuck her between him and the armor, and she could huddle there in safety, able to grieve without the rest of the world watching.

Is that what she needed?

If only he could offer her such a shelter. All he had was an empty hand. He slipped it around hers, brushed his thumb over her knuckles, and remained still at her side. Except the slight movement of her chin turning his direction, she didn't move.

Attention seemed to be the last thing she wanted. Except she didn't push him away.

~*~

A tap at the front door drew Cheryl's eyes away from the blank television screen to the entryway by the stairs, but she couldn't summon the motivation to answer it. They could come back later, whoever it was. Or not. Either way.

Her life looked just like that screen. Black and empty. Now she had no reason to stay.

She hadn't wanted to stay, had she? Not from the beginning.

She hadn't wanted to go back either.

Staring at nothing, she slouched back against the sofa and tipped her head against the backrest. The knocking sounded again. Again she ignored it. Even when the doorknob rattled, she did nothing. If it was someone entering, more than likely it was Ethan, and he could do whatever he needed to do. Didn't need her to play hostess.

Sure enough, the creak of the hinges announced the entry's opening, and footsteps soon followed into the house. Cheryl shut her eyes, hoping he'd think she was asleep, but the footfalls came toward her. Moving only her head, she sighed and opened her eyes.

Brock stopped in front of her, looking from her, to the shoes she'd kicked off near the couch, to the keys she'd flung onto the coffee table, and to her purse that lay on its side on the floor, open and spilling its contents. Eventually his attention came back to her.

He hadn't said a word at the funeral. Not a single one—just held her hand and wouldn't let go until she reached her car. She'd opened the door, stopped for a moment, but didn't look him in the eye, and said, "Good-bye, Brock." And that was it.

And here he was. Still not talking.

With a hand to her shoulder, he nudged her to scooch, and when she slid over a smidge, he lowered himself onto the couch close to her side. His hand drifted over her shoulders, down her back and up again, and then into her hair.

Cheryl savored every touch, logging it into her memory bank as one of those rare and fleeting moments of honest comfort. When he tugged her gently to his chest, she drifted to him willingly, and he adjusted his position so that she could lean against him in comfort. She waited for him to tell her that these things happen, that God had a plan, and her life would go on. That Nana lived a good life, and everyone loved her, and she should be so proud to be her granddaughter, and she needed to live in a way that would make Nana proud in return.

She'd heard the standard funeral spiel before.

But the gentle rhythm of his heartbeat and the quiet rush of his calm breath coming in and going out were the only sounds between them. His fingers twirled her hair, and his opposite hand took hold of hers.

"Aren't you going to saying anything?" she asked.

He pressed a kiss into her hair. "No. Not unless you need me to."

She shut her eyes and turned her face into his chest. He released her hand and pulled her into a secure hold.

Cheryl wondered where he learned to be so wise. As she drifted off into a dreamless sleep, she forgot to worry about when she would no longer be wanted by this amazing man.

~*~

Brock leaned against his headboard, his Bible open beside him. He thought it strange that Psalm 107 continued to call to him, as if something in it was important, that he needed to get it.

Such a bipolar hymn. Shouts of praise interwoven with stories of darkness. The *give thanks* parts he was familiar with, but honestly, he'd never paid attention to the other stuff.

Recently, however, the words demanded his attention. The goodness of God and the darkness of man...

Righteousness and peace have kissed...

Where was that verse? He'd only remembered it because the words had seemed...unusual. He flipped to the concordance section at the back of his study Bible, hoping he'd find the answer there. If not, he'd have to wait until he could get over to Mom and Dad's so he could check in their *Strong's Concordance.* Maybe it was about time he had one of his own.

Psalm 85:10.

Mercy and truth have met together; Righteousness and peace have kissed.

Brock stared at the words, still not making sense. He was no theologian, that was for sure. He'd ask Dad. But not tonight. It was eleven, and he was tired, and his heart still felt beat down.

It'd been a week since Nana Grace's funeral. In the limited time he could find, he'd gone into town every day since, just to be with Cheryl. They'd walk, her hand loosely in his, their long intervals of silence broken with occasional inconsequential stuff like "How was your day?" and "Are you up for a light dinner?" She'd been tired, understandably so, especially since she'd decided to keep the bakery going. That should have offered him hope that she'd be staying. Really, though, he understood the truth. She simply kept moving because if she was working, she'd be able to avoid the hurt.

Cheryl Thompson operated on an *if I ignore it, it will eventually go away* theory. Guess she hadn't learned yet that didn't work with things of the heart.

She was so lifeless. Not even the iconic Cheryl anger had surfaced, and that scared him. Did she really think that she could simply package emotions in a box and ship them off to oblivion?

Maybe it was time to push a little harder. Was it too soon for another real date?

They could just hang out with her brother and Brandi. Might be good for E too.

He had to do something to summon some kind of emotion.

"I think we're due for another date."

Cheryl glanced up from the counter where she was drizzling maple frosting over the fresh cinnamon knots. While thankful for the distraction from the heavenly aroma of baked goods, which were daily becoming more difficult to resist, she frowned at the man standing opposite her, his hands spread against the counter as he leaned her direction.

"What are you talking about?"

Transferring his weight to his palms, Brock leaned over the stainless steel work space and pecked her cheek. "You and me. We haven't had a date for a while."

Men were not sweet like this. Not in her world.

"You're after something."

He laughed, pushing back to his feet. "Yes."

"What?"

"You."

Her heart fluttered and then squeezed. Why had she stayed? Brock needed someone who didn't wear her past choices like iron shackles. He deserved a woman with a kind heart. Or at least an available heart. Hers was imprisoned, which didn't translate to available.

But...

The play-act could become real, couldn't it? She'd be his June Cleaver, and he'd be her Ward, only more progressive. And better looking. By far.

"Sherbert...oh, Sher-bert..." Brock cupped his mouth and used a singsong voice to softly call her back.

"Stop it." Cheryl grinned in spite of her attempted irritation. "You do that just to annoy me."

"No. I do it because it makes you smile."

"Not always."

He winked. "Usually."

"You're such a flirt."

A little-boy smile poked his dimple into his cheek, and he leaned over the counter again, pushing aside the tray she'd been working on as he moved. "Come here. I'll tell you a secret."

Eying him, she slowly leaned toward him. "What?"

His nose brushed against her cheek, and then he whispered, "I'm only a flirt with you."

She tipped her head away and lifted one eyebrow as if she didn't believe him. Brock playfully snagged her by the side of her head and brought her face back to his. Before she could push him away, he blew a sloppy, wet raspberry against her cheek.

"Brock!" Giggling, she grabbed his wrist and tried to wrestle it away. "Stop! You're so gross!"

His chuckle vibrated against her skin, and he dipped his mouth to the soft spot between her neck and shoulder.

"No!"

Too late. Another slobbery raspberry vibrated against her exposed skin.

Cheryl's laughter bubbled from deep in her gut, and Brock locked an arm around her waist, lifting her to the countertop and pulling her to his side of her work station. She continued to fight him away, though not with anything even remotely resembling a convincing effort. He pushed her hair to one side and planted yet another raspberry right behind her ear. She arched her back, still giggling, and reached for the wooden spoon she'd been using with the frosting. Weapon loaded, she brought it to his face and smeared. Maple frosting glazed his cheek, his nose, and his chin.

"You wicked girl." He pushed his nose against hers, and then his cheek, painting her face with the sugary glaze.

Nearly out of breath from squealing and laughing, Cheryl dropped the spoon and captured his face. "Okay, stop," she panted. "I can't breathe, and you're making a mess."

He gripped her wrists and held them against his chest, his nose still against hers. "I didn't bring frosting into this game."

Another laugh escaped as she settled against him. A sweet stillness enveloped them, and he released her wrists, moving his hands to the back of her shoulders. With closed eyes, he smiled as his weight rested gently against her.

"Will you have dinner with me tonight?"

Her eyes shut, and she felt her lips pull upward. "Yeah."

"Are you okay with a double date? E and Brandi talked about coming into town too."

"Okay." She spread her palms out against his shirt—another plaid-over-the-gray-T combo, and opened her eyes. "Think you'd better clean up first."

"Probably. Good thing I have a few hours."

She nipped at his cheek where frosting hung a little thick. "I could help."

Brock leaned back, a knowing grin puckered on his mouth. His hands moved from her shoulders, and one thumb slid over her cheek where he'd left a trail of frosting. He poked it into his mouth, made a noisy show of licking it off, and then reached for a rag on the counter. After wiping his face, he leaned back to her and landed another chaste kiss against her cheek.

"Someday, Sherbert, I'm going to hold you to that."

With yet another peck, this time on her lips, he dropped the rag back onto the counter and moved away.

"I'll see you at six thirty." He waved as he passed through the door.

Cheryl leaned back against the counter, reaching for the rag he'd just used. A tiny laugh wiggled her shoulders as she licked a smudge of frosting from her knuckles. She hadn't tasted something so sweet in years.

See? There was nothing to this make-believe. She hardly had to pretend at all. She and Brock could be happy. Even if she didn't deserve it.

Judgment is easy. Criticism comes as readily as rain from a heavy cloud, and seemingly harmless when you're the one carrying an umbrella.

What about those who stand naked in the storm?

Have you walked the path I've crawled? Do you know what terrified really is?

I know. You wouldn't do what I've done. And I deserve the consequences.

Believe me...I know.

Living with it is its own hell. Next to that, your judgment is another sword in my heart.

Does that make you feel better?

~22~

The Hi Way was hardly a date-quality joint. Not by LA standards. Although, Cheryl hadn't loved LA standards. In fact, there wasn't much of anything about LA that she'd been missing over the past three weeks. Her bed—because it was one of those expensive, high-end mattresses— but that was about the extent of her homesickness.

Home wasn't something she had, really. Except...

Cheryl glanced at Brock, who sat to her right. He'd been laughing at a story E was telling. A memory they shared about a race in their high school days. Apparently they'd gotten their entry bibs mixed up, and E had been awarded Brock's time. Or something. Cheryl had stopped listening halfway through the telling, suddenly struck by how much of life she hadn't been a part of.

Weird. She thought she'd taken a bench seat after that awful day. Now, listening to the stories the boys passed between them, she suddenly realized that she'd been a spectator most of her life.

Brandi, who had been laughing, fully engaged in the boys' conversation, brought Cheryl into the conversation. "Did you ever race, Cheryl?"

"No." Cheryl looked at her hands resting against the table. "I actually have never been snowboarding."

"Really?" Brandi tipped her head. "I thought everyone who grew up around here did."

"Nah." Ethan shook his head. "Sherbert isn't an extreme-sport kind of girl. She was a bookworm."

"Snowboarding isn't always an extreme sport." Brandi lifted a sassy look to her husband. "And I like books."

Brock laughed softly, covering Cheryl's hand with his. "Believe me— if you had ridden with E and me back then, you would know. It was always extreme or nothing with us. We were crazy. Cheryl was the smart one, and bless her for that."

No. She was the boring one. And no one blessed her for that.

"Ah." Brandi nodded and then redirected her attention.

What did that mean exactly? The woman was still evaluating her, doing some kind of clinical analysis. It made Cheryl uneasy.

"Can you believe this?" Brandi spoke again, gesturing toward the television anchored to the wall opposite them.

Cheryl glanced at the TV and froze. A report on the latest fiasco with a family planning organization had come on the news. Her vision blurred the image on the screen, and her stomach rolled violently. The muscles at the base of her neck knotted.

"I can't even imagine..." Brandi continued to talk, contempt edging her voice. "I don't know how you could do that and live with yourself."

Cheryl bit the inside of her lip. *They don't know...it's not about you, and they don't know...*

"Did I tell you guys that I was at a protest rally a couple years back when a woman screamed at me? Right in my face. Told me I had no right to tell her what she could and could not do with her body."

"Yeah?" Ethan stirred his ice with his straw. "What'd you do?"

Brandi tossed her hair to one side. "Looked her right in the eye and told her she was killing a *baby*. It's murder. I don't understand it at all. Like I said, I wouldn't be able to live with myself."

Cheryl's pulse throbbed in her ears, and black spots blotched her vision. *Breathe. In. Out. They don't know...*

How can you live with yourself? Murderer. God hates you. You're going to hell.

Suddenly the wailing from her nightmares joined the ringing in her ears. Pain jolted through her head, and she shut her eyes against the bright flash of white light that zipped behind her eyes.

They didn't know. They didn't know anything.

Anger trembled, hot and hard and fast from her middle. Her core shook, and she doubled her fists in her lap. They knew nothing.

She pushed against the table, sliding her chair backward so that she could stand.

"You okay, Sherbert?"

Her vision collided with Brock's, and for a moment she held. What would he say if he knew?

He'd condemn her. His silence already had, even if he didn't know.

"I've gotta go." She snatched her small purse and took a step to the door. She could feel their eyes on her back, the questions building in the silence.

Suddenly she was homesick for LA. There she was indiscernible. Just a face in the crowd. Nameless. Unaccountable.

Here she was condemned. Exactly why she'd never planned on returning and why she couldn't stay.

Quick steps carried her out of the sports grill and onto the sidewalk. Cool night air slammed against her body, and she shivered. The streets lay quiet, as if asleep for the evening, and the wind blew chilly from the peaks to the north.

Streetlamps stood indifferently as their light drenched the buildings in town. Some of them highlighted beauty—the well-built brick building that housed the bank. The rays played prettily with the glint of the gold-hilted lettering artistically spanning the polished windows, and the blond bricks glowed against the dark backdrop. Other buildings, however, sat miserably under the harsh beams of exposure— the rundown storefront that had once been a bookstore in years gone by. Without discretion, the light drew attention to the cracked windows and sagging wood along the doorframe.

Light didn't care what it exposed.

Beyond the streetlamps that lined Main Street, the dark sky stretched with a lonely invitation. Two choices in life. Stay in the light, where everything was exposed. Or step into the darkness, where the chill of loneliness was her only friend.

A hand to her back startled her, drawing her attention from the hopeless canvas beyond.

"Cheryl, what's wrong?"

She ached to lean against him. He'd wrap her in his arms, and she wouldn't feel cold. She wouldn't writhe with the loneliness.

Brock stepped closer, his chest brushing her shoulder. "Babe, are you okay?"

"I just need to go home."

"Another headache?"

"Yes."

"Okay, I'll go with you."

If only he could.

He slipped an arm around her waist and drew her close to his side, and they began down the walkway toward Nana's empty house.

Just one more day, she promised. *Let me have him for just a little longer.*

She wasn't sure God cared what she asked or promised. But she felt compelled to try. She stared beyond the town toward the looming shadows cast by the dark mountains in the distance.

Please, just a little longer. Then I'll go back to where I belong.

~*~

"How bad is the headache?" Standing at the doorway to Nana's house, Brock nudged Cheryl's hair away from her neck with his fingers and began to massage the base of her skull. He felt her relax against his side, and he turned to tuck her against his chest.

Something had happened in that restaurant. Granted, she hadn't been open and free, not like she was when it was just the two of them, but she hadn't been completely closed off either. Not until the moments right before she left. Did these headaches just strike out of the blue?

Seemed like something had triggered it. Maybe it wasn't prudent to search for the reason, but he simply had to know. That quest would require time and caution.

Cheryl cuddled against him, as if she was exactly where she wanted to be.

That made two of them.

"Better?" he whispered, his fingers still working.

"Getting there."

"Maybe these are tension headaches, not migraines." Was there a difference, practically speaking? He didn't know—wasn't a doctor. But if they could figure out the trigger, maybe she wouldn't suffer so much.

"Maybe." She didn't move, except to let her full weight lean against him.

"What if we go light the fire pit? The cool mountain air, the stars dancing overhead...maybe you could relax, and the tension would melt away?"

Sounded like a setup, even to his own ears. He probably should let her go crawl into her bed and sleep the pain away. But there had to be a cause...and if she'd trust him with whatever she was hiding, perhaps they could find a solution together.

"Sounds nice."

"Yeah?"

Her fists curled into his flannel shirt. "Yes."

He covered one of her hands with his and tugged. She followed willingly, staying snug at his side. Whatever had struck her back at the restaurant still bothered her—he could feel the mild and sporadic trembles that quivered through her small body. Somehow, he had to nudge the truth out of her. Brock led her to his truck, and they headed toward the ranch.

They stayed quiet on the way. Five minutes into the drive, Cheryl leaned across the bench seat and laid her head against his thigh. He wove his fingers through her hair until he touched the skin of her neck and began massaging again. When he glanced down, he found her eyes closed, but wrinkles rippled in her forehead.

"Do you need something for the pain?"

"I have Advil in my purse. I'll take some at your house."

"Maybe I should turn around, take you back home."

Her hand found his leg. "No."

"What if you get sick again?"

"It's not that bad. It might go away."

"Does that happen?"

She didn't answer. That'd be a no. What had he been thinking? Totally selfish. He'd just wanted more time with her to discover what was bothering her, but he should have sent her up to bed.

He moved his fingers from her neck to her shoulder and squeezed gently. "Promise you'll tell me if you need to go home."

Her hand wrapped around his. Somehow the move felt like she was reaching for a lifeline. His heart tugged, and in that moment he was sure there was nothing in the world that could change how he felt. The depth of emotion—it wasn't just adrenaline, chemistry. It was core deep. God given.

Would she freak out if he told her?

The last curve of his driveway passed under the truck's wheels, and he slowed into the spot in front of his garage where he always parked. Cheryl didn't move, even after he cut the engine.

"You're sure you're up for this?"

"Yes."

"Okay. How about you just stay where you are, and I'll get a fire going? I'll come back for you."

"'Kay."

He slipped out from under the slight weight of her head and paused. Dark hair fanned over her shoulders and draped onto his side of the truck. Her shoulders moved with the slow, rhythmic rise and fall of her steady breath. She folded her hands together and tucked them under her chin, shifting only slightly as she moved to a more comfortable position.

So pretty, when she wasn't scowling, snapping, or shutting down. Come to think of it, she was pretty even in those moments too. And those moments were dwindling.

Someday, they'd be few and far between.

~*~

Tell me if you need to go home...

Cheryl never would have imagined a simple, innocent sentence would nearly topple her emotional wall.

Home? Home was a dark and lonely place. Home was cold. Home had nothing that beckoned her back. Raw desperation clawed in her chest. Him. She just needed to be with him. What if, with him, she could redefine home? It would be tender looks, teasing smiles, warm touches. Home would be a happiness she hadn't dared to think she'd ever find.

Because she didn't deserve it.

Clenching her fist, she pushed the thought away. Brock liked her. That had to mean something. Even with her sharp personality and chilling people skills, he seemed to really like her. She'd be stupid not to snag that and hold on with everything she had.

The door at her feet opened, and Brock's large, warm hand rubbed her calf. "Are you up for this?"

She pushed against the seat with her palms, righting herself. The throbbing in her head was minor compared to what it could be. If she could shut out the image that had been displayed on that television, maybe this time a few pills, and an evening snuggled with this man, would be the cure.

"Yes."

He pushed a glass into her hand. "Water. For your meds."

"Thanks."

After a moment of rummaging, she found the bottle of painkillers, downed a pair, and slid out of the vehicle. His arm wrapped possessively around her waist almost as soon as her feet touched the ground, and that surge of desperation deepened. Whatever it would take, she needed him.

Brock had a quilt spread out on a small grassy slope near the fire pit. He let her settle on her back before he lay on what was left of the blanket next to her, one hand resting on his chest and the other arm tucked under his head.

"Remember in like fifth or sixth grade we had to study the constellations?"

She smiled, though she doubted he noticed, his attention focused on the sky.

"Yes, although I was a few years behind you, you know."

His soft chuckle rumbled near her. "Yeah, I know, kid. I'll bet you were a lot better at them than I was."

She tilted her chin and swept her gaze over the velvet night canvas above. "I remember a few."

"I don't remember any."

She glanced at him. "Oh come on. Sure you do." She pointed north. "See, there's Cassiopeia, right above the peaks there. If you follow the tip of her *W*, she'll point you to Ursa Minor."

"Ursa? I definitely don't remember an Ursa anybody."

"Yes you do." She lifted her head and propped up on one elbow. The throbbing had diminished to a gentle pulse, the pain dimming as the moments became more peaceful. "The Little Dipper. Polaris is in that constellation—the North Star. Everything in the night sky seems to rotate around her." Again she pointed, this time at the tail of the Little Dipper, and began to draw a trail over the sky. "And look—if you move from the Little Dipper to Ursa Major, you can find Leo just past that to the west."

Brock's low chuckle drew her attention back.

"What?"

"I knew you were better at it than I was." He looked at her with a grin. "You're so smart, you know."

"Was that sarcasm?"

"No." He pushed up to mirror her position on his elbow. "You are. And beautiful. And sometimes funny, when you're not hiding in your armor." One hand lifted, and his fingers trailed lightly over her hair. His eyes held hers captive, and the open warmth in them called to her longing. He moved, bringing her head closer, until his lips brushed against hers.

Not enough. She tilted her mouth to meet his again. He let a warm kiss linger before he leaned away to speak.

"The Hi Way." His thumb brushed her cheek. "How about you tell me what happened earlier."

Last thing in this life she wanted to talk about. Especially with him. But she banished irritation from her voice, keeping it soft. Maybe a tad sultry. "I got a headache."

"Why?"

She covered the hand that now rested near her ear and then trailed her fingers over his arm. "Don't know." Leaning toward him, she erased the small space he'd put between them and drew another kiss, this time deeper, from his mouth.

This song she knew...this dance she'd practiced several times over. He took what she gave, and she gave a little more with each offering until she had molded herself against him. For a moment he hesitated, separating their kiss.

"Tell me why," he whispered, his voice rough.

In the flicker of the firelight, she searched his eyes. The burn of longing smoldered there, but maybe not just for her body.

Her body was all she could give.

Please don't ask... She moved against him, and he fell to his back, matching her kiss for kiss, touch for touch.

In the end, all men were the same. This was really what they wanted.

~*~

You need to stop.

Cheryl moved against him, every touch threatening to topple his prior resolve. He knew what lay on the other side of those kisses—a pleasure not far out of reach—and the desire for it could overrule logic.

She had to know control was melting from his mind. No doubt she could feel his slide from thought to reaction.

Why is this so hard?

Easing back up, Brock focused his concentration on control. He'd let it go too far. Cheryl caught his shoulders as he gently pushed her away, her fingers digging for grip as her kisses kept the hot fire of yearning ablaze.

It'd be so easy to snuff out the tiny voice telling him to stop.

"Cheryl..." He rolled onto his hip, nudging her away. One more kiss, gentle and much more chaste, and then he completed the separation.

Her breath caught in a small cry of protest. "Brock." Her hand slid over the back of his neck, around his shoulder, and landed on his chest. "I want you."

Surely she felt the relentless pounding of his heart and the desire that still pulsed throughout his body. It wouldn't take much, and they'd be intertwined again, going somewhere he knew they weren't ready for.

She molded to his side, and her soft, warm lips slid against his neck.

God, help...

The groan that escaped his lips fueled her passion, but he caught her as she moved, not allowing her to melt against him again.

His voice came ragged, but he forced the words out. "We need to stop."

She pulled away, just enough to search his face. "Why?"

He sat up and examined her. She looked like a porcelain doll against the darkness of the night. The firelight increased the contrast of her dark hair and fair complexion. Exquisite. But in that moment, raw and vulnerable, he glimpsed the traces of scars that etched against her soul. Under her flawless beauty and her carefully constructed walls of perfection, she was a mess.

This wasn't going to go well.

She moved again, her mouth finding his.

His hands framed her head, fingers curving into her hair, and he tipped his face so that the kiss was broken, but his forehead still rested on hers. "Please stop."

She stiffened, stared at him for a moment, and then moved away.

Brock sat straighter and brought his knees up toward his chest. "Don't be like this, Sherbert. This just isn't going to lead us where we want to go."

"What does that mean?"

The hard lines of defense resurfaced on her face, the cold edge in her voice. He should have known better. He *had* known better. This whole deal—lying on a blanket under the stars next to a fire—what had he been thinking? Not anything with clarity.

"What do you want from this relationship?"

Her eyes pinched. "I don't know what you mean. Can't we just see where it goes?"

"Yes." He looked back at the fire. "But don't you have any idea, any hope, for where you want it to go?"

She sat wordless, and the silence built a thick wall of strain between them.

"Cheryl, I know what I want...and I'm pretty sure having sex tonight isn't going to get us there."

"You're not making any sense. I'm not trying to trap you into...into marriage or something. I just wanted to be with you."

She missed his heart entirely, because long-term commitment was exactly what he wanted. "Can I tell you something, and you promise you'll listen?"

Her beautiful lips, the very lips that had been soft and sweet against his mouth two minutes before, hardened into a cold line. "Sure."

Which meant she probably wasn't going to listen.

"I slept with Kayla on our third date."

"So this is sort of like our third date...you think it'll be unlucky?" Sarcasm chilled her words.

"No. That's not it at all. It did something to us." He rubbed the back of his neck and then picked up a twig and began poking the embers in the fire pit. "Like we felt obligated to each other, but not in a good way. I stayed with her because it was like I'd made a silent commitment to be with her, and when she didn't honor that unspoken code, it felt like she'd torn off a layer of my soul. Honestly, I'm not even sure I loved her, not like I should have, which is probably why we never set a wedding date, but after we'd been together... I don't know. Things just got complicated, not better."

She pulled in a long breath and then blew it out slowly, but when he looked at her, the chill in her expression remained.

"Cheryl." He reached to trace the outline of her face. She sat stoic.

Her attention shifted from him to the fire. He moved to bring her face back to his, but she pushed his hand away.

"Don't."

His heart dropped with a painful thud at the angry tone of her voice. "Don't what?"

"This was a mistake. All of it." She pushed off the ground to her feet, and she didn't look back as she slipped into the darkness.

Brock raked a hand through his hair and slunk back to the ground. Staring at the stars above, defeat pressed hard into his chest.

The growl of his truck cracked the silence of the night. The thief. Whatever. She could have it.

What was he doing with her? *Love her, Lord?* He'd never get ahold of her heart. She'd locked it up tighter than the federal penitentiary. He'd never have it.

Maybe it was best to let her go.

I cannot forget the wailing, no matter how much I wish to silence the memory.

Women, in pain. Physical agony. Emotionally shredded. Death hung heavy in the room.

No one warned us, and we cannot tell others. The code of silence cannot be broken.

Who would want to hear our story anyway?

~23~

Cheryl didn't bother folding the clothes as she threw them into her luggage—a stark departure from her neat-freak, control-driven norm. One thought propelled her past all of her carefully maintained rituals and through the pain searing her skull.

Leave.

She didn't belong there. She didn't belong with Brock. He wasn't the sort of man she could manage from a distance. He wouldn't be satisfied with her body and serving-sized pieces of her heart as she deemed fit. He wanted everything.

Except she knew for a fact he really didn't.

Not looking at what she was doing, she grabbed another fistful of laundry. Suddenly a hint of outdoorsy musk swirled in the room. She paused, hand in midair, ready to toss the wad of clothing into her bag, and studied what she'd snagged. Brock's hoodie. She hadn't returned it to him yet. Her body slipped into autopilot, and she brought the clothing to her face, burying her nose into the sweatshirt. Her eyes slid shut, and she inhaled deeply.

Why had he pushed her away? Couldn't he understand? That was all she had to give him, really all that he'd truly want. She would have been satisfied just to be with him, to let their bodies meld without making everything so deep and complicated. It was enough for her. Why couldn't it be enough for him?

A knock rapped against her bedroom door, and Cheryl ripped the sweatshirt away from her nose. Another memory she'd have to lock away. She'd leave his hoodie on the couch downstairs in the morning. Ethan would see that he got it.

The hollow tapping sounded again, louder this time.

"Sherbert, we need to talk."

He'd come for her? He hadn't chased her when she'd left the fire pit, and that had been hours ago. Why was he showing up now?

"I'm not kidding, Cheryl. Now."

She tossed his sweatshirt to the corner before she ripped the door open. "What?"

His eyes, hurt and serious, moved from her, to the bed where her suitcase lay open in the frenzied-packing mess, and back again. "Just like I thought."

"What's just like you thought?"

"You're running. Again. That's all you know how to do."

"I told you from the start that I couldn't stay here."

"Yeah, but you never told me why."

"This is why. You."

"Me? You can't stay because of me, because I want to be with you, to see you happy, and I want to do what's right?"

Cheryl spun away, marched to her bed, and began folding the clothes she'd flung into her bag. "Stop it. You're so self-righteous, looking down on anyone who might do life differently than you."

"What?" Brock left the doorway and followed her into the room. "Where is this coming from?"

"Oh, just go, Brock. Just leave me be. You're driving me crazy!"

"*I'm* driving *you* crazy?" He stepped between her and the bed. "I can't keep up with you. You make me dizzy. One minute you're tempting me, and the next you're leaving, and you don't give any space in between for me to get my head straight."

She glared at him and then reached around his frame to snatch another rumpled piece of clothing.

He stopped her attack against the sloppy clothes with both hands over hers. "Stop doing this and just talk to me. Tell me what's going on."

"You're asking too much." Had her voice just cracked? "Just let me go."

The air seemed to still as the weight of his look drew her into something like a trance.

"No." He pulled her hands to his chest and made her palms rest there. His head came against hers. "I'm not just letting you go. I love you." Slowly, he nudged her face until his lips grazed hers. "I love you."

Her fingers curled into his shirt, and the pounding in her head abated to a small throb. What if love, the kind of love Brock offered, was enough? If he knew, would he still feel like this?

"Are you hearing me, Sherbert?" His hands moved from hers and threaded through her hair.

Her lips quivered. "Yes."

What was this man doing with her? She didn't deserve him, didn't deserve his devotion. She could tell him she loved him too, which she was almost certain she did, but always there would be a piece of her he couldn't have. He wouldn't be okay with that. He would keep sifting until he discovered what she couldn't stand for him to find.

Or she could lay it out for him now and save them both the heartache.

Courage, where are you?

Don't say it...

The pain in her head flared.

Just tell him and get it over with.

Her heart hammered against her ribs.

No one else knows. He doesn't have to either.

She squeezed her eyes shut. Tears dripped from her lids to her nose.

"Cheryl?" His thumbs traced the wet trails under her eyes. "Just talk to me."

This man fights for those who have no voice. He stands against people like you. He'll never forgive you.

"You should go, Brock. You don't want me."

His head left hers, but his hands remained. She opened her eyes to find him scowling.

"Do you think I'm a stupid man? That I can't see the reality in front of me? I'm standing here telling you that you drive me crazy, but I love you. I want you to stay with me."

"Brock..."

"No." His fingers gripped tighter on her hair. "You're not sending me away. We're dealing with this, right here, right now."

Cheryl griped his forearms and shook her head. "You love those kids."

"The kids?"

"Yes. I can see how much you love them. You're their champion, and..."

"That's what this is about?" He gave a small, confused laugh. "You think I can't love you too?"

"No." Cheryl stepped back and pushed his hands away from her. "But I know how you think."

"About what?"

She sighed, wrapping her arms around her middle. "About me. Because...I...I should have one." A wave of fear crashed over her, and her voice shook.

"You should have one?"

Drawing her posture straight, she forced herself to look at him. "I got pregnant. Ten years ago."

Brock stared at her, and she could see him mentally filing through what she was trying to tell him. With a subtle step back, he scowled. "What happened?"

"I was...seeing one of my professors. His name was Michael." She wrapped herself tighter, but it didn't stop her body from shaking. "By the time I found out he was married..." She shut her eyes and drew a deep breath. "Anyway, he already had a family, and I was a student, so..."

Eyes wide, he continued to gape at her. "So...what?"

Her teeth sank hard into her bottom lip as pain exploded in her heart. There had been some bad moments in her life. Really horrible ones. But only two had been worse than this one, and this ran pretty close to those. Telling this man, this good man who said he loved her...

He'd walk. Turn around and leave her room and never look back. Worse, that love he said he had for her? It would crust over, freeze up, and turn into utter contempt. Because how could a man like Brock Kelly ever look upon a woman like her with anything else?

But there wasn't any turning back now.

She forced the truth through quivering lips. "I terminated."

Terminated...a clinical word for...

Though she didn't want to, she watched Brock as he sifted through the synonyms for *terminated*. His pinched expression told her exactly when he landed on the more common word.

Aborted.

She'd had an abortion.

In just a few more seconds, his *conservative pastor's son been pro-life since forever* mind would go to the next word. The one she couldn't place in her vocabulary when it came to that event. The one that had sent her reeling earlier that evening.

Brock looked at her, the deep love that had been in his eyes now replaced with horror. He'd found *that* word, put it over her name, and mentally branded her with it.

Agony seared through her. This was why. She'd sworn she'd never, never, never tell a soul. Ever. Because she knew how the other side thought. She knew what Brock was thinking.

"Say it," she seethed.

He took another step back. "What?"

"Say what you're thinking."

"I don't know what to think. I need to process…"

"Get out!" She flew at him, her hands colliding with his chest with a mighty shove. "I know what you're thinking, what you all think in your pristine church world. How could she do that? Right? How could she kill her unborn child? How can she live with herself? You don't have any idea what happened. I don't need your condemnation, so get out. Just leave, and don't ever come back."

She'd pushed him to the frame of her door before he finally caught her elbows and fought against her. "Stop this, Sherbert. I just need to think."

Her hand flew. In her rage, she didn't even feel the smack of her palm against his cheek. "Don't ever call me that."

He fingered the spot on his face that was beginning to turn red, and his glance measured her from head to toe. She didn't want to see the result of that calculation. The cool of the door filled her palm, and she flung it as hard as she could. Still shaking, she leaned against it with her back and slid to the floor.

She'd known it, should have listened to the warnings in her head. Not even Brock Kelly could love a blood-stained woman like her.

Stillness seeped through the hall beyond her door. *Leave, Brock.* The floor creaked under her, his weight shifting outside the halls. Guess she got her way. Her head fell to her knees as she wrapped her arms tight around her legs.

Something scuffled against the door behind her. "Cheryl." Brock's deep voice vibrated through the wood at her back. "I'm still here."

She winced. What was he doing? Waiting to convince her that she was a sinner? She knew. This everyday hell wouldn't let her escape that fact.

"I told you to leave," she screamed at the door.

"No, Sherbert."

With a fresh surge of fury she didn't understand but couldn't control, she jumped to her feet and ripped the door open. He jerked himself straight, and his hand, which apparently had been resting on the door, fell to his side.

"Didn't I tell you not to call me that? I hate you, Brock Kelly!"

He flinched and took a step back.

"Get. Out." She slammed the door shut again and waited until his footsteps echoed off the last of the wood risers below. Crumbling to the floor, she let the sobs loose. Life had been better when she'd kept her heart on ice.

~*~

Brock sat in his truck—Cheryl had left the keys tucked in the visor like he usually did—and stared out the windshield.

"What were you thinking?" The words left his lips in a whisper and floated around the cab until they seeped into his heart. Rage suddenly exploded, and he looked up at the laughing stars. "What were you thinking?" he shouted to the heavens. "I didn't ask for this! I didn't want a woman in my life again—I told you that. I didn't want her to rearrange my world, let alone grab my heart and turn it wrong side out."

He slammed a palm against the steering wheel, and a sharp pain shot through his wrist. It was nothing. Not enough. Balling a fist, he punched the dashboard over and over again until cool blood oozed from his knuckles.

Trembling, he gripped the wheel and fought for self-control. "I can't, God. You picked the wrong guy, and I can't do it."

With the heel of his palm, he wiped at the moisture that had trickled onto one cheek and then jammed the keys into the ignition.

JENNIFER RODEWALD

Cheryl could leave. He'd move on with his life. They weren't going to work, and somehow he'd get past the devastation.

People made choices every day, and they had to live with them. She'd made hers long before. That wasn't his fault.

I knew it was too good to be true.
Love has its limit.
You had to keep digging, searching, probing. You found the ugly.
And you did exactly what I knew you would do.
You turned around and walked away.

~24~

Fighting the leftover haze from her Mary Jane brownies, which were now legal in the great state of Colorado, Cheryl pushed back against the padding of her coach seat on the small aircraft. Just like she had on her flight into Denver, she tightened her fist around the letter that had started this whole stupid trip. She shut her eyes and let her mind circle around the mystery of why this mattered so much. She'd just left one of the worst nights of her life behind in Hayden. Why did she replay things from the past that were irrelevant?

I have no excuse, Cheryl. I treated you terrible. I have asked God to forgive me, for everything I did to you, to others, and for the rebellion I've waged against Him, and He has given me grace upon grace. But I know that I hurt you—I saw it in your eyes the day you told me good-bye. Please forgive me.

She was obsessed. That was the only explanation Cheryl could find for keeping Andrew's letter. The paper bore the marks of abuse. She'd crumpled the page and restraightened it at least a dozen times. It had landed in three trash bins, only to find its way back into her possession.

Andrew had been one of the biggest jerks she'd ever met—when he wasn't being charming. Mostly, the bad happened when he was drunk. Her research on his life had produced more of the expected dirt after they'd broken up. Dirt that involved the woman he eventually married. Surely Jamie, his bride, knew at least some of his offenses. There wasn't a way Andrew could hide them all. Two car accidents. License suspension. Probation at work... The list was too long for her not to have known.

Plus, that waitress seemed to know that he should *not* be drinking. She definitely gave him the *don't do this* scowl.

Jamie had to know Andrew's sins. There was no way around it. But she'd married him.

Why?

Indeed, that was the reason she kept thinking about it—the big *why* question.

Why did Andrew get another chance at life, at love? Was he so much less of a sinner than she? Were her crimes simply unforgivable, while his were able to be bleached?

Why were some forgiven and others eternally punished?

You're unfair, God.

Blasphemous. That was what that reckless thought was. She'd chosen the path of rebellion. God punished the crimes of a sinner. Wasn't that the truth?

But Andrew...

She pushed the arguments away. It didn't matter. Andrew's life had no bearing on hers. Some things were irrevocable, which meant they couldn't fit under the umbrella of forgiveness.

Apparently Brock thought so too.

I love you...

She pushed away the memory of the way his breath heated the skin on her face. Some kind of love. She'd pushed him to the edge, and he broke. From one skip of the heart to the next, his feelings changed.

Love was an illusion. She'd known better than to try to grasp it.

She should have known better...

The force of the aircraft as it pushed its way off the ground shoved her into the backrest of her chair. Nausea rolled, and she squeezed her eyes shut. A surge of panic sent her heart rate galloping as her vision skipped and blurred. She dug her fingernails into the seat beneath her and worked to steady her breath.

"I'm not a fan of flying either." The middle-aged woman next to her patted her arm, which was tight as a wire strung between power poles.

I'm not a fan of living.

No sense in voicing that thought. Cheryl swallowed, but her eyes remained shut. "I'll be fine."

"Sure you will, sweetie. Just rest." More patting.

Please stop touching me.

"I'll order you some ginger ale when we hit cruising elevation. You just relax, sweetie."

Sweetie... Her mother's voice touched her memory. *You're fine, sweetie. It looks scary, but this climb is amazing. A difficult but glorious path.*

Cheryl hadn't been able to see the *glorious* her mom had been talking about on that climb. She'd bowed to fear, and they went home defeated.

The theme of her life, it seemed. Someday, around her grave, the maybe one or two people on earth who cared about her would remember her in one phrase: *She bowed to fear.*

One. There would only be one person there. Brock had left her, so that left only Ethan.

The air in her lungs felt heavy and dirty.

Clean. I am desperate to be clean.

A surge of hot moisture gathered behind her eyelids. A drowning man may be desperate for air, but the longing for it wouldn't produce the oxygen for his lungs. Eventually he would succumb to the reality, and death would claim its victory.

Death. So tempting. *Maybe then I could hold her. Just once...*

That thought had been streaking through her heavily guarded defense of indifference way too often lately. It wouldn't happen. She'd sealed her sentence with one desperate mistake. Even if the Great Judge allowed a single moment with her unborn—which He wouldn't—why would she think that her child would ever want to see her?

No. She would be miserable in life and worse after death. There was no way out.

A voice next to her cut through the despair. "This lovely friend of mine needs a ginger ale."

Lovely friend? Lovely only if one looked on the outside, and Cheryl worked pretty hard to make sure that was all anyone saw. Strict diet. Religious exercise. Expensive beauty products. Everything to defer attention from her ugly heart.

Until Brock.

Her chest lurched with breathtaking pain.

Cool sweat beaded along her hairline and gathered in the small of her back. There were countless clubs in downtown LA, and hungry men for the choosing. She'd shower, change into something sultry, and lose herself to the varied distractions. Until morning...

Then what?

Not a big mystery. She'd been starring in this show for ten years. Clean up, go to work, fight against the bad guys, and hope Someone above took notice of the small amount of nobility she could muster. Evening would come again, and she'd start the whole cycle over. It'd been working for her.

Until Brock.

Shut up. He was just another man. With a quick intake of air, Cheryl sat forward and opened her eyes. A plastic glass of amber fizzed liquid sat on the tray in front of her. To her right, the woman who had ordered it for her sat quietly reading.

The title of her book caught Cheryl's attention.

Her Choice to Heal.

Something unraveled in Cheryl's chest, causing a mighty tremble to unleash in her heart.

Choice.

It seemed like a secret code—a phrase known to the inner circle of the silently miserable.

She had to be imagining things. It was a book title, not a calling card.

The book niggled, and she couldn't resist subtle glances at both the woman and her reading material. Emotion occasionally flitted across her face, but as Cheryl continued to sneak an assessment, she determined this was not her neighbor's first time through the words. Worn pages, some dog eared, spoke of previous use.

She studied the title again, and this time one word in the subtitle snagged her with a strangling grip.

Abortion.

Cheryl squeezed her eyes shut and moved so that she faced the window. Though her emotions were frayed and physically she was exhausted, sleep would not claim her. For two hours she focused on keeping her eyes shut, swatting at any invading thoughts about Brock, her neighbor, and that book.

LA, then shower, then clubs. That was her battle plan, sprinkled heavily with a dose of any kind of whatever she could drink, snort, inhale, or shoot into her veins that would dilute the power of reality. Nothing was off limits tonight.

The aircraft finally shifted, signaling their descent. Relief was coming closer. Next to her, the woman moved, repacking her travel bag, which meant it was safe for Cheryl to look away from the window.

Energy in the cabin buzzed as seat belts clicked open and the shuffling of papers and bags filled the air, lending Cheryl a sense of relief. Almost done. The woman next to her remained silent in her seat, almost pensive as she stared straight ahead.

Guess she had a lot to think about.

The wheels skipped on the ground, making that high-pitched scuffling noise. Muscles tense in her neck and shoulders, Cheryl stretched to her left and then to her right.

"Did you have a nice rest?" the woman asked.

"Yes." Civil lies were acceptable, weren't they? In her case, it didn't matter. She was black-marked by heaven either way.

Her neighbor nodded, her lips tight. The plane rolled to the terminal, and suddenly everyone was on their feet.

Except the woman next to Cheryl. Which meant she was trapped.

"Everyone is always in such a hurry," the woman said, "as if they think we won't all get a chance to deplane."

Cheryl forced a calm voice. "Anxious to be done, I guess."

"Hmm." The woman nodded, her expression still strained. Suddenly she drew a long breath and turned toward Cheryl. "I feel like I need to say something to you."

What the...

"You're never beyond God's grace. Never."

Cheryl drew back, pushing herself against the seat as if she hoped it would engulf her.

"I saw you glancing at my book—and I know that look." The woman leaned down, withdrew the paperback from her bag, and pushed it toward Cheryl. "I want you to have it."

Wide eyed and appalled, Cheryl didn't move, even when the woman set the book on her lap.

"There's hope, sweetie. I promise you—there is hope. Because the point of the Bible was never perfection. It is always redemption." With that, she rose and joined the line to exit the plane.

Cheryl sat trembling until the crowd was gone.

If I am forgivable, why am I forever condemned?

~25~

Misery didn't die quietly. In Brock's case, it wouldn't even stop screaming long enough to draw a new breath. Visions of Cheryl pushing him away, rage etched into the features of her usually beautiful face, continued to saturate his mind. He saw her when he shut his eyes, his peace entirely crumpled by her memory. When he walked by the piano in the dining hall, the music book he'd ordered for her pierced like a javelin into his soul. When he stood on the dock looking over the pond in the late evenings, a time he'd previously relished as his quiet moments with God, the tranquility was now interrupted by her anger.

The aching misery of being angry right back at her and yet heartbroken for her crumpled every part of his life, challenging his everyday normal. To play Frisbee with a trio of boys after dinner. To sing along with Brandi as she strummed her guitar. To lead the exploration at Fish Creek Falls alongside Ethan while Brandi took So-J over the mountains for visitation. He felt detached and empty. Like the colors of life had seeped away, leaving a monotone image as a depressing reminder of what had been.

Friday evening found him on the back portion of his deck, facing away from the voices that floated up from the pond on the other side of his house. He should have been down there, making s'mores with E and Brandi and So-J. But maybe this was better anyway. They were to become a new family, those three. They'd need every moment to begin solidifying what God was weaving together. Especially since So-J seemed determined to combat Brandi's every effort. Strange that. Brandi usually found a way with the kids rather quickly. But it was Ethan, and not his new wife, who seemed best at gaining So-J's more personable side. And that seemed to bother Brandi to a surprising extent.

Not his problem. Heaven knew he had enough of his own to worry about. Ethan and Brandi would figure it out.

That left Brock...alone. Except not really. He still carried Cheryl in his heart, aching in ways he couldn't understand.

How could she have done such a thing?

And yet, how could he really hold it against her? She'd screamed in her fury that he wasn't there—he couldn't know. That was true. He couldn't. Couldn't wrap his head around her choice, but couldn't let it lie either. And with every hint of judgment he felt rise within, an equally strong sense of conviction met it. Who was he to keep an account of her mistakes? The Bible said that rebellion was "like the sin of divination." Guilty. He'd gone his own way, took a gift that God had blessed him with and used it for his own self-serving glory.

And what about Kayla?

They'd spent over a year living together. What if...

Yes. What if? He'd probably never know. But now he was acutely aware that there was that possibility, and he'd have to live with it. He could call her, ask, but the thought gave him no peace. Either way, he'd gone down a path that led to destruction. He'd failed to be the man that God had called him to be.

There really wasn't a difference between him and Cheryl. He knew it, but when he'd gone back to try again the morning after she'd told him, she'd already left. For good. The hand-scrawled sign at the bakery said so. Still, he felt that divine imperative weighing deep within his soul.

Love her.

Straight up, he didn't know how. Clearly he had a whole lot of emotions twisting around concerning her, but love wasn't simply emotion, and he didn't know how to carry out the action. What would they look like together—a life intertwined from two lives that had been worn thin? The headaches, her aversion to participate with the kids, the constant underlying anger that surfaced so easily...all of it was coming into focus. How was he going to continue the life he'd carved into this serene piece of property—the life God had called him to after his own heart-shattering repentance—if Cheryl became a part of it? They weren't compatible, Cheryl and Kelly's Ranch. Was it wise to try to bridge the two?

The thread of questions took him by surprise. He'd let her go. Cheryl was gone. Why was he asking *how* questions when there didn't even seem to be an *if* in regards to any of it?

She was gone.

Gripping the deck railing, Brock lifted his face to the darkening sky. He'd been facing east, but he looked to his left, to the north. Cassiopeia rested against the peaks. A shiver crept over his arms. He'd looked up the mythology that was associated with that particular constellation. Not exactly a fairy tale. The beautiful queen suffered from vanity and arrogance, which led to another god's anger...and eventually to the sacrifice of her daughter, Andromeda, who was rescued from death by the mighty Perseus. Talk about twisted.

He turned away from the *W*-shaped constellation, his gaze traveling the width of the night sky. Why did beauty have to be marred by such tellings?

Why did life have to turn ugly sometimes?

The sound of footfalls against his deck redirected his thoughts. He released the railing and stepped away, leaving the stars and their beautiful, violent mysteries in the sky above.

"Hello?" He rounded the corner of his house toward the front door.

"There you are, son." His father stood with his hand raised as if he was ready to knock. "I wondered. Didn't see you with the group down below."

"Yeah."

Dad studied him for a moment, his eyes thoughtful. Brock's relationship with his parents had been restored over the past five years as he'd shed his arrogance and rebellious attitudes in the refining discipline God had recently put to him. Discipline that included the removal of a dream and being deeply wounded by a woman he'd thought had been committed to more than his career. Losses and gains. A renewed relationship with his father had been on the positive side of that equation. However, Dad simply showing up on a Friday evening was a bit on the unusual side.

Brock motioned to the two chairs he kept near the front door. A favorite spot for morning coffee. Dad's hand fell to his side, and he nodded before both men took a seat.

"Mom doing okay?"

"She's fine. Had one of those girly jewelry party things women do sometimes. You know."

"Sure. So you're on your own tonight."

"No. I'm here."

Brock looked as his hands, his knuckles on his right fist littered with crusted-over scabs. Discomfort began to throb in the silence.

"I could make some decaf or something," he offered, hoping his own needling emotions would stay below the surface.

"No. I'm good. Thanks." Dad leaned against his legs, folding his hands in between his knees. "I hear that you're not so good though. Wondered if maybe you'd want to talk about it."

He'd heard, huh? "What'd Ethan tell you?"

Dad chuckled quietly. "That something happened between you and his sister, and now she's skipped town and you're not good."

That about summed it up. Brock tipped his head, leaned the back of his skull against the house, and breathed deep.

"So what happened?"

"A lot."

He laughed again. "Sounds normal. What are you going to do?"

Brock squeezed his eyes shut and shoved a hand through his hair. In the next moment, he gripped both arms of the chair and stared out into the night. "I don't get constellations. Why, when what we see is so amazing, are the stories we tell so ugly?"

He felt his dad's gaze. Could guess his confusion. Dad sat still for a few breaths, allowing the silence to sort through their sludgy conversation. Eventually he turned toward Brock and nudged his hand with a knuckle.

"What'd the other guy look like?"

Brock glanced at his hand and tucked it into his lap. "Just the dashboard of my truck. Not a scratch." He pushed out a single laugh. "Hardly fair, right?"

"Guess it's better than hitting a brick wall. Or, you know, whoever you were mad at."

Unthinkable. Even when he'd literally shook with confusion and anger, what he wanted most was to hold the woman who'd set fire to his emotions. Strange. Only in that moment did that realization hit him.

"I don't know why our stories come out the way they do." Dad settled back into his chair. "Seems true to life, though, don't you think? But here's the thing: I'm sitting here under the same sky you are, looking at the same stars you're seeing, and I see something amazing, just like you. Maybe that's something to think about. The stories up there, they're not all great. But beauty shines forth from the darkness. Maybe that's what we call redemption."

Brock swallowed. "Does that mean we ignore the ugly stories?"

"No. I think that means we acknowledge them and then stand back. That's where the real wonder is. What man has twisted, God has redeemed. Really, that's quite something." Dad shifted again, this time to place a hand on Brock's shoulder. "And if we're really talking people here, son, and not stars, I want you to know that's how I see you. I am amazed at the man you've become, and proud doesn't even begin to touch what I feel concerning you."

Brock sniffed. "I really made a mess of my life for a while. Broke you and Mom's heart."

"True enough. But that's not what either of us see when we look at you."

There were no words. Emotions flooded—humility and gratitude and a fresh sense of wonder.

"Listen, Brock. I'm not sure what happened with you and Cheryl, but I do know that God has gifted you with a heart of enormous compassion. That's why you love what you do here at the ranch. Sometimes it's easier to give compassion to those whose troubles fell upon them undeserved. But those who've, from our perspective, tangled themselves up all on their own—they need compassion every bit as much."

You who are without sin, cast the first stone...

No one did. Because you can't grasp a stone while keeping a grip on grace. One or the other must stay on the ground.

Blinking, Brock stood. His father met him on his feet and put one arm around him, and Brock moved to meet him in a full hug.

"I don't need to know the details. Just know that your mother and I are praying."

He didn't wait for a response before he clapped Brock's back and moved away, leaving Brock to study the sky.

The beauty put him on his knees.

~26~

Endless silence enveloped her apartment. The sludgy black kind that told her this was her life. Forever. Through burning eyes, Cheryl let her attention drift from the letter she was rewriting. Back to where she'd been when this whole Ferris wheel started—quitting. It had to be the right thing to do. She couldn't go back to pretending anymore.

She could hardly function. Drunk didn't last long enough. The highs didn't either. Reality waited after every hit, every numbing binge. That reality screamed into every pore of her existence: *unforgivable.*

God would always be angry.

Brock had melted the ice, and even with his rejection—which she'd known would come—she couldn't summon a new cold front to numb her heart. So there she sat, no longer indifferent, shivering in the slush of what remained, and without a notion as to what was next in her pathetic little life.

If only she could stop feeling again. Or stop living.

Yes. Death, come, deliver your black relief.

How many times had she embraced that possibility, and with it a moment of relief? She could not count them. But the possibility brought only a wisp of hope, because on the heels of such thoughts came the ugly warning of what lay beyond the grave.

The Judge. He would look at her, rage seething in His glare. She heard the gravity of His voice, imagined the knife of His words falling upon her soul.

Your sin lies before me. You did not do enough.

Forever condemned. She could not face that. Death was not an option. Apparently, neither was life.

She scanned the skyline beyond her window. Lights glittered in every direction, a unique beauty she'd never seen until she'd moved to the West Coast city. So vast. So many opportunities. Cultural diversity. Activity. Cheryl sat, and for the first time in years, she let the view take her on a personal history.

Dad had pushed her toward law. Granted, he'd wanted her to go to the University of Wyoming. Not a chance. If she was going to move from Hayden, she had determined it would be as far away from her dad as possible. That left either the West or the East Coasts. So the negotiations ensued. He'd pay so much if she got accepted. Undergrad at UCLA it was, with the aim at continuing into law school. Dad probably had been banking on her not getting accepted into the UCLA law program—their qualifying percentages were pretty narrow.

Cheryl had made it her life ambition to prove him wrong. And then, to do as far as possible the opposite of what he'd wanted within the parameters of their agreement. He pushed for entertainment law or intellectual property. She pursued criminal justice. He campaigned for internships in private sectors. She only applied for public-practice experience. He wanted her to move back, to take the Colorado or Wyoming State Bar. She refused, planted her single taproot in California soil, and didn't budge.

If all of that had been what she'd actually wanted, it would have been great. But defiance for simple defiance sake didn't work out all that well. And the turn in her focus from simply practicing law to paying out meager peace offerings to the Great Judge twisted dislike into misery.

Brock's surprise at her chosen career niggled at her as she stared through those memories. What if she had stood up to her father on the things that had mattered to her, rather than manipulating as much money and frustration out of him as possible, just for revenge?

Perhaps her life would look very different right now.

Opportunities—thousands, possibly millions—literally spread out beyond her window in the vast sea of people and buildings and lights, yet none of them called to her. In the reflection of all that she'd lost, both within the past week and over the past decade, all of the beacons that littered the semidark skyline were gaudy flashes of false hope.

She'd left her real self somewhere behind. Possibly dead. Certainly unrecoverable.

Pushing aside the keyboard at her fingertips, she folded her arms and laid her head against them.

Where is hope?

Shutting her eyes, she let the words circle as if a prayer. No, not really a prayer. From her, those went no higher than the lofted ceiling above her head. God didn't turn his ear her way. He simply couldn't. The holy has nothing to do with the unholy. The righteous would not soil Himself with the stained.

And yet...

Ethan hadn't been an ideal man. He lived free. Brock said he too had been rebellious. Yet he lived unbound. Even her father, whom she knew to be a failure in many ways, seemed to live beyond the prison of guilt. And Andrew...

Was this freedom only to men? Or perhaps her sin was beyond the reach of grace. The latter seemed most likely. Who could forgive such an act?

~*~

Brock paused in the midst of the swirling rush around him. A monotone voice blared over the intercom, calling a name that meant nothing to him. People moved as though the world would shut down if they didn't reach their gate in the next breath. But in the midst of the scurry, Brock's reality slowed, focused, and steadied.

The little shop would be crazy expensive. All airport boutiques were.

Red roses say I love you.

He'd heard somewhere a while back that if you wanted to reach the heart of a woman, you had to speak her language. Which meant that something he may see as insignificant, and maybe even a bit of a waste, wasn't really a waste at all.

So he'd purchase a red rose bouquet.

It'd be a start. Maybe. He hoped.

~*~

Cheryl started, her rounded shoulders jerking before she lifted her head. Brushing the side of her face that had been plastered to her folded arms, she looked around.

Something had jolted her awake, which was interesting, as she hadn't realized she'd dozed off.

The skyline beyond her desk remained much as it had been in her last moment of consciousness—a million different lights gathered like a chorus in the night sky. She couldn't have slept for very long.

She was checking her bangle watch when the sound of a knock against her front door filled her home. Again. That was what had startled her awake.

After a glance to the door, she went back to her watch. Ten thirty. Who would come to her door at ten thirty?

She pushed against the desk and stood, stretching her neck from side to side in an attempt to relieve the tightness in those muscles. Foolish woman. She had a bed. A good one. There was no reason to fall asleep at her desk.

Inhaling, and still stretching, she shuffled toward the front door. Her neighbor, a man in his forties who still partied like he was in college, had people in and out of his home like he had a revolving door. Most likely, one of his many guests had the wrong apartment. Annoying, but harmless.

But she'd check the peephole just to be sure.

The hallway, what she could see of it, rested vacant. She could see the wall across the hall, and nothing moved to the left or right. With both hands against the door, she was about to push away when a flash of color drew her attention to the carpeted floor outside her entrance.

Red.

Her breath caught, and a wave of chills rushed over her shoulders and down her arms.

It could be a mistake. She could be imagining. Or misunderstanding. Or...

She unlatched the dead bolt and reached for the doorknob, silencing the possible explanations. With a tentative pull, she opened the door and crept toward the papered bundle on the floor.

Roses. A bouquet of red roses lay on the ground at her threshold. *Brock.*

The name caught in her throat, a silent sob capturing her whisper. He'd sent her red roses. She knelt, her hand trembling as she reached to finger the velvety petals.

"Hey."

Cheryl jumped at Brock's whisper, her eyes darting to the side of the hall. He stood, huddled against the wall on her side of the hallway, his expression tight with emotion.

He pushed off the wall and took a single step forward. "I wasn't sure if you'd open the door if you saw me on the other side."

Her bottom lip trembled, and she looked away from his face, back at the roses.

He'd come for her. She'd pushed him to the breaking point, and he'd come for her anyway. He'd brought her a red rose bouquet and laid it at her feet, knowing exactly what the roses would say to her.

Wrapping one arm around her middle, with the other hand she pulled the flowers toward her chest. *Oh God, why? I'm a wreck. He needs better than me...*

You are not beyond My reach.

Yes she was. Cheryl trembled, and the tears she had locked away suddenly surged to her eyes. Surely, she was.

But here was this man...

A cry broke from her chest, shuddering through her shoulders. In a breath, Brock was there, on the floor with her, his arms tightening around her, his frame covering hers.

"I'm sorry," she whispered, wetness covering her face. "Oh God, I'm so sorry. Please..." Another cry cut off her words.

She was turned into his chest, and then the arms that had covered her were suddenly carrying her.

Love tore down the last of her walls. She'd never felt more exposed. Or safe.

~*~

Brock had only heard that kind of depth in a sob once before. From her, in her nightmares.

Now he knew why. The last vestiges of anger evaporated, and his heart moved with a great ache. He only knew part of the history, but he could see the pain that lingered. What would anger do? Only damage. That was the furthest thing from his desire, because he loved her.

He'd nudged her front door shut behind him, not wanting her to feel like a sideshow as she broke down in his arms, and settled with her on her midcentury modern sofa. She turned into his chest, roses and all, and clung to his T-shirt, cries shaking her violently.

With a slight shift, he took the bouquet from her grasp and laid the roses on the spot beside them and then cradled her tightly.

"I'm sorry, Sherbert," he whispered into her hair. "I came here to say that I'm sorry and that I love you."

She sniffed, her head moving from side to side against him. "Why? You don't have anything to be sorry for, and you shouldn't love me."

"I should have responded differently. And I shouldn't have let you go."

Two weeks ago, she would have either pushed him away or tried to seduce him, and either way he'd have been frustrated. There, in that stripped-bare moment, she only shivered, tears still soaking into his shirt. All of it was making sense. Her control-freak approach to her body and appearance, her coldness, the headaches, the nightmares...layers of damage that had only ever been smothered.

But they could talk about that later. Right now, she was overdue a good, hard cry.

As the minutes added up, Cheryl began to calm. Brock loosened his hold and rubbed small circles into her shoulder with his thumb. She stayed huddled against him, but he felt her tension uncoil as her body grew heavier against him.

Oh, to stay there...

"Cheryl." His voice felt rough against his throat. Only then did he realize that he'd lost a few of his own tears.

Again she sniffed. "Yeah."

"You're tired. You should go to bed, okay? I'll be back in the morning."

She tipped her face up and pushed a hand against his chest so that she could look at him. Her eyes, the desperation in them, told him she wanted him to stay. For a moment, justification pushed against his conscious. He'd make sure she fell asleep. He'd be there if she had another nightmare. It wasn't wrong. They wouldn't cross any lines...

And then her expression changed. The request silently faded, and a look of respect took its place. She leaned forward, brushing her lips against his jaw. "You're such a good man, Brock. I didn't know men like you still walked the earth."

He inhaled deeply as her arms tightened around his neck. "Sometimes. Not always." He tucked his nose into her hair and breathed. "I'm all in, Sherbert. I want the good and the bad. All of it."

She hesitated before her nod moved against him.

Good enough for tonight.

~*~

Cheryl eyed the soft crimson flowers soaking in a vase on her coffee table. She was glad no one had ever given her the clichéd gift before. They meant the world coming from him.

Brock sat across from her at her bar-height breakfast table. He'd brought bagels and coffee from a shop he'd found between her apartment and his hotel. He looked tired, but his eyes held hers with that look—the one she'd been so desperate to keep.

The impossible had happened. He knew the truth, and yet he loved her.

She blinked against the tears. "How long can you stay?"

With one finger, he traced her hand. "As long as it takes." His steady gaze locked on her, wordlessly telling her that he wasn't leaving without her.

Love flooded her chest, so strong it actually hurt. "Brock"—she threaded her fingers with his—"why? Why me? Surely you know there's better for you out there."

"I don't know that." He tugged on her hand, and she left her stool willingly, moving so that he could secure her in his arms.

"But me?" she pushed. "You had no reason to fall for me. I'm...the ice princess. And a—"

"A sinner? Like me? And Ethan, and your dad, and the man who refused to be a father to your baby, and everyone else on this planet? Yeah, you're one of those."

She sniffed, burying her head against his neck even as she shook it. "You're the famous Brock Kelly, King of the Slopes. Pastor's son. Compassionate man extraordinaire. The pro athlete who gave it all up to run a camp for foster kids."

His chest moved with a small chuckle. "You forgot reckless rebel who dishonored his parents, basically ignored them for four years, lived with a woman who was not his wife. Consumed with himself, with his fame, with the idea that every woman alive must be dying for one of his smiles." He moved to frame her face, lifting it to look at him. "We're both a mess. We'll continue to be messy. I want us to be messy together. Can we do that?"

Even in the glaze of tears, which she simply could not shut off, she smiled. "I hope so."

One side of his mouth lifted, and then he pressed a kiss to her temple.

Cheryl slid her arms around him. "My letter of resignation is done, and I sent it this morning. There's nothing for me here."

A pause extended, and he fingered the hair that hung loose around her shoulders as he seemed to align his words. "I think we need some time in LA. Just a little."

"Why? My job is over. What about the ranch?"

"I've arranged for a small break. E and Brandi are adjusting to life with So-J, and they need the time off too. And I have my support agency looking for a manager for me."

She tugged away. "What? No. You *love* them. Those kids, your work. You're not leaving it for me."

Brock's gaze softened with appreciation. "That's a subject on hold for right now. I want you in my life—that doesn't mean trying to force you to fit into it as it is. It means finding out how to build one together. We'll figure that out when the time comes, but for now, this"—he motioned between the two of them—"is more important. There are things we need to work through, and we can do that here without distractions. Just for a while."

It was a tender gesture—no one had ever offered to give up anything for her, let alone everything. But as selfless and loving as it was, fear snaked through the love that had filled her heart.

Work through things...her past. The abortion. She didn't know how to work through that—hadn't ever wanted to. The whole point in doing it was so that she could leave the problem behind. Move on with her life. *You'll never have to think about it again...* That was what the woman had promised. It had been a lie. She couldn't stop thinking about it, even if her thoughts weren't conscious.

"You're shutting down on me." With a gentle finger, Brock lifted her chin.

Her lips trembled, and she pressed them together and shut her eyes.

"Sherbert..." He rubbed his thumb along the bottom edge of her mouth. "I don't know what I'm doing, and I'm scared too. But I know we, together, we have to work through this. The headaches, the nightmares, the anger, cutting yourself off from everyone...you have to see they're all related. Don't you?"

"I don't want to go back there again."

His chest caved inward as he sighed. "I know. And honestly, I don't really want to see you go through it, because I know it's going to hurt. But I think you have to."

"Why?" The question came out as a sob. "Why won't it just go away? God hates me. He's punishing me, and I don't think it will ever end."

That wasn't true—God couldn't hate her if He'd sent Brock into her life. It didn't make sense. None of this messed-up, tied-into-knots life of hers made sense. Why had God taken her mother? Let her dad abandon her? Let her get pregnant? Why did He allow her to do what she'd done? He should hate her for it. But then He gave her this?

Brock moved to cradle her again, fitting her head against his shoulder. "You remember Gramps's shoes?"

Weird turn. "Yeah?"

"They were the special kind—the kind he had to get at the pharmacy. I remember one time as a kid going with him to pick up a new pair he'd ordered. Thought it was so weird that he'd buy shoes at a drugstore."

She sniffed, the tears drying as Brock told his out-of-the-blue memory. "Okay..."

"He was a diabetic. I didn't understand until years later that his diabetes damaged the nerves in his body. He couldn't feel pain in his feet, and he had to be really diligent about taking care of them, or risk infection, deformities, or even an eventual amputation. I didn't know all of that back then, but I remember him telling me something I thought was kind of strange." Brock moved Cheryl so that she'd look at him again. "He said that sometimes pain was a gift. Really, really bad things could happen without it."

The gift of pain? Stepping away from Brock, Cheryl examined the idea as she surveyed the city beyond her window. The nightmares, they hadn't started right away. Actually, they hadn't started until after Andrew. And the headaches...those too. The other stuff, well she'd done that to herself. Cut ties with the people back home, kept herself away from kids, kept her emotions frozen. Survival tactics, because she was so ashamed.

But the others...why now?

She looked back to Brock, who had waited in patient silence. "God is trying to get my attention?"

"Does He have it?"

Her eyelashes fluttered. "Yes. But why?"

"I'm not sure. But if you're asking what I think, He doesn't want you to live like this. Apart from life. Separated from Him." He slid off the stool and took the two steps necessary to stand behind her. His hands covered her shoulders. "It's time to stop running, Sherbert. It's time to come home."

"I don't know the way back."

"He does."

Cheryl turned to face him again. "And you'll do this? With me?"

"Yes."

"It might be awful."

He took both her hands in his. "We'll get through it."

Drawing a long breath, Cheryl closed her eyes. *If you still want me, God, I want to come home.*

Brock stepped closer, and the moment Cheryl rested her head against his chest, his arms circled her shoulders.

Going home. The thought still seemed terrifying. But not impossible.

It might be worth the pain.

~27~

Brock stared over the sea of lights beyond the hotel window.

God, I'm terrified.

This thought from the great thrill seeker Brock Kelly. He'd ripped down slopes with his feet strapped to a board at speeds that could snap his neck instantly if he wrecked. Total rush. He'd ridden in the back country, where threats of avalanche were ever present. Didn't give it a second thought. He'd even jumped from a plane with a harness and a pack full of nylon as his only lifeline, just for the thrill of it. Heights and speed he could handle. Loved them.

But this?

He knew two things for sure. He loved Cheryl Thompson with a fierceness that shocked him. And he was scared to death to face the future with her knowing what lay in the past.

He'd never stepped into a crisis like this. A single question kept circling his mind, his spirit, relentless as it was unsettling.

Can you redeem even this?

It seemed faithless to ask such a thing. Theologically sound men didn't doubt like that, did they? God forgave all things. His blood covered all sin. Brock knew this.

It wasn't the forgiveness part that turned him inside out. It was the redemption. *To purchase or take back something by exchange.* Could God take this...this abortion and trade it for something good?

The days ahead looked unbelievably hard. While it was true that he was an adrenaline junkie, Brock wasn't an ignorant jumper. Informed consent. That was how he took on his adventures. Thus, he'd done some research.

Post Abortion Syndrome. PAS. Yes, there was a name for it, and he'd read about it before he came to LA. Agony streamed down his face while the information sank into his heart. Not only had he looked at the symptoms—and recognized several in Cheryl—but he'd researched the process through recovery.

It was long, and it was *hard.*

He pushed away from the window frame he'd been leaning against, moving to the king-sized bed. Heavyhearted, he dropped onto the mattress and let his head fall into his hands. Cheryl's body had felt like her own little earthquake when he'd carried her into her apartment the night he arrived in LA, so violent were her sobs. So much pain and regret. How could he ask her to do what seemed necessary—to face the truth rather than bury it? It was going to rip her up, and he'd go through the shredder right alongside her.

God, I don't know if I can do this.

But then what? If he didn't...if she wouldn't, then what?

Sometimes pain is a gift.

They could stay where they were, or pass through the fire. What was on the other side?

~*~

Sunshine warmed the pale sand under Cheryl's toes. Compared to the first two days after Brock's arrival, that Thursday afternoon felt like a vacation.

Actually, compared to pretty much her whole life, it felt like a vacation.

Brock had come to her apartment for breakfast, just as he had the mornings before, but his demeanor had been different. As if all of the yucky stuff they were swimming through had simply rolled off his shoulders. As much as she enjoyed the return of his easygoing laughter and teasing—even secretly relishing the raspberry he'd blown into her neck—she wrestled with a tinge of jealousy. He'd always be able to surface. The past didn't claim him and drag him under as it did her.

Because the ugly was hers and not his.

What she wouldn't give to be able to break through with him, to rise from the cold darkness and laugh in the warmth of the sunshine as he did.

But she could hardly begrudge it from him. So when he'd suggested a day at the beach, she summoned a smile, changed into beach-worthy clothing, and focused on the joy his warm hand around hers supplied her heart.

Small victories. Maybe, with time, they'd add up.

"Have you ever surfed?" Sprawled out in the warm sun at her side, Brock squinted at her and grinned.

Cheryl snorted. "Does that sound like me?"

He sat up, hooking both arms over the knees he brought to his chest. "I don't know how to answer that. What do you mean?"

"I'm E's boring little sister. Does surfing mesh with that, do you think?"

"I never thought you were boring." That impish smile made him look boyish. "I think I told you—I was rather fascinated by you."

"Hanging around to hear me play the piano does not equal fascination."

"Clearly you were never a seventeen-year-old boy."

Truly? Had he been interested in her back then? If only he'd acted on it.

"You still fascinate me." His fingers brushed over her arm, prickling tingles of pleasure. "Even if you don't want to go surfing."

She studied him, wondering at how he could blend fun and serious so smoothly. "You don't mind that I'm a chicken?" She meant to ask the question with a smile. Instead, it came out with an undertone of insecurity.

Brock leaned toward her, brushing her shoulder with his. "I want to see you live. That doesn't mean you have to live on the edge. You don't have to be your mom or try to be like Ethan. There's nothing wrong with preferring a book over the slopes, or music to the waves." He pushed to his feet and pulled her up beside him. "But you might have to compromise with me. I can't come to the ocean and not get wet."

Her hand still in his, she leaned away, trusting him to hold her up. "I doubt dipping your toes in the water will be the end of it. The thrill seeker in you won't be satisfied."

His eyebrows shot up. "Obviously you do not understand all the crazy things that happen inside of me when I'm with you."

Such a charmer. Her heart hiccuped and did its own little crazy, adrenaline filled cha-cha.

"Come on." He tugged.

She shook her head, biting a grin.

"Nope, not getting out of this." With one fluid motion, he had her swept up in his arms.

Hooking her arms around his neck, she joined his laughter, kicking her flip-flops from her feet as he walked toward the ocean. "You do realize the Pacific is not exactly the hot springs back home, right?"

"You do realize I've spent most of my life in the snow, right?"

Two more steps and his feet sank into the waves lapping against the beach. She felt his quick intake of air and chuckled.

"Cold?"

He smirked, continuing into the waves. "Deliciously."

She tightened her hold around his neck. "How deep are we going?"

"Deep enough to throw you in." The water moved above his knees when he stopped, and he swayed with the motion of the tide. His smile dared her to squirm. She simply locked her grip more secure.

One eyebrow lifted. "You don't think I would?"

"Oh, I know from experience you would. I also know that you'd go in with me, so..."

His expression changed, though he still smiled, gripping her with a security she was beginning to treasure. Loosening her hold, she slid a hand along his stubbled jawline. "I love that about you."

His nose brushed against hers. "That I'd throw you in?"

"No." She breathed a small laugh. "That you'd go in with me."

The arms that held her tensed, drawing her, if possible, closer into his chest. She could feel the words he'd said to her that last night in Hayden throb through his pulse. In spite of the truth she'd hurled at him, he still loved her. She realized she hadn't told him...

"I love you." Breathless, she let the three never-spoken-to-any-other-man syllables free. They floated on the salty air, swirled in the sun-soaked warmth, circled around them, binding her heart securely to his.

"That's good to hear," he whispered, brushing light kisses against her cheek, her chin, and finally her mouth.

Her hand curved around his neck as she responded to the gentle touch of his lips against hers. He shifted her, lowering her legs into the moving water. Her feet sank into the gritty ocean floor, and she shivered as the cold, salty ocean pulsed around her. The tide pushed her into him, and one hand spread across her lower back. When the undertow tugged her away, his grip strengthened, anchoring her closer, holding her steady.

His mouth broke away from hers. "I've got you."

She nuzzled his nose, toying with the hair that brushed against her fingers. "I know."

He reached for the hand that she'd curled around his neck and moved it until her palm settled against his chest. Strong, fast beats throbbed into her hand, matching the staccato rhythm of her own pulse.

"See? All kinds of crazy going on in there."

"Pull in here." Brock pointed to a parking lot to the right.

Cheryl complied, still confused. The day at the beach had been perfect. She couldn't help but feel nearly giddy as she wondered what else he had in mind. The quiet suburb he'd navigated her to didn't offer any hints. What was he up to now?

A few scattered cars dotted the lot, surrounded by three nondescript buildings strangely lacking overhead signs. Kind of a creepy place. Tension began to ebb in her muscles, replacing the wonder of their near-perfect day.

She parked her car and turned the key. "Where are we?"

Brock shifted in the passenger seat so that he could face her. The seriousness in his eyes caused the tension to grip harder. He reached for her shoulder as if he could see her pulling on her armor. "Don't get mad, okay?"

Not a good sign. She leaned away. "What are you doing?"

His eyes left her face and drifted to a door on the middle building. She followed his gaze. The small lettering stuck against the glass was hard to make out. She squinted to read the name.

Pregnancy Crisis Center.

With a sharp intake of breath, her shoulders curled, and she felt like a cat cornered by a barking dog.

"Sherbert..."

She swallowed, refusing to look at him, and reached to start the car. His hand caught hers and pulled it away from the keys.

"What are you thinking?" she hissed.

"Just listen, okay?"

"No. I'm not going in there. I'm not pregnant, and they don't have anything for me in that place."

"Cheryl, I've done a little bit of reading, and they have a recovery group that meets here—"

"No." She stabbed him with all the fury that had suddenly billowed through her. "I'm not going in there."

He sat motionless, his hand still curled over hers. His breathing seemed labored, as if he were fighting for control.

Why would he need to fight for control? This was her pile of crap, not his. He had no right.

She ripped her hand away from him. "I thought you said you didn't think I needed fixed. Remember that?"

"I'm not trying to fix you."

"Then what is this?" She flung a hand toward the building across the lot.

Sighing, he ran a hand over his face.

Cheryl didn't wait for an answer. Instead she turned the key and floored the gas.

Yep. Definitely should have known better. Fairy tales were always too good to be true.

~*~

Brock followed Cheryl into her apartment in the wake of her frigid silence.

Way to go, smart guy.

What had he been thinking? That they'd pull up to the center, the soft, teary version of Cheryl would emerge, they'd go in and talk to people who knew how the heck to handle this, and they'd both be all better?

Neat and tidy. Which would have been awesome, because he definitely did *not* know how to handle any of this.

Clearly.

Ice-princess Cheryl continued to rage in her fury. She stopped at the hallway to her room and spun around. "You have no idea what you're doing."

"I know that, Cheryl, but—"

"You want to fix me? Let's get honest then, Brock Kelly. Let's just dig out all the ugly. Wanna take a stab at how many times I've been high—totally stoned out of my head? Drunk?" She took a step forward, as if she'd turned into a predator and was ready to pounce on his already raw heart.

His fists clenched at his side, and his chest tightened. "Stop this."

She stalked forward until mere inches separated them. "No. You wanted to be Fix-It Felix. You're the one who's been probing around all the dark corners with a floodlight. You wanted full disclosure. Here it is. Do you know how many men I've been with in the last decade?"

The air seemed to thicken, and his lungs began to burn as if he were drowning. "Cheryl..." *I don't want to know—not like this.*

"At least a dozen, but you know what? I'm not really sure." Her voice chilled the room. "How does that sit with you?"

He shut his eyes against her fury, against the arrows she was ramming into his heart. *God, help.*

Silence locked around them. Brock forced his eyes open and searched hers. The fire there quickly died, replaced by the cold indifference he'd seen when she'd first walked back into his life.

They break my heart, and I let them.

Brandi's words whispered in his throbbing heart. Shaking, he unfolded his fists and lifted his palms to frame her face. She stiffened at his touch, and her expression morphed from the intensity of a predator to the fear of prey.

Help. An image swam through his mind, the memory of his father's face a little over five years before. *You can't force me into hating you, Brock. You're my son. You will always be my son, and I love you.* Words that in the weeks following had finally penetrated his hard heart. For all the arguments they'd had over the years about his choices and priorities—his rebellion—it was that pledge of unconditional love, and not all of the well-laid-out convictions delivered to him in debate, that had grabbed hold of him. He had not been able to escape the demands of deep compassion.

That was the message of the cross. Truth didn't change, and right was right no matter what people tried to do to manipulate it. But ultimately, the power of God was most astonishingly revealed in His unparalleled love.

Teach me to love.

The Spirit moved with an immediate surge, pouring into his heart both the emotion and strength that he hadn't possessed two seconds before. Closing the space between them, Brock brushed her cheekbones with his thumbs, ensuring that she was listening.

"I love you." His ragged voice wobbled.

Cheryl's lips trembled, and for a moment, he felt her lean into him. But it was a fleeting response. In the next heartbeat, she stiffened again, swallowed, and took a step back. "You can't."

Air rushed from his lungs as if she'd just kicked him in the chest.

"Leave, Brock. You don't want me." She turned, shoulders drawn tight and straight, and walked to her bedroom. The sound of the door latch clicking into place magnified in his ears, as if she'd just slammed a prison door, locking herself inside.

Iron seemed to lodge in his chest, and he slouched back against the wall, drawing a long, shaky breath. Thoughts swirled with dizzying contractions. Why did she keep rejecting him? He couldn't win with her. Love was supposed to win. She needed help—wanted help. Refused help. Why was she determined to live in misery?

He couldn't do this.

Pushing away from the wall, he stalked to the exit and jerked it open. His feet wouldn't move though, and with a hand still on the doorknob, he stood frozen.

If he left this time, that would be it. They would be done. He glanced down the hall where Cheryl had retreated, met by empty silence. Being with Cheryl was going to shatter his heart. It would be easier to walk away.

He squeezed his eyes shut. *God, I'm afraid it's going to hurt too much.*

I redeem.

The two words from heaven steadied his heart. With a soft push, he closed his path of escape, turned, and slid to the floor. He dug his smartphone from his back pocket and pulled up the information he'd searched out before on PAS. As he scanned the website, he thought over the trip to the crisis center. Seemed like a good idea at the time. What better way to show her that he was in this—that he'd be with her through this process, than to go with her to get help?

Apparently it was a terrible way—all it showed her was that he thought she needed fixed.

He didn't. Healed and fixed weren't the same thing. One was a project, the other was a person. One was about him, the other, about her. Not even close to the same.

Scrolling down to the ministry contact link, he tapped twice, and the screen opened to an e-mail form. After a moment of hesitation, and a quick prayer for wisdom, he typed out a short explanation of their situation ending with a simple, *I need help. What should I do?*

Who knew if he'd even get a response. But options being what they were—which was pretty much nil—he tapped the paper airplane Send icon and dropped the phone onto the floor next to him. Tipping his head back, he shut his eyes against the hard silence.

Except it wasn't silent. He could hear a small rustle coming from Cheryl's room. Sniffing. He sat forward. Cheryl was crying, reminding him that always lurking beneath the ice princess who drove him crazy was the heartbroken woman he loved.

He climbed to his feet and strode to the shut door of her room.

"Sherbert." He tapped on the wood. "I'm coming in, okay?"

Not a sound. With a firm breath, he fortified himself. She was like an unpredictable day on the slopes. Sometimes there was warm sunshine and great rides. Others...bitter winds and hard edges. With snowboarding, he could at least check the forecast. Cheryl... He'd have to take her as she came. He twisted the knob, and the door eased open. There on the edge of the bed, curled up in a tight ball with her hands covering her face, lay his heart, sobbing. Within four steps he was on his knees, taking her into his arms.

"I'm sorry," she cried, her voice breathless. "I'm so, so sorry. I don't know why I do the things I do."

"I know." He smoothed her hair away from her face and then tucked her head against him. "I shouldn't have sprung that on you. I should have talked to you—asked."

She leaned into him, one fist twisting a grip into his shirt as if she were afraid he'd go. Leave her.

He wouldn't. Couldn't. This well inside his chest sank deeper, love filling it with a surge of strength that he was certain was beyond himself. *Love her.* That was the heavenly whisper. He did. With everything in him, he did, and he *wanted* to take her as she came. The good and the bad, the beautiful and the ugly.

How could he show her he was all in?

There was one way he could think of. So many would misunderstand though. His parents. Her brother. To them, it wouldn't make any sense. And he'd already acted on impulse with an idea, and it proved to be completely the wrong move.

Better wait on it.

"Tell me what to do." He nudged her away so that he could cradle her face with a palm. "I'm lost here, but I'm desperate to make things better. What should I do?"

Her expression mirrored what he'd just said—that she was lost as well. How were they supposed to move forward when the path seemed indiscernible?

Three more tears rolled over her cheeks, and with the thumb he held closest to her face, he wiped one of the trails. He dipped his head, leaning it against hers. "I'll do anything. Just tell me what you want."

"Don't leave me." She raked a hand into his hair and held his head against hers. Her voice shook as she whispered. Pleaded. "No matter how frustrated I make you, don't leave me."

"I promise."

She pulled in a shuddering breath and moved to tuck her head into his neck. "Take me home." Her arms circled his neck. "I just want life to move forward. Please, Brock, take me home."

Back to the place where she'd insisted she couldn't stay. Brock didn't bother dissecting the irony. He'd promised her anything. Home was an easy place to start.

I never considered what my leaving cost you.
How much it would have hurt.
The shame was so heavy. I thought I'd die if you knew, and I couldn't look at you with the truth lurking in my heart.
But now that you're gone, I hate that I left.
I'm so sorry that I broke your heart.
You never quit hoping, praying, believing.
I'm coming home. I think that you know that already, and you are rejoicing with the God you have petitioned on my behalf.
He is drawing me back, sending His help, showing the way.
I am coming home.

~28~

Cheryl paused on the front step, her hand halfway to the doorknob. She inhaled, savoring the cool mountain air tinged with a hint of freshly mowed hayfields. The smell of summer in Hayden. Home. Her hand fell to her side, and with the other, she tugged her earbuds from her ears. The soft, high-pitched warbling notes of a mountain bluebird floated on the early morning air. Tomorrow she'd run without the earbuds. Maybe she'd go off road, take the footpath down by the river.

A small smile played against her lips. It'd been years since she'd paused like this, taken in God's nature and let His peace touch her heart.

Almost as soon as the thought formed, she folded it and tucked it away. She didn't deserve God's peace. Or this beautiful moment.

Or Brock.

Was this all a big tease? Maybe one of those crazy hallucinations where people who screwed up got to see what life could have been like if they hadn't been so stupid? Just to make reality that much more bitter.

Her phone vibrated against her hip, where she'd secured it in the waistband of her running tights. She tugged it free and checked the screen. New Text. From Brock.

Morning, love. Can you come out here for coffee?

And then there was that. How could he love her? *Her?* She'd seen his expression when he put *that* awful word over her name two weeks before. She'd thought it was hate, and maybe condemnation, that passed through his eyes. The typical response coming from a lifelong pro-life crusader. Replaying that horrible night a million times since, she was coming to see that his look wasn't contempt. It was agony.

And yet he loved her. He'd promised her anything, and then at her request brought her home. Did he mean anything beyond that? As in more? As in forever...

A hope she couldn't dare grasp. How painful would it be to feel the burgeoning promise grow strong and warm within her fingers, only to have it decay and crumble like dust falling from her hands.

Was God's anger that harsh? Was His punishment so cruel as to wrap her with the security of love, lead her out into the open, only to strip her bare before all to see?

Trembling, she turned and pushed quickly inside the house. After slamming the door closed, she leaned against it as panic seized her soul.

What if Brock didn't mean forever? What if he told her heinous secret to other people? She'd left the only other life she knew—granted, a miserable one, but it was safe. Here? Hayden was a small, tight-knit community. If Brock exposed her...

Stop. He wouldn't.

She fought through the raging thoughts, desperate for an anchor. *Deep breath in. Long breath out. Just breathe. Steady. Easy.*

God, do You hate me? Her bottom lip quivered. *Surely You hate me.*

She slid downward against the door until she was a crumpled mess against the wood floor. *God...*

The phone she still held vibrated again. Through blurred vision, she made out the new text.

I love you.

Wrapping her arms around herself, she lay against the cold planks, aching for it to be so. Without the ice around her heart numbing her to all emotion, she couldn't deny it. She was utterly desperate for those words to be true.

Of both God and Brock.

~*~

Brock wiped down the length of the stainless steel countertop while Cammy finished loading the last of the dishes.

"You're sure this is a good move?" Cammy talked while she worked.

Brock stopped pushing the cloth, and he looked up at her. She looked tired. No wonder. He'd pretty much abandoned her and Brandi and Ethan last week, leaving only an explanation that he needed to take care of some personal stuff and wasn't sure when he'd be back. And oh, by the way, he was looking to hire a manager for the camp.

Talk about insecurity. And worse, he still couldn't give them an explanation, because doing so would betray the heart he loved.

So he had only to fake some confidence. "I'm sure. We could use all the help we can get."

"But you manage this place just fine."

"Thanks." His chest tightened. He really didn't want to give it up. But right now... "I just need more full-time help. It's going to be good for all of us, I think."

Cammy rested both palms against the counter and sighed. "Okay, Brock. My selfishness and aversion to change aside, I'm worried about you. What's going on?"

Brock held her look. What if she knew? The Cammy he loved would take Cheryl in. Show her the compassion and grace of God.

His tongue nearly unhinged, until he imagined Cheryl's reaction. Brutal anger. Followed by a torrent of tears. It wasn't his story to tell, and he couldn't force Cheryl to, nor could he betray her.

"Brock?" Cammy frowned.

"It's personal, and I really can't share. I need you to trust me right now, okay?"

"Are you in trouble?"

Some days he felt like he was drowning. That wasn't what she meant though. "No. Just working through some things, and they're going to take some time."

Cammy's concern etched into her expression, and the ache to share pressed harder. What if Cheryl had a friend, besides him, and she could see that life was messy for everyone?

"This has something to do with Cheryl, doesn't it?"

Obviously. He'd left without explanation and came back with her, a moving truck, and all of her things.

"Cammy, please don't press this."

She examined him closely and then dipped a slow nod. "She's good for you, you know? You're softer."

"Softer?" He was kind of a wreck, he knew, but soft?

"With the leaders—especially the women. You talk to them, don't give them the cold shoulder. It's like the bitterness from before has finally drained."

Cammy saw all of this? "I was that big of a jerk, eh?"

"Not to everyone. In fact, I think the fact that you're so kind to the kids made your aversion to the female leaders all the more obvious."

Brock tugged on his ear, which felt exceptionally hot, and then shoved a hand into his jeans pocket. "I'm sorry—and thanks, I guess." He forced a wiry grin. "But I still can't tell you more."

Cammy looked to her hands for a breath and then back at him. "Tell me what you need from me. I won't ask why, but I want to be helpful."

There was the grandmotherly woman he trusted. "Just accept her. Love on her. No matter how hard she pushes against it."

Cammy inhaled, her posture stiffening as if she were fortifying her heart for the job. "I can do that."

"I know." He felt a half smile push his mouth. "And it would mean the world to me."

~*~

Cheryl snuggled against the cushions of Brock's sofa, a warm mug of decaf cradled in her hands. Brock had gone out to do night check—which apparently had been a standard part of his everyday life. Lights out at 9:30. Night check at 9:45, and then all should be quiet at Kelly's Ranch.

After a sip of coffee, Cheryl studied Brock's world beyond the front window of his cabin. A post lamp near the dock bounced its light off the gently swaying waters of the pond. In the distance the dark outline of the rugged peaks to the west met with the softer black of the night sky, heavily jeweled with diamond stars, each one vivid on this dark, clear night.

The black sky set the canvas for the shimmering glitter of light. Who knew darkness could be so beautiful?

I make the night beautiful.

Was that the divine whisper of God? The words moved in her heart, soft and gentle, like the caress of a loving promise. Could that be right?

"God..." Her call lifted from her lips, broken and barely audible.

The door latch rattled, and she blinked, pushing away the rush of emotion. A moment later, Brock stepped over the threshold, letting the screen slap shut behind him.

"All is quiet." He crossed the small space of wood floor and lowered onto the spot beside her. When he pressed a kiss to her temple, she closed her eyes and smiled, leaning into him.

He settled back, one arm secure around her, and a gentle silence cocooned them. Cheryl's attention drifted back to the night sky outside, and her thoughts pulled the silent whisper back. God made the night beautiful. He pierced the blackness and gave it purpose—it became the canvas for the diamonds of beauty.

Hope surged through her heart. She settled into Brock's arm, snuggling against his shoulder.

A soft, satisfied rumble came from his throat, and he bent his head to rest against hers. "I love you, Sherbert," he whispered.

Every time he said that, it was like a precious stone poked through her loneliness. Beauty. In her darkness.

It stole her breath. Who was she to be loved? To possess real beauty?

"Why?" Wonder lifted her voice, fringing the question with breathlessness.

"You make me a better man. You chip away my arrogance and force me to see people—all people—with eyes of compassion. And"—Brock moved, turning her with his arm and lifting her chin so that their eyes met—"I see your heart, Cheryl. It is beautiful. Full of music and laughter and life that is longing to break free. To live."

For all her efforts to hide, he saw her. But even though he knew the truth, he didn't seem to see what she had been afraid to expose. Sudden tears pressed hot against her eyes. "But I..." Her throat closed, cutting off the words. She swallowed and pushed them out. "I killed my baby, Brock. How could I do that?"

He winced. Her heart tore, and a shudder gripped her body. She didn't want to talk about it, to see him writhe with the pain of her past, but for some horrible, unidentifiable reason, she had to. "How could you love me knowing what I am?"

Tears glazed his eyes. Yes, her choice pierced his heart. Deeply. But when she expected him to move away—to reject her at the point of her darkest shame—his hand came to her face, cupping her cheek with a gentle strength that communicated his own ache and desperation.

"I believe in redemption."

~*~

Music filled Cheryl's mind as she slowly awoke. Faint light pressed against the window opposite her bed. Time for her morning run. Today though, rather than her iPod, she'd listen to the melody that played inside her mind, and to the songs that rustled through nature. To God.

Her chest quivered at the thought. Still, even after Brock's assurance of his love, of his belief in redemption, Cheryl could not shake the fear that it would all crumble. God would reject her. He wouldn't be able to forgive her. Not completely. She would live forever with the guilt, this horrible shame of knowing what she had done. Perhaps there were degrees of redemption. If the sin was great, the redemption would only cover so much.

Maybe that was true. But even if God could forgive her a little, to give her a small portion of life and joy with Brock by her side, it was better than the black death she'd lived with before. Maybe for her, the darkness would remain, but God would see fit to give her small diamonds of light. Little portions of redemption.

She'd take it. Even small servings of light were more than she deserved, and she'd be grateful.

That made sense as she tugged her long-sleeved running liner over her head. Her life would never be the all-out joy that someone like Brandi would get to embrace, but she could live a little. It was better than dying all over again every morning for the rest of her life.

Cheryl focused her mind on gratitude as her feet pounded against the cement. At the edge of town, she took to the narrow dirt-packed path, focusing her mind to listen to the music that she'd awoken with. It had been the song she'd played after the "Feather Theme," the one Brock sang by her side. What were those words?

Be still my soul...the Lord is on thy side...

On her side? Probably not. She had thrust herself among those who rebelled against God, against life. God was willing to forgive, maybe, but to be on her side? It was more like the Lord was not set completely against her.

Perhaps, though, there were ways to ease the Almighty's frown. Penance that would give Him more reasons to poke holes through her black existence. Something like...

Piano lessons for a foster girl.

Cheryl stopped jogging, settling her hands on her hips and surveying the place where the mountains met the sky. Could she do that? What if a migraine hit her in the middle of it? What if the girl triggered another nightmare?

Not like she didn't struggle with both either way. Perhaps it was worth a try.

Was this why Brock did what he did? Was he working his way back into God's favor?

The thought struck a flat tone in her mind. Though Brock said everyone had regrets, he didn't seem to be haunted by his. Then again, he hadn't stopped a beating heart, so all of his mistakes combined couldn't possibly amount to her one great regret.

If piano lessons would earn her greater favor, then piano lessons it would be.

~*~

"Wait, what?" Brock studied Cheryl's blue eyes. She wasn't ready for this. He knew it all the way through his gut. Those migraines were triggered by stress, and kids triggered reminders and guilt and all sorts of stress.

"You thought giving So-J piano lessons was a good idea."

He drew in a breath, measuring his words. "That was before I understood."

Cheryl looked to her hands, folded in her lap as she leaned back against his sofa. Her brows drew down as she mashed her lips together. Brock tried to read her expression in the lengthening silence. With one hand, he covered both of hers, brushing the knuckles under his thumb.

"You don't have to do this for me."

He waited. She swallowed, her attention pinned to her lap.

"I mean it, love. This camp—"

"Is your calling. Your life." She raised her eyes to meet his. "And I want to be a part of it."

"You are. And I can adjust." Brock scooted closer and gripped one of her shoulders. "In fact, I wanted to talk to you about something. Tell you, actually, that I think I found a camp manager."

"Why? I told you I didn't want you to do that."

Shouldn't the answer be obvious? *Just spit it out.*

Confusion passed through her eyes. "Brock—"

"I think we should get married."

Cheryl's eyes rounded, confusion morphing into alarm. Yep. That was how a guy *just spat it out.* Very smooth. So romantic. Brock's heart shrank into a too-small ball, while at the same time it pounded unnecessarily hard. After a long draw of air, he lifted his hand and fingered the locks of dark hair that framed her face. Her eyes softened, and her bottom lip quivered.

Maybe this hashed-up proposal could be saved. He dipped his head until his gaze was level with hers, and whispered, "I want to marry you."

One trembling hand touched his chest and then curled into a fist, his shirt caught in her grip. Her eyelids closed as an expression of disbelief fell over her face.

"Why?"

"I want to be there when the nightmares come, to hold you until they pass. I want you to know that I'm here, that I'm in this with you, no matter what. I want us to do life together."

She pulled away just enough to look at him.

He covered her cheek with his hand. "Because I love you."

Her hand covered his, still cupping her cheek, and she wove her fingers with his. "I don't want to change your life."

"Too late." He smiled and tipped her face for a gentle kiss.

"Brock..." Warmth from her breath spread across his lips as she breathed his name.

He hovered just above her mouth. "Marry me."

"I want to." The hand still fisted at his chest uncurled, her palm flattening against him as she gently pushed him back.

Was she refusing him? He studied her eyes again. Sheened, they whispered conflict.

"Then say yes," he said.

"Not until you tell me why you think you need a manager for the camp in order to marry me."

"I want to take care of you. To be with you."

"I moved back. I'm here."

"I know, but I need someone on site at all times. I can't do both."

"Why would marrying me mean you couldn't be on site?"

He tipped his head. Was she saying she could move—live there, at the camp, with him? With all of the kids that came and went on a weekly basis? That wouldn't work. "What about the headaches? Kids are here all the time, Cheryl. All. The. Time."

"I know."

He shook his head. "No. I'm not asking you to live like that."

"And I'm not asking you to abandon something that makes you the man I love."

Brock straightened. This mattered to her? He'd expected *her* to ask him to walk away from the camp—and he understood why. The daily reminders, the pressure of guilt. Who could live like that? "We could live in town. At Nana's house. You could help Ethan with the bakery, if you wanted. Or not. Life can look like whatever we want."

"This is where you belong, Brock, and I—" Emotion cut her sentence short.

Brock waited, possibilities swirling in his mind. Honestly, he wanted to stay. Giving up competition boarding and establishing this camp had been his hands-wide-open, palms-up offering to God, and he felt like God used him there.

But that didn't mean God couldn't use him elsewhere. Sometimes dreams, plans, shifted. Life bent, and they'd adjust. That was okay.

"I want to try, Brock. Please let me try with So-J."

Eyebrows furrowing, Brock continued to examine Cheryl. "And if piano lessons are too hard?"

She picked at the paint on her fingernails and shrugged.

"Why do you want to do this?"

Her jawline trembled as she fought for enough control to answer him. After a long draw of air, her voice came again, rattling with emotion. "What if there's healing in it?"

Push through pain...maybe there was some wisdom in that. And on the other side, redemption? That was the point of forgiveness, was it not? Love swelled in his chest until breathing hurt.

Brock covered her hands and waited for her eyes to meet his. "Are you going to marry me or not?"

Slowly she lifted her face back to him, and when their eyes connected, the strain in hers melted. She smiled. Heat raced through his veins as he leaned to meet her forehead with his.

She lifted her hands and traced his mouth with a finger, breathing a gentle "Yes" before her lips brushed his.

One question answered. Only about a thousand more to go. But they'd figure it out. Together.

~29~

"Dad, I need some advice." Brock leaned forward, settling against his arms, which rested on the table in his parents' kitchen. The site of many discussions over the years. Some hard. This could be one of those.

With both hands anchored on his mug, Dad waited.

"Cheryl and I..." He shifted. "I asked her to marry me."

A grin grew against his father's face. "And..."

"We want to get married sooner rather than later. She doesn't want a wedding."

Dad's smile faded, his brows gathering.

"It's not what you're thinking, what it looks like." Brock's words stumbled over each other.

"I'm not thinking anything, except it's unusual for a woman not to want a wedding."

Brock squirmed again. How could he explain without exposing Cheryl? "She's not a usual woman." He sighed, rolling his shoulders back. "Look, I can't tell you everything because..."

"Because you'd be breaking her trust."

"Yes. But I feel uneasy about it all."

"About marrying her?"

"No. Not that." Brock lifted his head, meeting his father's eyes. "I love her, and I'm certain that God has brought us together. But she's mentioned eloping, and I guess I would feel guilty about it, and I don't know why. Would it be wrong?"

Dad studied him, his eyes thoughtful. "I don't know that I'd say wrong. Marriage is really before God. But there's something to having people there to witness your vows, an element of accountability that we see patterned in the Bible. And personally, your mother and I would be a little disappointed not to be there when you get married."

That was the real pinch. He'd already disappointed his parents with so many of his choices in the past. Marrying Cheryl—he wanted more than anything for them to back that decision and to be a part of their life together. She needed family more than she could grasp.

"Son?"

Brock's attention locked back on his dad.

"Is that your only hesitation—the actual wedding?"

"Yes."

"Cheryl seems..."

"I know. Dad, there's a lot there, and like you said, I can't break her trust. But I know what marriage is, and even though there are still some murky waters ahead, I know that I don't want to do life without her."

Dad sat, his finger tracing the rim of his mug, while he filtered through what Brock had shared. His chest expanded with a long draw of air, and then he nodded.

"Brock, I trust you. Whatever you decide, whatever you believe God wants for you and for your soon-to-be wife, your mother and I will be behind you."

Unending grace. That was what his dad kept handing him, certainly originating from the hand of God, because he didn't deserve that kind of unreserved trust. Love always gave more.

Brock blinked and sat back against his chair. "Thank you, Dad. Can I ask you one more thing?"

Dad nodded, looking like he was prepared for anything. Probably he wasn't, not for the truth, but that wasn't where Brock was going with this. "Love her. The way you love me, love Cheryl."

"It's not even a question, son. We do."

~*~

Marriage. To Brock Kelly.

Couldn't be real. Cheryl looked down at the light fabric of her country-style summer dress.

White eyelet.

That had been a mistake. Brock had helped her pick it—though he hadn't seen it on her, it had been his favorite. Simple. Clean. Pretty.

Not fit for her.

Her bottom lip trembled, and she couldn't face the woman in the mirror. This whole thing had been a mistake. They could have slipped off to a courthouse, spoken their vows in front of a justice of the peace, and come home married. She didn't need a wedding and definitely should not be wearing this white dress.

But a small wedding had been important to Brock. For accountability. And healing?

That still made little to no sense.

Cheryl shivered in the lonely room Brock had cleared for her. That man, so kindly stubborn—this was his room, soon to be theirs, which held a surreal sense of wonder all by itself. But instead of allowing her to use the women's washroom in the lodge as her bridal room, he insisted that he'd use a cabin and she take the house. The whole of it.

Because it's yours, love. That was what he'd said.

Hers. She shivered again and reached for the dark denim jacket that she planned to wear over her white sundress. Just to add a bit of reality to this scene. She was hardly an all-white kind of woman. Not a pure bride.

A soft knock against the door had her pause, midmotion, as she was pushing an arm into the denim sleeve.

"May I come in?" Lydia Kelly stood just outside the door, her head poked around the opening.

"Sure." Cheryl tightened her fist.

What must the woman think of her? This little harlot of a woman marrying her son. Even if Lydia didn't know the whole of Cheryl's story, she knew enough—certainly must have heard enough—to make her wish for a different daughter-in-law.

Cheryl would forever feel unworthy in front of the woman who had raised such a good man.

"Ah." Lydia passed through the door, her purple dress floating as she walked. "My son has found himself a lovely bride. You look beautiful."

Her son had found himself a train wreck of a woman and seemed to be bent on loving her anyway. Cheryl looked at her boots, feeling like she could ball herself up on the bed and cry.

"I don't believe in flattery, Cheryl." Lydia stepped right beside her and captured her chin in between two fingers. "I mean what I say."

Cheryl's lip quivered, and heat glazed her eyes. "This doesn't seem right."

"Why not?"

Words would not slip past her swollen throat.

Lydia stepped in between Cheryl and the mirror. "If you have doubts about marrying Brock, then you should well be scared. Don't do it. But if this is about something else..."

A tear slipped over her eyelid, and she shook her head.

"Tell me, then, sweet girl. Why do you tremble?"

Cheryl drew a breath, long and shaky, released it, and then pulled in a second. "I shouldn't be wearing this." One hand tugged at the side seam of her dress.

Lydia smiled and then laughed. "Oh, goodness. The dress? You look beautiful. Brock will love it."

Brock did love it—already told her so. Cheryl ducked away from the woman's probing look.

"It's white. That's what bothers you, isn't it?" Lydia hummed a sound of thought, shook her head, and then took both of Cheryl's hand in hers. "Oh, hon. Once upon an arrogant time, I thought only a virgin should get to wear white at her wedding. Such a pious woman I was. But you know, I studied history in college, and still do from time to time. Do you know where the white dress tradition comes from?"

"The Bible?"

Lydia made that humming sound again. "No, ma'am—perhaps the tradition was in ancient cultures as well, but the tradition in our culture comes from a different source. Queen Victoria. The whole pomp and flourish of a wedding, the lace, the veil, the dress...it was all founded in the showing off of one's wealth. There's nothing biblical in it. And the white dress? Just a fashion the queen chose because she had some white lace she adored. Nothing about her virtue was calculated into any of it."

Cheryl looked to her with a mild sense of wonder and disbelief. "But doesn't the Bible talk about a virtuous wife wearing white?"

"A virtuous wife, yes. And your past doesn't mean you can't be one. As for the white...the only thing I can think of that resembles that idea is when the church is referenced as Jesus's pure and spotless bride." Lydia stepped around Cheryl, her hands still enclosed within, and tugged her to the foot of the bed. "Here's what strikes me, Cheryl. We know the church is made up of people. People who can be ugly. People who do ungodly things. But people who are forgiven. When Jesus calls the church pure and spotless, it's because He has washed those people clean, not because they came to Him clean. And"—her voice wobbled, and she tipped her head so that it touched the side of Cheryl's—"I love this...when I see Brock with you, I see that picture. He looks at you with love. He doesn't see your past. He sees you as the woman he wants to spend his life with. I think it's a small, granted incomplete, but beautiful picture of how Christ sees us. How He loves his church."

How could that be so? Couldn't be right. Could it? Another tear escaped down her cheek as Cheryl processed through Lydia's words.

Lydia patted her hands. "Don't misunderstand. I'm not saying Brock can be your savior—or that he's by any means spotless himself. We know full well our son has made plenty of his own left turns. I'm just saying...he looks at you with a pure love, and I know that you love him too. So you go on and wear this lovely white dress, knowing that you are his chosen bride. You will receive no condemnation from us."

Brock kept his promise. The ceremony was short, the gathering small—his parents, Ethan and Brandi, and her dad. She was almost ready to forgive Brock for that last part. He'd insisted they invite the man who'd first abandoned her—even making a point to call her father himself, to ask properly for her hand. Old-fashioned chivalry met hot mess. That about summed up their story.

But during the wedding, such as it was, Brock stayed right by her side, and she felt sheltered beside him. No dance meant her dad couldn't beg for a turn, and a limited reception sent them on their way to their honeymoon within an hour.

And now she stood trembling in the suite's bathroom.

This part...it was nothing new to her. Why was she terrified? She'd pushed for intimacy before, and Brock had stayed her. Now he waited, ready to take that consummate step, and her stomach rolled with apprehension.

Sharing Brock's bed would be so much more than sex. That quivered through her being. She wanted him to have everything, but was scared to death to give it. There would be no going back...

He's not one of them...

For sure, Brock Kelly was not the man who'd preyed on her young vulnerability and taken her virginity all those years ago. He wasn't all of the Andrew Harrises she'd had in her life after that. He was her husband.

Leaning toward her reflection in the mirror, she touched her trembling lips. "He loves you," she whispered to the pale woman before her. "He won't reject you."

"Cheryl?" A soft tap sounded on the door. "Are you okay, love?"

She shut her eyes. No more delaying. Pushing from the granite countertop, she pivoted and moved to open the door. Still in his suit, complete with his tie, although that had been loosened and the top button to his collar undone, Brock leaned against the doorframe. With one hand, he reached to brush a knuckle down the side of her face.

"I have something for my bride." He pushed up from the frame and stepped so that she could see the bed they'd share.

On the comforter, a small gift bag waited, the white tissue paper tugged decoratively and exposed.

Just the right size for a teddy. Heat coiled in her stomach, and the muscles in her shoulders tightened. She pushed against the anxiety. Lingerie was a perfectly legitimate gift for a husband to give his wife. She shouldn't feel...disappointed. Swallowing hard, she stepped toward the waiting gift. But when she tugged it toward herself, it drug too heavy for a slip of sexy fabric. Confused and curious, she pulled away the tissue paper.

A Bible. Brock had bought her a small Bible for their wedding night?

His hand slipped around her waist, and he secured her against himself. "I didn't imagine me and you, and I didn't expect this marriage, Sherbert, but I can't tell you how happy I am. I wish I could be more—that all the things that you're dealing with I could just take away. But I'm just a man." He turned her and tipped her chin upward to his face. "My mom said something to me at E's wedding, when she knew that my heart was already gone. She said not to forget whose armor I wear."

When he paused again, he took both her hands and stood just as he had when they'd spoken their vows. "I know this for sure, love. If you and I are going to make it, we need an anchor."

She followed his glance back to the bed, to where the Bible still lay. Relief and humility drained every misgiving from her body, and she sagged against this man she'd somehow managed to marry.

Truly, he wasn't like any of the others.

I'm not sure who I am.

Am I the cold creature, numb to emotion and life, that I've been for the past decade?

No. The ice has shattered, and I am left exposed.

What now?

A wife? Yes. But it didn't fix the ache. Not like I'd hoped.

My knight is just a man. Good, but just a man. He cannot give me life.

I long for music, for laughter, for warmth.

Do I dare seek them? How?

~30~

The honeymoon was over. Time to face reality. She preferred the fairy tale.

Cheryl clenched her fists, her nails biting into her palms, as she stood outside the lodge door. Today. She'd reenter her life of restitution today. With a little girl Brock called So-J, a little girl he clearly adored.

A little girl who seemed a lot like her. Locked up for some unseen reason, only letting the world see the hard, sharp edges. Porcupines raised their quills for a reason—for protection. Brock had enough compassion and wisdom to know that, and she loved him for it. Now, to take both that love and that knowledge into the room beyond the door.

God, please don't let it hurt too much...

The prayerful thought slipped through before she could filter it. Who was she to ask for something not to hurt? She deserved the pain. And this was restitution, after all.

One last lungful of air, and Cheryl pushed through the door. A tight bundle of aggression in the form of a dark-eyed, dark-haired ten-year-old girl glared at her from the piano bench.

"I ain't here because I want to," she spat, her arms crossed in front of her chest.

"Good to know." Cheryl wasn't necessarily either. Although, she wasn't sure what she wanted. She crossed the space between them and sat on the bench.

"Can't you get your own chair?"

"I could." She sat, eyebrow raised. "We'll see if you can convince me."

So-J scowled. "What's that supposed to mean?"

She had sass down to a fine art, complete with a defiant look, hard, threatening voice, and ramrod posture. That took practice.

Cheryl's shoulders tensed, and the spot at the base of her head began to knot. "I'm a lawyer. Did you know that?"

"What are you doing here then?"

"I married Brock."

"And I figure in how?"

"Not in that equation." Kind of a lie. *Sorry, God.* "But he mentioned that you seemed to like the piano, and I know how to play. Here we be."

"Yeah. And you're still in my space."

"Hmm. Keep trying." Cheryl cocked her head, partly in an attempt to cut off the knot tying in her neck, and partly to look at the little mouthy kid. "Here's the thing, So-J. I've learned that to get what I want, I need to know how to make people see things my way. With my words."

"So what?"

Cheryl hiked one eyebrow. A hint of understanding flickered in So-J's eyes before the girl had a chance to mask it with cold anger. Aha. They were communicating. Cheryl thought about the quick run-through of tips Brock had given her the night before.

They need to learn how to think rather than to just react. How to communicate their needs with words. Most kids her age have been taught this skill through modeling and appropriate correction. So-J hasn't, so she's operating on the only survival mechanism she knows: fight. She also doesn't trust women, so limit contact physically. She's a tough kid, and she'll take a swing at you if she feels threatened.

Probably should have paid closer attention to that last bit and should have chosen a different place to sit in the first place. However, this was where they were, and maybe a place to start. Careful to maintain a thread of distance between her and So-J, Cheryl lifted up a silent prayer. *Please don't let her explode.* A strained silence lengthened between them in the otherwise abandoned room. Cheryl fought the urge to bite her lip, putting on her courtroom face as she waited. It was highly possible the kid would downshift to that fight mode Brock warned her about. But he was just in the next room. He'd know what to do...

"Please move."

Though mumbled, Cheryl understood So-J's words, and fought the urge to smile. "Good job. Almost got it. Now look me in the eye and say it again, and I'd be happy to."

So-J's voice stabbed the air. "Why?"

Oh, Cheryl was definitely pushing the limit... "Because then I know that you respect both me and yourself enough to make eye contact, and I will be sure to understand exactly what you need."

So-J stared at her, her eyebrows drawn together. She made a show of widening her eyes, keeping them focused on Cheryl's face. "Please. Move."

Not really respectful, but it'd work for now.

"You got it." Cheryl stood, and as she turned to grab a chair from the table behind her, she caught Brock sandwiched in the kitchen doorway. He lifted half a smile and winked.

Guess that meant she was doing okay. She smothered a sigh.

"Okay... Wait." Cheryl sat in the chair she'd just positioned by the piano. "Do I call you Sonja or So-J?"

The girl's mouth pushed to the side as she gave a not-so-friendly look. "I'll tell you when we're done here."

"Fair enough. How about you show me what you know?"

"I have a better idea—"

Cheryl leaned forward. "Eyes."

So-J turned her head and gave her that exaggerated wide-eyed look. "It's *rude* to interrupt."

"True. I'm sorry. What's your idea?"

With a lift of her chin, she maintained eye contact. "You're the one s'posed to know everything. How 'bouts you prove it?"

"You want me to play for you?"

"Boom."

"Not convinced. Try again."

"Are we doing piano lessons or manners school here?"

Smart kid.

"Depends on the need. Did you want something?"

Wide, owl eyes set on her again. "Would you *please* show me how you play?"

Still ever so sassy. Baby steps.

Cheryl rolled her shoulders, trying to ignore how stiff they'd become. "Sure." She stood and snagged the music book Brock had bought for her, handing it to So-J. "What shall I play?"

Oh no. Shouldn't have asked. *Anything but the* Sabrina *song...*

So-J stared at the book without taking it and shrugged. "Whatevs."

Slowly exhaling the bundled breath she'd held, Cheryl nodded. "May I sit on the bench, please?" Kind of like talking to a judge. Funny.

The girl slid off her seat, and with an exaggerated gesture of her hands, she offered the bench.

"Thanks. Okay, since you don't want to pick, I'll play my favorite." The "Feather Theme" it was. She began with the bass clef solo, and by the time her right hand joined her left in the song, Cheryl was able to breathe normally, and some of the tension left her neck. She'd been practicing since that first day Brock had heard her play. The notes didn't stumble—they sounded like music. Like joy. By the time the final chord came off her fingers, Cheryl felt a small piece of her old self flicker.

In the silent moment following, a breath of healing touched her heart.

"Almost convinced." So-J mocked Cheryl's earlier words. "One more. I'll pick."

And that breath vanished. *Please not the* Sabrina *song...*

So-J snagged the music book off the piano and flipped through the pages. "These must be oooold." She continued thumbing.

Cheryl's chest tightened, and her head throbbed. *Please...*

"This one." So-J set the music in front of Cheryl.

Her heart lurched, and she squeezed her eyes shut. A high-pitched squeal pierced her ears. *Why?*

"Hey." So-J's voice came through the ringing. "I thought we had a deal?"

"We did." Cheryl opened her eyes, focusing them on "Theme from *Sabrina,*" and then nodded. The music in front of her blurred. She blinked, cracked the knuckles on her right hand, and then touched the rough keys with her trembling fingers.

It's just a song...

Her hands moved as she concentrated on the notes, trying desperately not to hear the song she played. She didn't make it through the fourth measure.

Brock had been right. This was too hard.

~*~

She hadn't played that song before. Brock knew, because just like he had back in high school, he hovered near whenever she played.

Something had gone south fast, and it wasn't because of So-J. Cheryl winced as she focused on the notes in front of her, her fingers stumbling over the chords. Her chin quivered enough for him to notice from the kitchen door, and her hands abruptly fell away from the keys. In the next heartbeat, she was on her feet and hustling toward the exit.

Brock waited until she pushed through the opposite door and then wandered into the dining hall toward the piano.

"Dude, I swear I didn't—"

"I know, So-J." He rubbed a palm over the back of his neck and sighed. "Did she say anything?"

"No." So-J's brow furrowed. "What's wrong with her?"

Brock studied the girl who had so easily gained his heart with her calloused wounds. His mother's words at Ethan's wedding replayed in his head. *God has given you such a tender heart toward those who ache... Just remember whose armor you wear.*

Didn't seem like he wore any armor, because his heart felt run-through. Sometimes, though, you had to take a deep look at the pain before you could begin to grasp it. You had to let the hurt of another shatter your heart before you could learn compassion.

And then...

Then maybe he could walk a path of healing alongside those he loved.

"Mr. Brock?"

His attention, which had wandered toward a window, returned to So-J. He connected with her dark eyes, wide with real concern. He could keep it simple, and she'd understand. "You know how there are things in your past you wish you could forget?"

So-J's face pinched, and she looked at her lap. "Yeah," she whispered. "Lots of things."

After a few steps that brought him next to her, he rested his palm on the curve of her head. "Cheryl's got some too."

A loaded silence fell between them, and Brock let his hand slide over her hair and then to his side.

"Will she get better?"

That wasn't the question Sonja really wanted to ask—Brock could tell by the desperation edging the girl's voice. What she wanted to know was would *they* get better.

God, please...

He blinked against the burn in his eyes. Answers didn't come, and he wasn't going to lie. Instead, he squeezed the shoulder closest to him, and when Sonja looked up, the look they shared was like a bond for life.

"This is a good place, Mr. Brock, especially for people like us."

People like So-J and Cheryl. The broken, the rejected, the hopeless.

Not hopeless.

Cheryl was here, and she'd volunteered to teach piano to a child she couldn't even look at a few weeks before. So-J was sitting there, suddenly more open hearted and compassionate than he'd seen from her yet.

Definite signs of hope. He just had to look for them.

Cheryl sat on the bench in the sun, the slick wrap of the paperback book cool against her palms.

Why had that woman on the plane given it to her? How did she know? Cheryl had sat by dozens of people on as many planes. Never once had a stranger nailed her for what she was.

Post abortive. That's what the book called it. The minor chords of the music she'd just attempted to play strung together in her mind, the music fluid, vivid, and painful.

God, I don't want to remember...

But she must. Something strong and insistent inside her declared it to be so.

Why?

There is a time to mourn...

Wasn't that a song? No, it was in the Bible. A time to laugh and a time to mourn.

It had happened ten years ago. Why must she shatter over it now? She'd told Brock—her greatest fear—and he'd come back for her.

Loved her, married her. That should mean that life could move forward, shouldn't it?

Footfalls sounded with a dull thump against the decking around the front of the house. Cheryl turned the book over between her hands, wondering what Brock would think about her having it.

Shouldn't be a question. He'd wanted her to seek some kind of help. Group. Counseling. Something. She hadn't seen the point. It was done. Nothing could change it.

But this book said that she could heal. Offered hope...a hope she was too terrified to really grip. As the footsteps came nearer, she tucked the paperback under her thigh. Just not now. Maybe not ever.

"Hey, love." Rounding the corner of the house, Brock closed the three feet between himself and the bench where she sat and lowered himself to her side. He traced the outline of one side of her face with his thumb and then leaned back, relaxing against their shared seat.

Cheryl hesitated a moment before she let her head rest against his shoulder. "I'm sorry."

He pressed a kiss into her hair and then wrapped an arm around her. "I'm not angry, and neither is So-J. You did really well with her. If anyone understands the impulse to run, it's her. Trust me—she gets it."

Fear twisted in her chest. "Did you tell her?"

"Only that you had things you wish you could forget. Like I said, she gets it. Probably just gained her trust more than anything else."

Cheryl squeezed her eyes shut and buried against him. "Why can't I forget?" Such a ludicrous question. As if she had any right to.

Brock didn't respond. The tips of his fingers trailed along the length of her arm, and the rise and fall of his steady breathing moved gently against her cheek, but beyond that he remained still.

In the silence, the music she'd tried to escape began drifting through her mind. It hinted mystery and brokenness, and yet, oddly enough, beauty. She'd loved that song, second only to the "Feather Theme." It had reminded her of her mom—a woman she'd not been able to understand but had admired with her whole heart. Mom had been strong and beautiful. Kind and firm. Gracious and determined. The harmony of the life Mom had lived seemed uniquely beautiful in Cheryl's memory, and through the years Cheryl had ached to know that beauty. To be that beauty.

All through high school, she'd resented that Mom wasn't there to teach her, to show her how to be brave and strong and fun all at once. She'd had to figure life out on her own, and she'd failed. Longing for someone to notice her, to love her, she'd found herself in the arms of a man who knew neither faithfulness nor love.

All beauty shattered.

And yet, here she sat, held by another man. One who, though she hadn't seen it exactly before, embodied all that she'd adored in her mom. Courage, kindness, joy.

Brock was bringing the beauty back into her life.

God, I don't deserve it...

Brock's hushed voice interrupted her silent musings. "Have you read Psalm 107?"

The Bible he'd given her still lay largely untouched.

"No."

"I've been poring over it. I think you should."

"Why?"

"It's about redemption. God coming for His people."

His people. The clean ones. The perfect ones—or at least the forgivable ones. Her chin fell toward her chest. "People worth coming for."

Brock's chuckle bounced under her head. "Not really. Rebellious, stubborn people who exchanged freedom for bondage."

That wasn't in there, was it?

"Here's what keeps resurfacing in my mind." Brock rested his chin on her head. "Let them give thanks to the LORD for His lovingkindness... For He has shattered gates of bronze and cut bars of iron asunder."

A bubble of hope grew in her chest, and this time she couldn't pop it.

"When I started to get really good on the board, back about my junior year in high school—do you remember?" He paused. She nodded against him. "My dad said something that I couldn't shake. He said, 'Slavery doesn't always look ugly from the outside.' Man, I was so mad at him. I thought, *Dude, God made me good at racing, and I'm gonna use it.*

"I was the one who didn't get it. God's gifts are supposed to be used, but for His glory, not mine. I got caught, you know? Like there came a point when I knew I wasn't okay, but I didn't know how to get out of it. I'd surrendered to bondage."

"But you did get out. And anyway, what you did wasn't that bad when you look at—" Her. Her life, her bondage. She couldn't get those words out.

"Do you know what God says about rebellion?"

He sure knew a lot about what God said. Did this come from being a preacher's kid?

"Divination. He matches it with witchcraft. And He hates it."

Cheryl fisted the gray T-shirt beneath her hand, afraid to look at him, to allow the hope breathing life into her spirit to grow any more. It wasn't the same. Her sins...

"Sherbert—"

"Don't, Brock." She winced. Killing hope hurt. "I don't want to talk about it, okay?"

She felt his chest cave in as air drained from his lungs.

Apparently he felt the puncture wound too.

When I was a child, I believed.

Saved seemed so wonderful. So secure. Especially when my mom died. Heaven was a promise, and I owned it.

But then I found out something horrible. There are some things in life that simply cannot be forgiven.

Not just unforgiven. Unforgivable.

There is no greater agony than to be that woman.

~31~

You're unforgivable.

Cheryl stared at the image on the overhead screen. That wasn't actually what the printed words read. But that was what she heard. Felt. Believed.

Even as Brock's wife—with his devoted love surrounding her new everyday reality—she couldn't dislodge the conviction.

The sign overhead said *abortion is murder*, and she couldn't argue the point. Her baby, who should have been going on eleven next month, was dead.

Unforgivable.

Tightness gripped her chest, and the muscles in her neck and shoulders contracted. Sharp pain traveled from the base of her skull into her brain, sending violent flashes of light into her eyes. She squeezed her eyelids shut just as the ringing in her ears began.

This was why she had quit church. But Brock's dad—now her father-in-law—had been such a gentle and gracious man. His mom had brought her into her heart and family with unreserved love. She never would have guessed this would be posted in their church.

A gentle touch against her neck nearly made her bolt from her chair. She forced her eyes open as the large, warm hand of her husband cupped around the base of her head.

He leaned until his nose brushed just above her ear, and whispered, "I'm sorry." With his thumb he began to softly knead the cramped muscles in her neck. "We can go home."

Cheryl pressed her lips together, her eyes drawn to the public announcement still glowing at the front. Though the Kellys didn't know—she knew Brock would not betray her ugly secrets—she felt as if those bold, jagged words had been posted just for her. To make sure she wouldn't ever forget.

Suddenly a voice in her head, vile and fierce, took aim at her festering wounds and let the fiery arrows of condemnation loose with deadly aim.

I know the truth. Brock does too. He can't love you. It won't last. You're too ugly, too dirty. There is no salvation for you.

Brock's hand moved until his arm curved around her shoulder. With gentle pressure, he pulled her securely into his side. "Let's go, love."

He can't love you. Frozen, Cheryl tried to blink.

"Stop looking at it, babe. We're going home."

You're too ugly, too dirty.

Her head throbbed, and it seemed that she could not pull in a full breath. The world began to tilt, causing her stomach to lurch. Brock stood, pulling her up beside him. Bending, he reached across her to gather her purse and the Bible he'd given her, and then with her anchored under his protective arm, he led her outside.

Her head thumped with stabbing pain and nausea blurred her vision as Brock drove her home.

~*~

Brock knelt beside the bed, a glass of water and four Advil in his hand. The plate of toast sat untouched on the bedside table.

"Sherbert, you need to eat. This stuff will rip up your stomach if it's empty."

She opened her eyes and slowly tilted her head to look at him.

Agony had a look that ripped a heart in two. Pain knifed through his chest, followed closely by anger. What had Dad been thinking? Didn't he understand—

Of course he didn't. His dad was just like he'd been two months before. So set on the righteous cause to protect the unborn that he hadn't considered the post-abortive woman.

Setting the medicine on the plate and the glass to the side, he pushed his fingers into Cheryl's hair. "Can I lay beside you, or will that make it worse?"

Her eyes slid shut, but she lifted a hand to cup his jawline, her touch speaking in her silence. *I need you.*

He hadn't bothered to change when they got home, so in his starched button-down shirt and good jeans, he slipped beside her on their bed, careful to keep the jostling of the mattress to a minimum. She rolled to her back, her face tilted slightly up and her eyes shut. Moisture lined her dark lashes, and when a bulb of a tear emerged from the outside corner of one eye, Brock's emotions ruptured. His hand trembled as he moved to brush her tears.

"Sherbert, they don't know." Hoarse, his voice wobbled in his throat. "You have to believe me, love. If they knew, they would never—it wouldn't have happened like that."

"If they knew, they'd hate me. They'd be so disappointed for you."

He cradled her face with one hand. "No. They'd feel terrible about today, I promise. Cheryl, they just don't know how it hurts. Forgive their thoughtlessness, just like you forgave mine. In their zeal for the unborn, they have missed the women who walk away completely shattered. But if they knew—"

Her eyes opened, panic sparking in them. "No. Please, Brock. Please don't."

She was wrong. He was certain. He knew his mother—she'd tear up for Cheryl's heartache, take her into a death hug, and beg for her forgiveness. And his dad...he'd understand, and the depth of his ministry would grow. Compassion marked his parents, despite what had happened today. They would shift with the revelation, and it could change lives.

He knew. Because his life was shifting.

"Brock." Cheryl gripped the fastened buttons at his chest. "Promise me..."

Her blue eyes pleaded, making his heart hurt more. Leaning close, he brushed her face with his own.

"Promise." Her whisper cracked.

Right or wrong, he couldn't deny her. It was, after all, her story to tell. Or not.

"If that's what you want. I promise."

~*~

He knew that cry. Brock moved against the mattress, his eyes adjusting to the dark.

His wife lay at the edge of their bed, huddled in a tight ball, arms clenched over her ears. Brock pushed to an elbow and reached for her trembling body, pulling her against his chest. Cheryl was locked in another nightmare. Why did this continue?

Another moan escaped from the bundle in his arms.

He pushed the hair from her face and moved to whisper near her ear. "I've got you, Sherbert. It's over, love. It's all over."

God, why won't you set her free?

Cheryl shuddered, and her tears seeped warm through his shirt. "Please...please...I'm so sorry..." Broken words lifted from her throat, chopped by breathless sobs.

She was forgiven. If God's Word was true, and if He was the God Brock knew Him to be, then she should be healing. Recovering. Not still writhing with this unbearable guilt.

Please, God. I beg You on her behalf. Set her free.

The verses he'd been poring over lifted to his mind.

It was for freedom that Christ set us free...

He rescued us from the domain of darkness and transferred us to the Kingdom of His beloved Son...

They were true, weren't they? God's Word was true. All of it. So why did this continue?

"Cheryl, wake up. It's just a dream."

A dream that should have stopped. *God, why won't you take them away?*

"Please make it stop..."

"Cheryl." He shook her shoulder. "Wake up. You've got to let this go."

Was that it? She was trapped. How could she let it go? She didn't choose to have these nightmares. She didn't choose to live in defeat. People didn't choose that kind of life. She ached for healing, longed for freedom.

Where was Truth? If Christ set her free in His forgiveness, then why was she not free?

With a sharp inhale, Cheryl stiffened in his arms. Brock tightened his hold.

"I'm right here. I've got you."

She pulled in another staggering breath.

He pressed a kiss to her forehead. "It's okay."

Her body relaxed, and then she tucked her head into his chest. Brock leaned back against his pillow, pulling her with him. Her hands anchored behind his shoulders, and he felt her whimper against him.

"Same dream?"

Her answer came breathless. Hopeless. "Yes."

"Tell me what happens."

She buried her face deeper against him. "I am there again. At the clinic. It's dark and cold, and I hear a voice telling me not to go through a steel door. But I go anyway." She stopped, and a soul-deep cry ripped through her. "He warned me, Brock. It was God, and I ignored Him."

Brock fisted the hair he'd been stroking as his throat closed over. He shut his eyes against the burn of tears as her desolation sank through him. How could she overcome such regret when it continued to spear her conscience?

Believe.

With all his being, Brock believed she was forgiven. He believed God could heal her of this festering wound. Why didn't He?

Cheryl pulled in another quivering breath and continued. "Then I am alone. I hear the sad minor chords of the *Sabrina* theme, and then the cries begin to take over."

The *Sabrina* song. The one song she couldn't get through in the music book he'd ordered for her.

"Why does that song make you cry?"

"I was playing it when I realized I was pregnant."

Brock's chest seemed to cave.

"But I'm not the one crying in my dreams."

No, she wasn't. She always begged for the cries to stop.

"Babies," she finally whispered. Though her tears came on full force again, words tumbled fast. "I hear the wailing of babies, and I know mine is among them. I cannot escape their accusation."

She paused, and another quake of agony seized her body. "They cry because of me."

Brock's jaw clenched tight as his lips trembled. *Oh God... Where is Your forgiveness? You said You redeem. When?*

~*~

He didn't respond. Cheryl felt the muscles beneath her face tense as Brock's arms wrapped tight around her. But he said nothing.

This was harder than he'd thought, this being married to a woman with a past like hers. Waking him up with her nightmares. Making him watchful and sad with her headaches. Provoking his tears with her regrets.

She shouldn't have let him talk her into this. Marriage for Brock Kelly should be all joy and gooey smiles, and their most intimate moments together in this bed shouldn't be laden with tears of guilt.

The bride who wore white because he'd wanted her to hadn't yet changed. She still felt as filthy and wretched as before, and she'd brought it to his bed.

Brock continued to hold her, though his grip lessened. One hand cradled her head, and he began stroking her hair again. He sniffed, the sound telling her what she'd feared. She'd made him cry. She'd taken the life of another into her own hands, as if she could see the future, known what was best. As if she had been God. Did women in that clinic imagine the everyday death they would live with after their choices? Maybe they didn't live with it the way she did. Maybe somehow those other women found a way to stymie the shame.

Maybe she alone was cast out.

"Sherbert." Brock's hand paused, resting against her back. "You're forgiven. You know that, don't you?"

Forgiven by Brock—that was something. But it wasn't everything— wasn't enough. What of her baby? Or God? God was the giver of life. Cheryl had taken it. Was that even forgivable?

Brock moved to his side and rolled her to her back. The hand that had been caressing her hair came to cup her face. "Cheryl, look at me." With his thumb he tipped her chin so that she would comply. "God doesn't lie. When He says that He forgives, He forgives. Completely."

Her jaw tightened. "I know, but—"

"But what? Do you think you're the one sinner on the planet who His grace cannot reach?"

A tear escaped from the corner of her eye, carving a path against her skin until it dripped onto her hair.

Brock leaned over her, his nose brushing next to hers as he spoke. "Tell me what we just read the other night. In First John. What did it say?"

Cheryl's throat closed over as tears rushed from her eyes. She couldn't form the words, though she could faintly recall them in her mind.

Brock waited two breaths. "We confess. He forgives." He pulled away just enough to trace the streams on her face with his thumb. "I was there, Cheryl. I heard you. You begged, through your tears, for His forgiveness—and I'm guessing that wasn't the first time you'd done so. He hears you. I *know* you are forgiven."

"What if this isn't forgivable?"

"Then the Bible lied. Do you think that's possible?"

She sniffed, searching his eyes in the semidarkness. "Lied?"

"King David was a murderer. Psalms tell us he was forgiven. Peter was a deserter. Also forgiven. James was a mocker who didn't believe until Jesus came back from the dead. Thomas was a doubter. Paul was a persecutor of the church. All were forgiven. Do you think the Bible lies?"

King David was a murderer... She had forgotten that. The man after God's own heart had taken a life to make his own easier. Just like her. He had been forgiven.

"Cheryl." Brock's voice surged with conviction. "You think that your sin is too big. But it isn't the degree of the sin that determines God's forgiveness, but the greatness of His love."

Stillness replaced the passion of his voice, and Cheryl lay soaking in his words. Every example he'd given, every claim he'd made—they were true. The Bible said that God forgave.

Oh, how greatly she longed for forgiveness. Brock was right. She'd begged for it. Repeatedly. But this guilt...

"Why do I still feel unforgiven?"

Brock came back to nestle by her face, his lips brushing the moisture of tears that still remained. "I don't know, love. But I don't think this guilt is from God. I think the enemy knows exactly where to hit to knock us down, to keep us in the ditch."

Either way then, she was stuck. "I can't fight that, Brock."

He pushed away, his hand covering his forehead as if he had a headache. Or he was praying.

Praying was likely. That was the kind of man she'd married.

After a moment he looked back to her, the zeal of conviction back in his voice. "Believe God, Cheryl." With both hands, he held her head. "The voice telling you you're unforgivable isn't Him. He says you're forgiven. He calls you beloved. Believe Him. That is your shield."

~*~

Believe...she did believe in God.

I call you forgiven. Redeemed. Friend. Do you believe this?

Cheryl examined the words on the page. This book of recovery...the very one she'd been hiding. It offered her exactly what Brock had held out to her. Hope.

Hope rooted in the Bible. God called her forgiven. Redeemed. Friend. With her Bible on the other arm of her chair, she flipped through the references listed above that statement. Ephesians 1:7. Romans 3:24. John 15:15. Every time, Truth said she was forgiven.

How then did she crawl out from under the weight of guilt?

Believe Him.

She'd had to come to a point where she really believed that Brock loved her. She'd hurled every ugly detail of her crimson-stained life at him, certain he'd reject her. He hadn't. He loved harder. It had changed their relationship. She began to trust him, love him more honestly, and even feel a little more whole with him by her side. Could this be the same kind of thing? Could God be calling her out of darkness, waiting with an outstretched hand for her to simply believe?

Her attention went back to the book.

Sometimes when we despise what we have done, we determine how much God can forgive. But you and I, we are not God. He is so much more than we can imagine, and when He offers His forgiveness to you and me, it is complete. God's forgiveness is where the greatest amount of freedom is found, because when we begin to take hold of it, we will learn to live in forgiveness, and we will become able to forgive others and to forgive ourselves.

Freedom in forgiveness. From God, and from her baby, whom she'd read in this book was now perfected in heaven and able to forgive her because of the grace of God. Brock had forgiven her, and maybe his parents would too, if she'd give them the chance. Maybe it was time to step into that forgiveness, to live there, and to give it. To herself and to others...her dad, to Michael—the professor who'd fathered her baby—

to Andrew...the list would get long. But one by one, she could let go of resentment and live more fully in love.

Cheryl pulled in a staggered breath as she felt her very soul shift. The thawing continued, and she felt as if, in her heart, she could reach up to the heavens.

God reached back. Pulled her near, and with that silent, divine whisper, He confirmed the Truth.

You are forgiven.

The last of the ice broke away.

I've been angry with you all this time.

In my heart, I couldn't understand why you left us when we needed you most.

I kept thinking, just give me a reason. Let me understand.

Maybe if I understood, it would be easier to forgive.

Maybe not.

I don't know. But I am learning something new.

It is not for me to understand. Perhaps there was a reason. Perhaps not. Either way, it doesn't matter.

It is only for me to forgive.

So, I'm doing that...and I'll keep at it until it is complete.

I'm forgiving you.

~32~

Steam curled from the two mugs in Brock's hands, their misty white swirls drifting into the early morning air.

Sleep had finally claimed him somewhere in the middle of the previous night, holding him in gentle silence well after the sun had crested the eastern peaks. He couldn't know if the same had been true for Cheryl. Probably not, as she sat in an Adirondack chair on the dock below.

Pausing at the path's entry leading down to the pond, he studied his wife's profile. She was stunning, with her dark hair dancing in the breeze and the sun tickling the soft skin of her cheeks. But she was so much more than eye candy, even if she didn't understand that yet. She made him better. Cammy, Ethan, and his mom all saw it. She'd been God's tool to cut away the lingering bitterness and mistrust birthed by a relationship he hadn't any business being involved in in the first place. She challenged his arrogance, keeping his feet and head where they needed to be. And she continued to grow compassion in his heart by sharing her pain.

They were well matched. The yearning for her to know so stretched in his heart.

Cheryl paused in her reading—probably the book she'd been working to hide from him—and tipped her face skyward. Her eyes slid shut, and after a few breaths of healing silence, her fingertips brushed against her cheeks.

Tears. *Oh Lord, let them be the good kind.*

Her attention went to the wide arm of her chair, where another book waited. After lifting a pen, she seemed to pause, to draw in courage, and then began to write.

He should leave her.

Brock turned and took two steps toward their home and then stopped again. Glancing over his shoulder at her, a compelling urge to be at her side gripped him.

What could he do for her? Nothing. She didn't want to talk to him about it.

Go.

But...

No. No buts. This was why he'd married her in a way that seemed to the rest of the world rushed and foolish. He hadn't wanted her to walk through this alone anymore, even if she continued to lock him out of it. He would go through it with her.

Resolute, Brock returned to the footpath and followed it to the dock where Cheryl continued to write in the morning sun. So lost in her page, she didn't notice his approach until he knelt at her side. She sucked in a breath and turned startled eyes on him. He smiled, and with one hand pushed a mug of coffee her way.

"Morning, love." He leaned to press a kiss to her temple.

Pink crept over her face, and she looked at the drink. "I didn't hear you."

Brock smiled, stood, and moved to the chair at her side and sat down. "I didn't hear you get up this morning. I guess that makes us both sneaky."

"You were tired." She settled back, subtly covering her book and journal with her free hand. "I'm sorry I woke you last night."

"Cheryl, I don't think you're getting this." Brock bent to set his coffee onto the dock. "You and me, we're doing life together. The places you have to go"—he touched her head—"here"—he moved his hand to meet the soft beat of her heart—"and here. I'm going there too."

She shut her eyes and inhaled. After a moment, she wrapped the hand he'd placed over her heart with her own and brought it against her cheek. "Aren't you afraid?"

"Yes."

She opened her eyes and searched his face. He could only hope that she could read how full his heart was for her. With another long breath, she moved to retrieve the book she'd been hiding, slowly passing it to his knee.

"When I flew back to LA, I sat next to a woman who was reading this. She gave it to me after we landed. I don't know why. I pretended to be asleep the whole flight, but she said she felt like she was supposed to give it to me."

Brock shifted his attention from her face to the book. Two words screamed for his attention. *Abortion* and *Healing*. He wanted to crumble to his knees with relief.

"Why did you think you needed to hide this?"

"I told you I didn't want to talk about it."

"Why? I mean I already knew, so why are you afraid to talk to me?"

She looked away, her face toward the dock at her feet. "I don't know. What if every time you're reminded that I've had an abortion, you love me less?" Turning to look at him again, desperation filled her eyes. "You've stripped me of every piece of armor I've kept, and now I'm defenseless. To lose you—"

"You won't." Brock moved from his chair, scooped Cheryl from hers, and settled her on his lap. "You're not going to lose me. You choose, Sherbert. You choose to be forgiven and to forgive. You choose to be loved and to give love. You are not locked into a future of bondage."

Cheryl's brow furrowed the way it did when her thoughts ran deep and troubled. Brock tugged her against himself and cuddled her close, praying that she wouldn't close up yet again. If only this time she'd let him—

"I believe."

Her whispered words cut off his thoughtful prayers. What did she mean, she believed?

Their fitful night returned to him. *Believe Him. Believe God.*

Brock's shoulders sagged, and he leaned back against the chair. Faith was their shield.

Thank you, Jesus.
At last. The real journey could begin.

~*~

This is long overdue...
But I forgive you.
We were both a crazy, tangled-up mess.
Alcohol had an iron grip on your life, and shame kept me wrapped up in ice.
I am glad you found truth. You found healing.
You found love.
Thank you for seeking me, for your apology.
You showed me what redemption looks like.
I am sorry I came to you with vengeance and resentment.
Is it too late to ask for your forgiveness?

Cheryl reread the last three lines she'd just written. She reclined against the sloped back of the chair where she'd spent most of the day. Brock had held her for a glorious eternity that morning. Every minute of their beautiful silence spoke his strong love to her fragile heart. This life...beyond her hopes. So much more than she deserved.

Brock believed in redemption, and now she was beginning to take hold of it too.

Andrew had shown her what redemption looked like. Was that irony or grace? Irony, in that Andrew's letter had brought her home. Grace that it brought her to Brock.

Why me, God? Why even this? Tears clogged her sinuses as she felt the words lift to God.

I am more than you imagine. I redeem. It is My power and My pleasure. I ask only for you to believe.

The words pressed so firm in her mind she could nearly hear the great, gentle voice from heaven speak them. With one outstretched hand lifted toward the sky, she leaned forward until her face touched her knees.

I do believe. Help me to believe more.

She remembered the day Brock had told her he believed in redemption. It had hit her like shards of ice. Painful, cold, and cruel.

Because she didn't think it possible. How could God redeem what could not be undone?

But maybe redeemed didn't always mean undone. It didn't always mean no more pain, at least not on this side of heaven. It might mean that now she could breathe again. She could live and love and feel joy, even through the pain.

And it might mean that she give others the chance to show her grace. Like Brock's parents.

With her vision blurred, but her determination locked, she took up her pen and found a fresh page in the notebook she'd been writing in. Terrified, she took in a courageous breath and thought of her mother. A woman who gazed at fear and refused to bow. Maybe today, Cheryl could be her daughter.

The words tumbled from her heart through her pen, her handwriting shaky and at some points barely legible. She'd never be able to speak them and probably wouldn't even be able to deliver the letter in person, but she'd give her in-laws a chance to prove themselves. Brock had every confidence in them, which strengthened her budding courage. He was, after all, their son and the best man she'd ever met.

Her knight. In God's armor. Maybe he learned it from them.

You upended all my strongholds...
I believed You didn't want me.
I believed I was beyond Your reach.
What I believed didn't make it true.
You came for me...
And You sent one who would show me what was true.
Love came for me.

~33~

Cheryl slid the daypack from her shoulders, lowered it to the lightly vegetated ground at her feet, and stretched her spine.

Brock stopped at her side, resting his hand on her back. "Doing okay?"

She looked at the formation in front of them. It happened here, somewhere on the rock face that climbed toward the clouds in front of her. She swallowed as a small tremble waved through her core.

"I never climbed with her here." She looked up to him. "I never climbed a real face with her, actually. Only ever went to the training walls. I was always too scared."

Brock listened, his attention moving from her to the Rabbit Ears formation and back again. "It's not for everyone. Looks pretty intense to me. There's no shame in that."

"I know." Cheryl sighed. "I guess I just always felt like maybe she was disappointed in me."

"Doubt it." That charming half smile lifted one corner of his mouth, and then he leaned to kiss her temple. "Time to let it go," he whispered.

Yes. It was. That was why they'd taken this hike. Cheryl bent, taking up her pack again, and unzipped the front panel. Two folded letters waited, and she tugged them both free.

"Would it be weird if I read them out loud?"

Tenderness passed over his expression, and he squeezed her shoulder. "Not at all."

She nodded, drew a long breath, and unfolded the first note.

"I never said good-bye. I was mad, and I didn't want to.

"But I know that it wasn't your fault. You lived the life God intended you to live. You followed your passion for nature and climbing, and you never let life sideline you.

"I'm not like you, with a heart for adventure. But I want to live like you in my own way. To be who God intended. To believe Him. To be willing to take risks.

"To live.

"But to do that, I have to say good-bye. It's overdue, and I'm sorry I held on to my anger for so long. But here it is, Mom.

"I love you, and I do know that you loved me. Someday, I hope to hear you say it again. But for now..."

Cheryl paused, tears choking the words in her throat. Brock's arm came around her, and he anchored her to his side. She cleared her throat and began again.

"For now, I hope you'll say it to my daughter. Say it for me. Tell her I love her, that she's never left my heart."

Cheryl sniffed as she folded the letter, brushing a tear with her free hand. Brock squeezed her against him, and he leaned to graze another kiss on her hair.

She gulped in another breath. The hard had only just begun. But sometimes the only way out of pain was through... She shuffled the second letter to the front, and her hands shook as she unfolded it. Her voice barely worked, but she began to read anyway.

"To the little one I never held.

"I'm sorry.

"You are my deepest regret. Not that you were, but that I denied you. I hope, because you are perfected in heaven, you can forgive me. It seems unfathomable that I should even ask, but here I am, asking you to forgive me.

"I don't know why I think that you were a girl. If you're not, forgive that too. I've called you Sabrina, because every child should have a name.

"I wish I knew what you looked like. Do you have my blue eyes? My dark hair? Do your cheeks dimple when you smile? Are there freckles across your nose?

"Questions that someday will be answered with a simple glance.

"Someday.

"I imagine you walking with Jesus, your hand in His.

"Healed.

"I am holding His hand too, and He is healing me as we go.

"I wish I'd chosen a different path. You would have been worth every struggle.

"But some things cannot be undone, and there is only I'm sorry. And forgiveness. And love.

"You are loved.

"Really, that's what I want most for you to know. You are loved."

Her face soaked, Cheryl moved away from the arm that held her up, and stepped to the base of the rock formation. Brock followed—she could feel his presence as she touched the rough, volcanic stone. He shuffled behind her, unzipped the pack that he'd carried, and knelt by her side. A flash of green and red contrasted with the dark charcoal stone, and Cheryl looked down.

Red roses. Brock had brought her mother and her baby a red rose bouquet. Cheryl came undone. Crumbling to her knees, she sagged into his arms, and together they cried.

"Thank you, Brock," she breathed between sobs.

He pulled away enough to look at her, the tears trickling over the rough, sandstone stubble littering his jawline. "I love what you love." He wiped at the trail of her tears. "And we'll walk this path together."

Leaning into the hand that cradled her face, a prayer lifted from her heart. *Thank you for this man.*

Shifting again so that he sat, Brock let her go and reached into his pack. "I told you I don't know what I'm doing in all this, so I hope that this is okay—good and not hurtful." His hand came out of the fabric holding a small box. With his palm open, he held it out to her. "But if it's not, just say so. The last thing I want to do is add more pain."

Cheryl took the small gift—a jewelry box—and slid the lid off the top. Laying against pink velvet was a charm of two tiny feet clasped to a delicate silver chain. With a breath of emotion, a cocktail of heartache and love, she fingered the charm, lifting it from the box. A rough texture on the back drew her attention, and as she turned it in her palm, she found that Brock had it engraved.

Not forgotten.

Her fingers closed around it, and she leaned into his chest.

"Is it okay?" Hesitation hitched his question.

"Yes." Her voice wobbled. "I love it."

His arms tightened around her. "I would have loved to meet her. I would have taken her as my own."

Beyond a doubt, Cheryl knew it was the truth—bittersweet, but she loved him for it. A nod against him was all she could muster. That was enough for him as he sheltered her in his arms while the intensity of all that had been, all that shouldn't have been, and all that was tore through her one more time.

The storm didn't leave her devastated though. As the swirling winds of regret calmed, a gentle rain seemed to take over in her heart. Washing. Resculpting. Sinking in deep. Giving life.

Cheryl moved so that she sat next to Brock, her head against his shoulder as she faced the world that lay beyond the mountain. The valley to the west was stunning. The Yampa meandered with its gentle curves, water gleaming in the late afternoon sun. Green pastures lay deep and rich and inviting. Blue peaks gathered around as if to protect the rare treasure of the high plain.

A view she'd never seen before, because she'd lacked the courage to come to this place. Breathtaking. With a long draw of clean, thin mountain air, she let her chest expand, and her heart seemed to grow.

"Will it be easier now, do you think?" She didn't look at Brock while asking the question.

He rubbed her shoulder with one hand and then squeezed. "I think there will be good days and there will be bad days. I think we'll have laughter and we'll have tears. We'll come back here and grieve, and we'll go back down and dance. I think that's the way this life is."

She nodded and then looked up at him. "But we'll do it together."

"Yeah. Every day, together." A gentle smile preceded his tender kiss.

A breeze danced around them, rustling the roses Brock had placed against the stone to their right. The movement of color caught Cheryl's attention, and his kindness once again tugged on her heart.

Kindness that had been sent by the Healer of her heart.

She blinked, a small smile tugging on her mouth. "I didn't know how much I wanted Him to come for me." She turned to look up at Brock. "But He knew, and He sent you."

Brock's silent look said it all. He loved her. Because God gave him a love for her. Because he chose to love her. Because he was willing to look at her brokenness, listen to the pain, and let it break his heart.

He loved her.

All of it seemed beyond comprehension, but she sat in that shelter, overwhelmed by the reality.

"So that makes me, like, your knight. Right?" Leave it to Brock to bring laughter to her tears.

She lifted her lips to his, kissed him softly, and pulled away. "Don't let it go to your head. I need you on the ground."

With a chuckle, he zipped up the packs and stood, pulling her to her feet with him. "E said you'd keep me humble."

"Apparently someone is supposed to."

He dropped another kiss against her forehead. "I can live with that." His hand slid around hers and squeezed. "Ready to go home?"

"Yeah." She followed him as he made his way back to the trail. The footpath took them south before it curved back west and then began to descend. Cheryl paused at the elbow, once again looking over the valley. So amazing.

Ten feet down the path, Brock stopped and turned back to her. Backlit by the sun, he seemed washed in the intensity of warm light. But she could make out the love in his eyes.

"Coming?"

She remembered that image she'd seen so many weeks before, the one of the two diverging paths. One stale, cold, and hopeless. The other dipping into an unknown, but somehow surrounded by life. She'd taken the path that dipped.

Apparently it climbed too. It wasn't all dark. There was light after the darkness. Hope on this difficult but glorious path.

You were right, Mom.

"Yes." She took another step toward him, and he continued to wait for her.

When she reached his side, he took her hand and led her into the sun.

Heal me, O LORD, and I will be healed;
Save me and I will be saved,
For You are my praise.
~Jeremiah 17:14~

THE END

Dear Reader,

I didn't see this one coming. Honest. As I was going through the final editing stages for *Blue Columbine*, I got to the scene where Cheryl leaves Andrew in his downtown loft—livid, frozen, and completely unlikable. Something whispered to me, "She has a story." Probably that "something" was Someone.

Great, I thought. *Series sell, so let's do it. What's Cheryl the Ice Princess's story?*

I fiddled with some ideas, sketched out some plot possibilities.

Nothing stuck. That was okay. I was in the middle of completing *The Carpenter's Daughter*, so it could keep.

A few months down the road, my hubby and I somehow managed to snag a night on our own, and we decided to watch a movie. I'd purchased *October Baby* over a year before, but honestly, I knew the story, and on the rare nights that we could choose our movies, that hadn't made it to the top of the list. But my hubby doesn't do reruns that well, and it was one of the only movies we had in the house that we hadn't seen. And so we began...

There is a scene where we see the birth mother. Most remember her as cold, stiff, and indifferent. That wasn't what grabbed me. Truly, of that whole movie, what I remember most vividly was the ten-second sequence of seeing that woman shatter.

Her, the Whisper said. *That's Cheryl, and you need to tell her story.*

Truth? God couldn't have laid this story on a more unqualified woman. So I argued. *I don't know anything about this. I don't want to do this. I will completely mess this up.*

But Cheryl...she wouldn't leave my mind.

There was nothing easy about this story. I found myself shredded through the process of research—something I usually love to do. Sitting down to write her story came with a sense of heaviness and a strong dose of fear. Still, her story would not let me surrender.

I am so thankful. I loved when Brock said that his life was shifting. My paradigm has shifted too. I don't write so that I can preach. I write so that I may be changed.

I am definitely not the same. *(We) cannot escape the demands of deep compassion.* Truth. And it has opened my eyes.

Sometimes, as we saw with both Brock and Cheryl, you have to be willing to look at the brokenness and to allow another's pain to break your heart before you can truly learn compassion.

Thanks to Cheryl, my heart has been shattered. I am better for it. Because of that, I am so thankful for the things that I hadn't seen coming.

I pray that you are as well.

Thank you for traveling this road with me. Until we meet again...

JEN

Note from Sydna Masse

Dear Reader:

As a post-abortive woman, I read Jennifer Rodewald's book *Red Rose Bouquet* with my heart in my hand. After over twenty-four years in helping women find God's healing, I am surprised to say that *Red Rose Bouquet* kick-started a deeper healing in my soul. This excellent resource can do the same in your heart.

From the very beginning, I related to every aspect of Cheryl's journey toward God's amazing healing. The emotions of self-loathing and an inability to accept or give love often overwhelm the post-abortive heart into the extreme "ice princess" position. Brock's gentle ability to hear and obey God's voice allowed Cheryl access to unconditional love that she simply never expected from anyone.

As the leader of an international abortion recovery program, I am blessed that Jennifer allowed God's Holy Spirit to touch this story at an anointed level. Though never experiencing abortion, Jennifer offered God's healing balm to parched souls, outlining the typical post-abortion experience. Her desire to help post-abortive women discover the safety of addressing this pain with God's help will bring peace to our world.

The journey that Cheryl experienced in *Red Rose Bouquet* is a common one. Few choose abortion with any understanding about the long-term impact. Abortion is packaged cleverly as a "safe and legal" response to an unexpected pregnancy.

Sadly, many women are pushed into making this choice by those who may never endure any emotional, spiritual, psychological, or physical consequences. Abandoned and alone, post-abortive hearts often flow into other sinful behaviors, falsely believing they have committed the unforgivable sin. Often, alcohol and drugs help numb their pain.

To those who have experienced abortion, please understand that there is no sin that God cannot forgive. Like Cheryl, you may have more trouble forgiving yourself. The pain and grief of this form of pregnancy loss is often denied, muted, or simply ignored. Yet abortion memories can reignite at any moment, causing the post-abortive individual great pain.

Abortion doesn't solve any problems—it only creates new ones. God's redemption is available to anyone who would humbly confess and seek out His healing. There is a way to find healing and peace.

If you can relate to Cheryl, know that God has a plan for your life. Here are steps to begin healing any pain that may reside in your heart:

Understand you are not the only one that chose abortion—Abortion providers outline that one in three American women have experienced abortion. Of those who choose abortion, as many as 44 percent may go on to have additional abortions.

Realize that tears rid the body of toxins and bring healing—Many falsely believe that if they begin to cry, they won't be able to stop. Tears are part of grieving and can help begin the process of healing.

Research the symptoms of Abortion PTSD—If you relate to three or more of these symptoms, an abortion recovery class could help your heart.

Discover your local abortion recovery ministry—Pregnancy centers offer these services, along with physical, emotional, and psychological support to those in unplanned pregnancies. Visit Ramah International's directory (http://ramahinternational.org) to find your closest center, and contact it for more information.

Obtain a copy of *Her Choice to Heal: Finding Spiritual and Emotional Peace after Abortion*—This resource includes details on the pain many experience after abortion, along with chapters that help begin the healing process.

To those who love a post-abortive person—Understand that God can use your prayers and compassion to help her find His healing. Brock knew very little about Cheryl's specific agony but was led by God to simply provide unconditional love no matter what sins were shared. There is no condemnation in Christ.

Sydna Masse,
President/Founder at
Ramah International, Abortion Recovery

JENNIFER RODEWALD

Made in the USA
Middletown, DE
14 April 2021